CW00496093

Benedict Kiely was b(
Dromore, Co. Tyrone. H(
to school in Omagh and is a Freeman of that
town. Apart from some years in the United
States, most of his life has been spent in
Dublin. He graduated from University
College, Dublin and worked as a journalist,
broadcaster and lecturer. He is past-president
of the Irish Academy of Letters. His first
book of memoirs *Drink To The Bird* was
published by Methuen in 1991.

IN A HARBOUR GREEN

By the same author

Benedict Kiely

IN A
HARBOUR GREEN

In a harbour grene aslepe whereas I lay,
The byrdes sang swete in the middes of the day,
I dreamed fast of mirth and play:
In youth is pleasure, in youth is pleasure,

Robert Wever

MOYTURA PRESS • DUBLIN

First published in 1949 by
Jonathan Cape, London

This edition published in 1992 by
Moytura Press, Ormond Court,
11 Lower Ormond Quay, Dublin 1.

© Benedict Kiely 1992

BRITISH LIBRARY CATALOGUING IN PUBLICATION DATA

A catalogue record for this book
is available from the British Library.

ISBN 1-871305-09-8

Printed in Ireland by
Colour Books Ltd, Dublin

Contents

In memory of
PHILIP ROONEY

Introduction

Three young men, in this novel, in an Ulster town in the year before the Second World War began, or blew up, walk past an old mansion that is to be taken over by the British troops. Those young men sense, "the end of something, the beginning of change in their world as they had known it, a wind sharper than the wind of early Spring and blowing from some unknown place, beyond Ulster, beyond Ireland, beyond Britain and mighty London."

For that old mansion I had vaguely, in my mind Knocknamoe Castle just outside Omagh, a house more than a century old, where the Campbell family lived, in my time thereabouts, and which is now an hotel. In the years after Pearl harbour it was taken over by the U.S. Army and in one of its rooms Eisenhower and Montgomery are said to have met, and discussed something or other, on the eve of D-day.

Pat Rafferty, at home on his father's farm, thinks that if "you listened carefully you could hear, through that green Spring silence, the movement of life over there, a restless giant turning in his sleep." Even the Bear Mullan and Joe Keenan, in their hideout in an abandoned haunted house, fear that someday, they will hear the crash of falling trees, the roar of military lorries and the blaring of bugles: "Something was happening to the world when even a ghost could not be sure of his peace".

Something certainly was happening to the world. Leaving school (secondary) in the late 1930s had about it an extra-special feeling of finality. But Keenan's wish to survive the ancient (imaginary) guns around and to blow the town to hell was what so many young people were to feel, and say, with increasing emphasis in the postwar period and, more particularly, over the last twenty years.

In the beginning I had meant to call this novel "Echoing Green", borrowing the title from William Blake. But Cecil Day-Lewis had used that title for an anthology of verse for young people and Jonathan Cape pointed out to me that while there was no copyright in such (quoted) titles, it was also true that two books with the same title did not help each other in the bookshops. So a friend opened at Random the Oxford Book of English Verse (Quiller-Couch) and came on The Wever poem: which is sometimes attributed to nobody in particular. That fine writer Denton Welch whose youth was marred by tragedy, was to take a title for a book out of the same verse: "In Youth Is Pleasure".

This forty-three years ago, was my second novel and my fourth book: and my first personal experience of the Dublin Censorship of Publications. It was adjudged to be, in the phrase that was, at that time, scattered far and wide and frequently: "In general tendency indecent or obscene." Pamela Hansford Johnson, who was rather nice about it in some London review, thought that it would make pleasant reading for a sixteen-year old girl. And at the same time as it was banned in the mostly Catholic Twenty-six Counties of Ireland it was reprinted in London by Christina Foyles Catholic Book Club. Are you right there, Martin, are you right?

One of the comicalities of the blanket-censorship of that time was that you could begin to feel there was something wrong with you if you were not banned. Everybody else, almost, native and foreign, was banned: and I can think of only three or four worthwhile Irish writers who were not. One of them, I feel, escaped only because The Censors did not realise that he was in a way, writing about them. The novelist I refer to was Francis MacManus and his study of the perverted, agonised spinster in, "The Fire in the Dust".

Yet, while being on the banned list could make you feel that you belonged to the best club, you had to pay for your privileges. You lost money, And back at home in rural places the old people assumed that you had taken to destroying young girls and/or running away with other mens' wives. Irish writes were supposed to have a name for that class of carry-on all the way back to Eoghan Rua O Suilleabhain: who wasn't so bad because he did it long ago and in Irish. Or through the medium.

At the time of the publication and censoring of this book I was employed as a leader writer on a Dublin daily newspaper never notable for its red, revolutionary opinions. When I joined the staff a colleague said to me: "You have two topics. One is Godless Russia. The other is the Ratepayers' Burden. Any given night write three hundred words on one or the other. Entitle the result what you like. But, for God's sake, do not come to any conclusion about anything."

In addition to shaping public opinion in that fierce fashion I also wrote theatre notes above my initials. The two previous theatre critics, David Sears and Niall Carroll, had been, as Niall cheerfully said to me: "Shot down for Communism." They had, that is, been over-zealous in their agitations for the National Union of Journalists. Even more cheerfully Niall was later, when my turn came, to say to me: "But you were shot down for filth."

To be fair to the editor and the management I could see their point. A man on their staff, a leader writer, an authority on Godless Russia and the Ratepayers' Burden, a critic of the theatre, had written what the Censors said was a dirty book. So they quickly stopped asking me to go to the theatre.

When I asked the editor (a decent man whose one worldly ambition was to get a papal honour before he died) if my demise as a theatre critic was because of the banned book, he said: No. But later he told me, more in sorrow than in anger, for he had a genuine concern for me, that he couldn't give the book to his wife to read. This amazed me as it may amaze and/or amuse you if you persist in reading to the end.

But he was, as I have said, a fair man, and he compromised: I could continue to write the theatre notes if I did not use my initials at the end of them. This, for obvious reasons, I preferred not to do. It did, too, seem comical that a man who had written a dirty book could still be trusted to write anonymously about Godless Russia and the Ratepayers' Burden. There was, too, some question about a play that I had praised for the force of its language, and so many pious Dublin people had written in so many protesting letters that the editor told me quite genuinely that he wouldn't print them, or even show them to me, in case I'd be upset. Little did he know the hardened scoundrel who stood before him. The play in question was Farquhar's, "The Recruiting Officer".

The editor then said to me, almost in these words and my memory is fairly good: "Suppose you go to a play in which, in the back of a motorcar, a middleaged man puts his hand up a young girl's clothes. If you praise the play I will have letters of protest. If you condemn the play I'll be told you're a hypocrite because you put just that into your novel."

No doubt about it, that was a dilemma. He suggested another compromise: if I saw a play that seemed morally doubtful then I should mention the matter to him before I wrote the review. So we went on, until I left that newspaper and went elsewhere: although that modus operandi, or scribendi, did lead to one comic discussion over Donald Wolfits presentation, in the Gaiety Theatre, of Ben Jonson's "Volpone". During which, and at the attempted-rape scene, an outraged father herded his two handsome daughters out of the theatre. They were, obviously, a lot less shocked than was Papa.

So I told my good editor what had happened and, to the best of my ability, tried to explain who and what Ben Jonson had been. He said: "Yes, A classic. Compress him into a paragraph." So at his request Ben Kiely compressed Ben Jonson, who was himself skilled in compression, into a paragraph.

Aodh de Blacam, or Hugh Blackham, a scholar and a gentleman, an Ulster man and proud of it, a convert to Irish nationalism, the Irish language and the Roman Catholic Religion, once said proudly that no Ulster writer had ever been banned by the Censorship. This novel gave me the doubtful distinction of being the first.

It all seems so comic and so far away. That seduction under the bridge seems, as the poor slavey said about her unexpected baby, to be only a weeshy little seduction. But censorship was not so comic at that time. It was an annoyance to Irish writers and an even greater annoyance to Irish librarians who were trying to promote Irish writers. The type of mind that created such absurdity is still with us, and with everybody else. The ultimate in censorship may be the bomb in the street just because somebody wants to make a political point. On the other hand, I grow weary when I hear, as I once did on a BBC programme, that Censorship in the Twentysix Counties was on of the causes of the troubles in the Six. Or Contraception or the lack of it: an odd double-negative. Never did I hear that the Orange lodges were great promoters of Irish literature. Nor the Queen's paratroopers.

It was, naturally, a different world in a northern town before

1939. As it was everywhere else.

As for this novel: Too many people in my own hometown (and, as towns go, it was and is a tolerant place) identified, quite wrongly, people and places described in these pages. A legal friend said to me, in jest, that, in Fiddis and his misdeeds, every lawyer in the town thought that I meant him.

Fiddis, by the way, in so far as he was a politician at all, would have been an Irish nationalist of the old style: and cynical at that. Who, in those days, could have foreseen John Hume or Gerry Fitt or Seamus Malin or Austin Currie and/or the Alliance Party. Ian Paisley had been there for a long time.

But then, in Belfast, a young girl could still go shopping without having her legs blown off. The stagnant pool had not been stirred. Not all the wise warnings, much later, of Fitt and Hume and others, as to what might one day happen could make Westminster turn and look, "towards the way of the North : and behold on the north-side of the gate of the altar the idol of jealousy in the very entry."

There still was an Empire then, and the old stupid arrogance, and still some money, to underwrite it.

The ornamental sentries, toy-soldiers, no longer parade in that way outside the Courthouse. The sentry at the gate of the barracks could not muster a smile if you gave him in a package deal, Brigitte Bardot, the crown jewels, and the right numbers for the lottery. The towny boys no longer play soccer in the Soldiers' Holm. But even then the ancient sword that the boys found in the river was, as swords are, the symbol of violence, and they, as they rescue it from the water, know all about revolvers, and R.U.C. raids, and documents and illegal organisations.

It seems odd now to realise that Fiddis who had everything of that sort, did not have colour-television. It wasn't there.

The old monsignor and his attitude towards Sean O'Casey, something I reported verbatim, may seem a long ways away from the contemporary Dublin theatre-festival.

The Campbell family (by no means the above-mentioned) lighted gas-lamps when they sat down to table in the evening. And out on the streets a lamp-lighter did his rounds.

The young people had not travelled much beyond Bundoran or Belfast or Dublin. Fairdays were still fairdays. The horse-and-trap and bicycle were still as much in use as the automobile.

Now I remember that about the time this novel was first published a German refugee from the Nazi's said to me that, outside Ireland, the world was a madhouse. If I knew where he was now I'd ask him again for his opinion.

1

A Moment

WHEN the photograph was taken the little red- faced photographer came so suddenly from the shelter of his black cloth that the fifty-nine boys laughed simultaneously. Still laughing the thirteen boys who had squatted cross-legged on the thin strip of matting jumped to their feet. Still laughing the sixteen boys who had sat on chairs stood up, balanced the chairs on their oiled and carefully-combed heads, went up with them through the sloping garden from the tennis-court to the schoolhouse. The eighteen boys who had stood on the ground put on their jackets over the white shirts that were part of the school-choir uniform. They were big boys. They didn't laugh too easily. Six of them had broken voices and long trousers and didn't sing with the choir any more. They were there merely to balance the photograph.

And the twelve boys who had—standing elevated on the wooden forms—made up the back row, carried the forms up the garden, tugged and shouted and pushed each other, fell once on the green grass at the edge of the path, then saw the frown of the supervising Christian Brother and went the rest of the way in disciplined quietness.

Next week the photograph was developed: fifty-nine boys in four rows, fifty-nine boys in white shirts, black pants and black-and-white belts, black stockings with black-and-white tops, fifty- nine boys smiling mechanically at the camera. Behind them was a high wall and a green hedge and thin trees, roofs and high spires seen between the trees: fifty-nine boys who had gone up through the garden from the tennis-court to the schoolhouse, down through the empty playground and a narrow laneway from the schoolhouse to the town, out along the streets of the town and the

1

roads around the town, and, after a few years, out from the town over the roads of the world. But a fading, unframed photograph in the shop of the little red-faced photographer held for ever that moment of mechanical smiles. For that one moment the movement of time and the wheeling of the world had stopped dead in the tennis-court at the foot of the sloping garden. A little man with a red face had that moment in fifty-nine lives for ever in his power.

But he had no power over the things that happened afterwards, over the ways they went home through the coloured evening, over the homes they went to, over the homes they left a few years later like a flock of birds separating and whirring off every way into the air.

Fifty-nine boys, and a single moment on a quiet evening, and fifty-nine lives continuing, and some staying for ever in that town, and more going out into other places, and little news of some of them ever returning, and peace ending, and the world at war, and some of them dead or drowned in strange spots far away from the tennis-court and the garden and the playground and the high wall, and the green hedge and the trees, and the spires and the roofs seen between the trees, and the happy moment when the black cloth was flung aside and a little red face and tousled hair set the small boys laughing like silver.

2

Murder

I

THAT evening there was a crowd waiting outside the court-house. A man had murdered his wife at a place eight miles outside the town. Coming down the playground Gerry Campbell said the man was guilty and would be hanged. Jim Collins said the man had been tried twice already, the second time in Belfast, and each time the jury had disagreed, and how the hell did Gerry Campbell know better than two juries that couldn't make up their minds either one way or the other? Then there was an ugly moment of argument where the narrow gate in the grey wall of the playground opened out to the narrow lane. The boys gathered around, interested and afraid. Gerry Campbell didn't like Jim Collins and Jim Collins didn't like Gerry Campbell, and they were both big fellows with broken voices, and the whole school felt that some day for some excuse or any excuse they would come to blows.

They might have fought that evening to find out whether the man had or had not killed his wife. But big Pat Rafferty came down the playground wheeling his bicycle according to the regulation that said no cycling until you were through the gateway and out safely into the lane. Big Pat had a broken voice, and nailed boots, and a fist like the head of a sledge, and nearly six feet of hard bone and sinewy flesh, and a gentle face, and black hair that stood up straight and stiff like the prickles on a hedgehog. He pushed his way through the crowd, using the front wheel of his bicycle as offensive weapon.

He said: "What's the row about?" A dozen voices told him. Jim Collins and Gerry Campbell stated their theories and appealed to him for support.

Pat said: "The whole country out our way says he's guilty. He only lives across the river from us, the first farm below the stepping-stones. But no jury will ever convict him."

Jim Collins said: "There were extenuating circumstances," and a thin voice in the crowd called jeeringly: "Who ate the dictionary?"

Gerry Campbell said: "Murder is murder, any day of the week."

"Anyway," big Pat said, "fighting here won't hang him or acquit him. I know him well. The man's all right only a wee bit odd. They say out our way he had a lot o' trouble."

His superior knowledge and height and weight led the crowd down the narrow lane to the street. He led them up the slope of Tower Street, past the talking women at the door of Smith's shop, past the smell of the piggeries oozing up the dark entry of Duncan's yard and the smell of herrings from the barrels and cases in Gallagher's. The small boys held their nostrils and groaned and walked with affected indications of suffering. Above them on the hill were the ruins of the old tower, and higher than the ruins the walls and spires of the church. He wheeled his bicycle, and Gerry Campbell walked on his right and Jim Collins walked on his left, and they went down Wood Street to the place where the crowd was waiting outside the courthouse.

The ground was soft with sawdust that deadened the sounds of feet and hooves and wheels, and deepened the silence around the solemn slow mysteries of law and trial and judgment. High up in the great wall was the statue of a judge, his stone wig white with bird-droppings. The spring sunshine slanted across the high windows that gave light to the public gallery. They pushed their way through the waiting, casually-chatting crowd, round the corner of the building into the Diamond where they could look up at the great pillars guarding the entrance, and down through the Diamond into High Street and the long straggling town, and shops and monuments and moving traffic, and the distant piled greenness of trees with the red-brick of the County Hospital showing among them like a patch of flame. Two soldiers walked up and down on the path at the foot of the pillars, nine steps away from each other and then nine steps towards each other. Their nailed boots on the pavement were painfully audible in the saw-dusted silence. Their shining fixed bayonets were at the same time a protection and a challenge to the slow majesty of law. The voices of the crowd were hushed by their

4

nearness to that heated, hidden room where bewigged men talked wearily around the puzzled, grey-headed man whose home was only across the river from the home of big Pat Rafferty.

"I'd like to hear what they're at," said Gerry Campbell.

"You wouldn't get in there," said Jim Collins.

"Anybody with long trousers gets in," said little Chris Collins, looking enviously at the six, long, cloth-covered legs of Jim and Gerry and Pat. Gerry Campbell said: "We got in before. The time the two brothers put the water bailiff into the river. And the time the wee daft girl prosecuted the fellow, and he had half the boys in his townland to witness that it wasn't him."

A man in the crowd said: "They cleared the court this morning. The jury are out this long while."

"They'll never hang him," big Pat said. "My uncle that lives on the far side of the water was a witness for the defence."

The crowd moved, pressing closer to the marching sentries and the pavement at the foot of the pillars. The murmur of voices rose suddenly higher. Black-uniformed policemen formed a square under the pillars and around the court-house door, pushed their way through the crowd and cleared a laneway across the street to the door of the police barracks. The murmur of voices died as suddenly as it had risen and there was a terrible, waiting silence. Above them the court-house clock struck five slow strokes. The sunshine moved away from the high windows. The sentries ceased marching and stood stiffly to attention, as if the sound of their nailed boots had been devoured by the ravenous silence. Only far away in the High Street was the noise of traffic and the movement of life.

Then abruptly the quietness cracked. Around the corner in Wood Street a motor engine roared, and a woman on the edge of the crowd cried piercingly: "The dirty blackguard. They've slipped him out the side door." The cordon of black policemen was laughing without restraint at the disappointed crowd, and, above brown uniforms, the sun-tanned faces of the sentries creased in smiles. The crowd moved, rushing around the corner, crushing into the narrowness of Wood Street. A shawled, toothless woman stumbled and fell, grabbed in her falling at the tails of Tom Nixon the grocer's black coat, tumbled him with her on the dry sawdust. The crowd cleared a circle and laughed at the discomfiture of the respectable grocer, at the vision of unattractive underclothing displayed by the woman as she was helped awkwardly to her feet. The car was gone from the side door of the court-house.

Somebody said, a voice loud in the disappointed silence: "He's half way to Derry by this time. The bloody murderer."

"No murderer," a policeman said. "They disagreed again."

"Jaminty God," Tom Nixon said, brushing the sawdust from his clothes, "the twelve of them between them couldn't hang a picture."

The crowd laughed. Commenting voices spoke suddenly from every corner of the gathering.

"Disagreed again. Then he's a free man. . . ."

"Sure the two Crawfords should never "a" been on the same jury. They couldn't agree about anything. . . ."

"If ever a murderer missed hanging. . . ."

"Maybe he's innocent. . . ."

"Innocent me backside. . . ."

"He's a free man anyway. As free as you or me, Mr. Nixon. . . ."

Tom Nixon said: "That wouldn't be hard."

The crowd shouted. But there was no knowing whether it was a shout of anger for a dead woman unavenged, or a shout of joy for a grey-headed man sitting between two policemen in the back of a motor car, driving towards freedom with his own memories in a farmhouse across the water from the home of big Pat Rafferty. The shout trickled out in a few isolated voices, like the last bursts of floodwater going down a river. The crowd cracked into groups, melted away down the Diamond, or up Wood Street, or along the flat curves of Devlin Street.

"There'll be rejoicing out our way," big Pat said. "The poor man, they say, had a hard life." He threw his long, right leg over the saddle of his bicycle, his strong left boot still steady on the ground. He said: "So long boys. I've eight miles before me."

They watched him free-wheeling recklessly down the Diamond. Then Gerry Campbell went walking down the slope and Jim Collins turned right along Devlin Street. They didn't speak to each other.

II

The sound of the great sliding-door of the garage being slowly closed was, every evening, the signal for the Campbell family to sit

6

down to tea. Old Campbell was a man of regular habits and when the two hired mechanics were closing the door he was always half way up the stairs that ascended from the back of the garage to the ground floor of the dwelling-house; and, always, when he entered the dining-room his two sons and his two daughters were seated impatiently at the table and his sister solemnly pouring out the tea. The presence of visitors only meant that there were more people sitting at the table and that Jinny, the maid, was fussily interfering with Aunt Aggie's slow solemnity. That evening there were two visitors and everybody, even Aunt Aggie who always said the cinema and the Sunday papers would bring the curse of God on the rising generation, was talking about the murder trial. One of the two visitors was a tall lean, dark-haired, dark-faced priest, home on holidays from a parish in California. He listened patiently to Aunt Aggie saying she didn't know what the world was coming to. He said: "'Tis little we know about the world here in Ireland." He savoured slowly the first sip of tea. "Outside this country," he said, "the world is under a shadow. The world's a mad-house."

The second visitor was Fiddis the solicitor, and because Fiddis was a travelled man he smiled the smile of a man hoarding mysterious and mischievous knowledge. His eyes moved around the ring of faces at the table, lingered for an appreciative moment on the sun-tanned face and graceful breasts of May Campbell; and he smiled, maybe at Aunt Aggie or maybe at the priest from California.

His voice was soft and patient and tired, like a silk dress rustling around slowly-moving limbs: "I suppose, Father, a murder more or less wouldn't be noticed in the United States." "Would you believe it," said the priest, "there are people out there and murder is the main part of their business?"

"There's some I could name in this town," said Aunt Aggie, "would be at it if they could." She compressed her lips, shook her head with the air of a woman restraining herself with effort and for the highest motives. Her sallow hairy face always looked comic to her nephews and nieces when she did that. May and Dympna and Gerry and little Dinny laughed suddenly, suppressed their laughter hurriedly when the priest began to speak.

"I'll give you a concrete example," he said, "and it's not a million miles from our presbytery. What they call out there a roadhouse.

Well, a man goes in and sits down to have a drink, and no sooner is he sitting than a strap of a girl sits down beside him and says "Hi, bud."

"The young women of the present day," said Aunt Aggie, "are not what young women should be to be pleasing to God."

"If the man's foolish enough he'll answer "'Hi, babe" and they get friendly. When he's ready to go, she's ready to go, except that she says her jealous boy friend is waiting with a gun outside the front door. So she points to the back door and asks him to wait outside."

Across the street one of the town's small dissenting congregations began its nightly public meeting with a rousing hymn. The words tramped, a procession of militant Christians, through the open window behind Aunt Aggie: "Everybody ought to love him, everybody everywhere." Dinny's feet, high above the floor, began to move like pendulums to the rhythm of the music, his small mouth puckered and began to whistle. He said: "Bishop Thompson the butcher gives free meat to the Hamiltons because they go to his Sunday school." Across the table Dympna laughed and Gerry laughed and Fiddis the solicitor smiled, but May nudged Dinny, and old Campbell said: "Quiet, boy," and Aunt Aggie said: "Mind your manners, Dinny."

The words kept marching, an army of the saved ignoring the delightful dangers of talkative girls in Californian roadhouses, passing on through an Ulster town to the everlasting brightness of the celestial city.

"No sooner is the fool of a man out the backdoor than something clips him behind the ear, and if he ever wakes up it'll be in a ditch miles away—robbed of every cent." "The moral," said Fiddis, "is not to go out the back-door."

"The moral," said Aunt Aggie, "is not to go in the front."

"Well said, Miss Campbell," said the priest.

"You don't want to mind Mr. Fiddis," said old Campbell to the priest. "He'll have his wee joke about everything."

"Joke," said Aunt Aggie, with mock indignation "The views of that man and his opinions are enough to bring brimstone on this town." "The town is safe," Fiddis smiled, "while you're here, Miss Campbell. If you'd been alive then, the Lord would have spared Sodom and Gomorrah for your sake."

8

He relaxed his wide, neatly-clothed shoulders against the back of his chair. He wiped his rimless glasses with the coloured silk handkerchief out of his breast-pocket, and smiled slowly at Aunt Aggie the smile of a man who knows how well slow smiles become a handsome face as yet untouched by the first frost of age.

"If you were the Lord you'd spare everybody," old Campbell bellowed laughingly.

"Didn't he try to argue down my throat," said Aunt Aggie, "that old Maxwell was right to murder his wife?"

Fiddis raised a restraining right hand. "Now, now, the court has this day acquitted the man."

Gerry said: "A fellow called Rafferty who goes to school with me lives near the place where the man murdered his wife."

His sister May was suddenly thoughtful, her neat white hands, her neatly-manicured nails resting quietly on the table. She asked: "That's the big black-headed boy who stands in the door of Kerrigan's gramophone shop listening to the girl playing the new records?"

"That's him." Gerry was enthusiastic. "He picks up all the new songs that way. He's the strongest fellow in the school. He can hold a bicycle out straight in his hand . . . like that." He demonstrated, extending his right arm at right angles to his body.

"Strength and a love of music," said Fiddis, "should go well together."

The remark meant nothing. It was meant to mean nothing, and, in the silence that followed, the words of another revivalist hymn could be heard marching, Onward, Christian Soldiers, across the darkening street.

Aunt Aggie said: "Jinny, pull across the curtains and put a match to the gas."

"The evenings are drawing in already," old Campbell said, "and the Summer hardly over."

"It wasn't much of a summer," May said. She was thinking of the strong, dark-headed fellow standing in the door of the gramophone shop and listening to the music. Her thoughts were not clinging or tender, but she liked music and she admired strength, whether it was strength of mind or body or of worldly position.

She said: "I love the summer."

"The autumn's nice too," said Dympna.

"The colours of the fields and trees are loveliest in the autumn," the priest said.

Little Dinny said: "My birthday's in the autumn."

Old Campbell said: "I used to like the autumn when I was young." His heavy, double-chinned face was grey in the gaslight, his eyes restful with memories.

Little Dinny had been born in the autumn. His mother had died in the autumn. Success was there and the biggest garage in the town, and four fine children, and Aunt Aggie, tall and ugly and pre-destined to live and die unmarried, to rule the house. But the yellow-and-gold autumns were not beautiful any more.

Little Dinny asked: "Aunt Aggie, may I ask Chris Collins to my birthday party?"

"You may not," Gerry said.

Dinny's white head and blue eyes were defiant. "I asked Aunt Aggie. Not you."

"Aunt Aggie wouldn't let people like that near this house."

"Chris Collins is my pal."

"I don't think much of your pals."

The voice of the priest was smooth with pacification.

"The Collins family," he said, "seems to be a controversial topic."

"They're all right," Dympna said, "only Jim Collins beat Gerry in an examination."

"That's a lie," Gerry said.

Aunt Aggie's knuckles sharply rapped the table.

"Children," she said. The rising roar of a preacher echoed across the street. "The Collinses are excellent," she said, "in their own place, and that's the British army. But they belong to Barrack Lane and not to High Street. They're what we call here, Father, the leavings of the militia. The sons, all except two, are privates in the army. The father was a private in the army. His father was a private in the army. All the uncles were privates in the army."

"And all the aunts took in washing," said Fiddis.

"Or worse," he added, half to himself.

From anyone less distinguished than Fiddis, the solicitor, Aunt Aggie would have resented the interruption. Instead she smiled stiffly and said: "He's off again."

"Maybe it wasn't such a terrible thing to belong to the British army," he said. "Maybe some day soon we'll be glad of the British army."

"Over in the States," the priest said, "we think that if Hitler starts he'll take a lot of stopping. The dough-boys will be needed again."

"It's a long way from here to the States," Fiddis said.

Aunt Aggie said: "There'll never be another war."

"It wouldn't. help the motor business," reflected old Campbell.

"It wouldn't help anything, much," Fiddis said.

An engine hummed in the garage where behind the closed doors a mechanic was working late. Across the street the holy people, the Christian soldiers, were singing their last hymn. Fiddis rested the tips of the fingers of his right hand against the tips of the fingers of his left hand, scratched his high forehead with the joined fore-fingers. His fingers were long and white, and square at the tips. War, if the world came again to war, wouldn't help anything or any place or any person: a little village that he remembered in the English Cotswolds; a forgotten medieval corner of gallant Paris; a narrow street in a German town where the air was always in motion with the chiming of ancient bells; his own town, lazy, sprawling streets, six thousand peaceful people living by a shallow river in a quiet Irish valley.

He raised his teacup and said: "Here's to peace."

The shadows were thickening in the street, the darkness gathering over the houses as the darkness was, maybe, gathering over the world.

"You could drink to a good cause in a better drink," said Aunt Aggie. She stood up to her full tottering height. She was as tall and thin as a hungry witch. She walked to the fireplace and tugged determinedly at the enamelled bell-pull. When the door opened she said: "Jinny, the drink," and before Jinny had fussed back again with the two bottles, amber for whisky and dark red for wine, she said: "Now children, your homework."

She didn't pour the drink until the door had closed behind the vanishing children: Dinny and Dympna and fair-headed Gerry.

III

Fiddis the solicitor walked home through the quiet deserted streets of the town. He had taken more than enough of Aunt Aggie's tremendous whiskies, but he wasn't drunk. He had been hilarious in seven capital cities, in Dublin, London, Paris, Madrid, Rome, Berlin and Warsaw, but he had never once been drunk or sick or obstreperous. The fact that he could remember the names of the seven cities in which he had been hilarious was a sure proof that he was as sober as a judge. Fiddis the solicitor was as sober as a judge.

He stood for a while on the edge of the footpath, his back to the closed doors of one of the town's two cinemas, looking across the street at the three lighted windows in Mrs. Graham's hotel. One of the three lighted windows was in one of the bedrooms on the second floor. That meant that somebody was going to bed, or sitting reading in bed, or . . . in Mrs. Graham's hotel a lighted window or an unlighted window might mean anything. Two of the three lighted windows were beside each other on the first floor, and that meant that Mrs. Graham had a friend or friends in, still drinking or card-playing or doing any of the interesting things permissible under a roof that like God's sky arched indifferently over the just and the unjust.

If he crossed the street, opened the door with one of the keys always provided for Mrs. Graham's special friends, went through the darkened lounge-hall and up the wide stairway, he would—he knew—be made very welcome. Alice Graham would take both his hands, would possibly embrace him, her painted face becoming alive with genuine joy, her voice, a little husky with gin, saying: "Bernard. You look younger every day. You make me feel like an old hag. Why don't you drop in more often? You're one of the few bright spots in this Holy Mary of a town." Rocking backwards and forwards on the edge of the pavement he calmly considered the prospect. There was, mind you, a lot to be said for Alice Graham. She had a good heart. He knew that, because he had been her friend ever since the day she had arrived in the town, coming from the wicked world in which, according to rumour, she had left three divorced husbands. She had a good head, because in spite of that initial rumour about the husbands, and in spite of other rumours that later accumulated about the goings-on in the hotel, she had made a very solid financial success of the place. She drank too much and she smoked too much and she painted too much, but her tall body was still very attractive. For the prudent men of a prudent town, the way she walked and the way she dressed, the good perfume she used and the gin she drank were all challenges waving like flags above a gateway that opened into another world. But she chose her intimate friends carefully, and avoided prudent men as they prudently avoided her.

Fiddis crossed the street and stood for a moment fingering in his pocket the key that would open the door. Then he changed his mind and walked on along the footpath towards his own home. There was nobody on the street to notice the peculiarity of his conduct, the hesitating way he walked, his halts to stand looking up vacantly at the vacant night or to stand, leaning on his silver-topped walking-stick, looking into some lightless shop-window. Tonight he was not in the least attracted by Alice Graham. The smell of perfume, the sweet smell of gin would have sickened his soul dreaming of fresh beauty as lovely as a rose after light rain. A painted cheek would only have set him more madly desiring to touch a cheek shaped perfectly and innocent of everything but the sweet colour of life, or an arm bare to the elbow and resting on the edge of her father's table, or white fingers playing with the little cross that hung on a chain around her neck.

He crossed a bridge over the shallow, whispering river, went along a wide road lined with high houses until he came to the northern limits of the town. Ahead of him and behind him the long road was deserted. The sound of his feet on the pavement was solitary and forlorn. He was man, respectable man, as lonely as the soul is lonely, walking quietly through the darkness to the quiet of his own monotonous home; civilized man walking modestly in suburban roads and dreaming of holy valour or unholy violence and hoping for something to happen; for the wind in the trees to become suddenly the voice of God, for all the silent windows to fly open and scream to the night about secret loves and hates.

North of the town and beyond the last of the high houses the road forked. Fiddis turned to the left, crossed an old stone bridge that arched humpily over the twisting river, turned again to the left along a dusty by-road, walked twenty yards to the wide, white gate of his own garden. The house faced to the south, looking over the river and towards the town and beyond the town to the lazy, blue curves of the mountains. With the light of day you could look down a steep, tree-covered slope, could follow with the eye the river bending

13

through the flat, green fields and vanishing into the grey blur of the houses. But in the darkness there was only the sound of his feet crunching on the gravel of the avenue, the sound of the wind, the voice of God, moving in the trees, the sound of the river far below rattling musically over the shallows. The avenue curved, almost completing a semicircle, to the wide, flat steps leading up to the door. The back of the house towered solemnly above the by-road.

He tiptoed, carefully avoiding the furniture, across the wide hallway, and as softly as possible up the creaking stairs. Judy, his housekeeper, disapproved of late hours and of steps that moved unsteadily. She knew her place better than to shape her disapproval in words, but her little circular nervous face would bunch and harden like a clenched fist. Judy had worked for his parents. Judy had known him in short pants; and, although most of the time she annoyed him intensely, he respected her and preserved her as he considered the civilized man should respect and preserve all established traditions. In his own room, with his books and his prints of good pictures and his radiogram and his gramophone records, he was safe from the disapproval of Judy, safe from the influence of the town in which, half unwillingly, his life had been lived. Still, he kept his diary securely under lock and key. It always struck him as particularly appropriate that the key to the lock of the drawer in which he kept the accumulating black-bound folio pages should be neighbour on his ring to the key that opened the door of Alice Graham's hotel. There were three ways of escaping from the town and from his life in the town: escape by going on a journey, escape by seeking the society of Alice Graham, escape into this room to the careful writing of the things he thought and the things he did. With the one exception of Alice Graham, those pages would have scandalized the population of the town. It was old-fashioned, he knew, keeping a diary, like a model husband in the seventeenth century writing the log-book of his hidden infidelities. It was, possibly, even more old-fashioned than thinking all the time, from morning to night, until thought was a vicious burr sticking to the soul, of a girl nearly twenty years younger than himself.

He wrote: "Tonight I had tea with the Campbell family. A prosperous household. That big, stolid, red-faced man must have made thousands out of the garage business. He's worried now about the possibility of another war. Thinks it might seriously affect

14

supplies of petrol for civilians. I suppose he knows what he's talking about. His bank-balance is there to prove that he's not as stupid as he looks. He hasn't much to complain about. Prosperity, and no loneliness in his life. There was another visitor there, a priest from California, some relation of the dead Mrs. Campbell. Telling us all about the big bad world. And, of course, we talked about the Maxwell murder trial. For weeks the whole town has been talking about that—the boil bursting out on the smooth skin of our quiet even lives. I wonder where on the body will the next boil burst out, and when will it happen, and will it be a murder or a robbery or a baby begotten on the wrong side of the blanket? Old Campbell's family are growing up. The eldest is a fine-looking young woman, just twenty and called after her mother. . . ."

He stopped writing, screwed the cap on his fountain pen, a desperate firmness in his large capable hands. He could not write down the eleven letters that made her name. If he wrote it once he might go on writing it, line after line, page after page, like a young boy in first love or a poet scrawling some woman's name in every one of his poems. He dreaded that possibility, as the respectable man would dread the degradation of indecent exposure. This germ in his blood, this worm in his bones had this night already closed against him one of his paths of escape. He could not allow it to close another, to threaten his security here in this room above the tall trees and the winding river. The whispers that would go from lip to lip through the town, giving a new malicious life to the old grey walls!

He closed the book with a bang. The early saints had fled praying into the desert. His head was bowed, his face hidden in his cupped hands, but his mouth was hot with prayers prayed in the ancient world, before the saints had fled from the pleasures that the world offered.

IV

The boys at school called Chris Collins the cricket. He was thirteen years of age. He was small for his age: thin, bony wrists blotched with large, pale-brown freckles, thin legs that when he ran flickered like thirty legs, a small, snub-nosed, freckled face, a shock of reckless, red hair. But his thin legs could run faster and his bony knuckles hit harder than the legs or knuckles of any boy up to the age of fifteen.

He leaned over the parapet of the old humpy bridge to the north of the town and showed Dinny Campbell where the tangled ivy had caught and held the falling body of Eddie Masterson. Dinny's fat placid body struggled, breathing heavily, to the rough top of the parapet. He brushed his white hair off his forehead, widened his blue eyes, looked down at the ivy and far below at the flowing water.

"Only for the ivy," Chris said, "Eddie would 'a' been killed stone dead. He'd 'a' fallen down there." He indicated the water, sparkling into the sunshine, bursting out from the shadow of the arches like springwater leaping from the darkness of the ground, spreading out into a wide, shallow pool rimmed with restful green trees.

"That ivy must be as strong, as strong. Eddie's a big heavy man."

"He's the biggest man in the town except for Paterson the butcher with the greasy apron."

In silence they straddled on the grey stone, contemplating the strong ivy, the flowing water, the peaceful trees.

"Up there Mr. Fiddis lives," Dinny said. "He was in our house last night." Through a gap in the greenery covering ground that rose steeply above a bend of the river they saw the sunshine reflected from a wide window, the blue smoke rising slowly from a thin chimney.

"He has pots o' money," Chris said.

"It's a lovely place to live."

"He's a gas man too. A girl that lives up our way says he followed her up the town one Saturday night and tried to put his arm round her at the big gap where there isn't any light. She says there was an awful smell of drink off his breath."

"Could you heed what a girl would say?"

"I suppose not. Anyway you'd want to be drunk to put your arm around some o' the girls in this town. That's what my brother Jim said."

"You'd want to be drunk to put your arm around any girl," said Dinny; and again in silence they contemplated the ivy, the water and the trees.

Chris leaned out further from his perch on the parapet. He stared down into the shallow pool. He said: "I see a trout." They stared together until Dinny also saw the brown back, darker than the sand but not as dark as the pebbles on the bottom of the pool, the tail moving gently with the motion of the water. "I can see it better," Dinny said, "when it waggles over the bright thing there."

Out of the half-darkness of the shallow river something shone, too bright even for a bright pebble, as bright as silver but much too big, Chris said, to be a silver coin, now shining clearly upwards, now lost for a moment as a wind-shadow thickened the water.

"I'm going to see what it is," Chris said.

They climbed over a barbed-wire fence, slithered down a steep slope to the bank of the river. They took off their shoes and stockings and rolled up the legs of their trousers. A motor lorry panted across the bridge and on up the road away from the town. Standing in the cool water and looking upwards the bridge seemed twice as high, grey with age, draped with dark green ivy, and through the shadowy arches they could look up the river as far as the flash of broken water at the weir and the salmon-leap and the high white walls of a mill. From the level of the water it was no longer possible to see the silver flashing of the object on the bottom of the river, but Chris had exceedingly sharp eyes and a good sense of direction. Half way across the river, the water lipping coolly around his thin bare thighs, he slipped off his jacket and gave it to Dinny to hold, rolled up the sleeves of his shirt, bent down and groped among the sand and pebbles, straightened up again with the object held proudly in his two hands.

Freed from the crystal water and seen in the candid air it no longer glittered like silver. It was a sword, a curved sword with a hilt of intricately twisted metal, scabbard of some black material that was harder than leather and not as hard as wood. With long lying under the water the scabbard had burst in one place to expose several inches of the broad blade, clear enough from rust to have reflected through the glassy water the light of the sun. They looked at it, silently savouring the delight of discovery. Drops of water fell from the twisted hilt and from the dark scabbard.

"What'll we do with it?" Dinny panted.

"Take it home with us. What else?"

"You couldn't walk through the town with that."

"Why not?"

"Everybody'd be after you. And what about the police? It's a weapon. An' we don't know who it belongs to. The owner might claim it."

"If it has an owner he doesn't live in our town. Why didn't he come an' take it out of the river himself? What'd he put it there for anyway? An' by the cut of it, it's in the water for years."

They were unanswerable arguments. Dinny waded slowly back towards the bank, feeling with his toes for the smooth, sandy patches on the bottom. "Anyway," he said, "it's a weapon. We'll have to be careful."

It was a weapon. Chris considered the point as he waded slowly, carrying the weapon, after Dinny. Johnny Hughes that worked in the bakery had got two years in jail because when the constabulary raided his house they had found him in possession of a revolver, a box of ammunition, and documents proving that he was a member of an illegal organisation. Chris remembered the phrases because his brother Jim was the devil for rolling such phrases across the table at the Scottish lodger who was working in McCanny's butcher shop. This thing in his arms was neither a revolver nor a document nor a box of bullets. Still, if it was polished and sharpened you could cut off the head of a man with a swipe and, maybe, the head of the biggest policeman in the barracks with two swipes. There was no doubt about it. It was a weapon.

On the grassy bank they dried their feet with their stockings, then slowly pulled on stockings and laced shoes. Dinny whistled softly to himself. Chris, considering every detail of the problem of concealment, wrinkled his brown face, pulled his laces tightly, knotted them securely. "If I had even a bit of paper," he said.

"Brown paper or white paper?"

"Any colour from pink to puce."

"All the paper in the town wouldn't wrap up that thing."

"A middlin' big bit would do the job."

They stood up, the sword lying between them on the grass. They looked up at the wide window still reflecting in its high place the light of the sun, at the blue smoke still rising gently from the thin chimney.

"Fiddis is the sort of a man," said Dinny, "would have cartloads of paper about the house." Chris stooped to pick up the sword. He said: "You couldn't show him the sword. He's a solicitor."

"A solicitor isn't the same thing as a policeman. An' he wouldn't

18

tell. We'd be safe enough."

"As long as we're not wee girls."

"That's a dirty thing to say, Chris Collins."

"That's what the people say."

"The people should mind their own business. Mr. Fiddis is all right."

"If he's all right for you, he's all right for me," said Chris Collins. He led the way up the steep slope to the road. His thin legs were hard with energy. His brown stockings bunched untidily around his shoes. His thin body could bend and straighten again with astonishing speed, could fit through surprisingly small spaces between threatening strands of barbed wire. He dumped the sword on the grass at the roadside, came back to help Dinny, puffing and panting, up the slope and over the fence. Side by side they walked to Fiddis's gate, through the gate and up to the first bend in the avenue. Then Chris and the sword waited in hiding behind a high laurel bush while Dinny went on up the avenue and pulled the bell-knob beside the front door.

The bell rang, loudly and solemnly, like the swinging bell in the belfry beside the church. Dinny wasn't alarmed by the solemnity of the bell, or the size of the great house towering above him, or the perfection of green lawn and blossoming flower-beds on the terrace above the river. He had seen it all before, doing messages from his father to Mr. Fiddis or from his Aunt Aggie to Judy the housekeeper. Judy frequently had tea with his Aunt Aggie: a small, soft round woman and a thin, yellow, hard woman sipping tea and crunching digestive biscuits and ripping and rending the reputations of everybody in the town. Judy wasn't bad. She gave him apples and gooseberries and tea for his trouble, once in a while. She would give him all the paper he wanted, and wouldn't ask any awkward questions. When he heard the hard heels of a woman's shoes hammering across the hallway he decided that the problem of the sword was as good as solved.

But the tall dark woman who opened the door was certainly not Judy. With his mouth opened to speak he stood wordless, his nostrils filling with the sweet smell of her perfume. The tall, dark woman had never sipped tea or gossiped with his Aunt Aggie. More often than not she had been gossiped about when Judy and Aunt Aggie came together. He knew who she was. He had a vague notion that there was something about her of which Aunt Aggie disapproved, something terrible, for once Aunt Aggie had said that the doings of that woman would bring fire and brimstone on the town. He closed his mouth and backed away from her. Was the smell of burning brimstone strong and sweet like the smell of her perfume? He looked up at her face, her red lips, her red cheeks, her long straight nose, her dark eyes, her high square forehead. Aunt Aggie said once that woman would be a fine house-keeper in hell. Maybe, above the high forehead and hidden by the crimped black hair were the stumps of horns like the horns of the devil. Then she smiled a friendly smile. She put out a thin hand, heavy with rings, and too terrified to move he felt her gently patting his head. She spoke, and her voice was musical and kind and not at all the sort of voice to raise itself above the howling of hell.

She said: "Hallo young Campbell. Looking for somebody?"

His courage returned with a rush. Anyway, Chris, armed with a sword, was waiting behind the hedge. He said: "Is Judy here, Mrs. Graham?"

"Judy's out for the evening," she said. "Wouldn't I do as well?" The words she spoke were shaped differently, slenderly and daintily, from the words spoken by everybody else.

"I was looking for Judy."

"What has Judy got that I haven't got?" She fluffed her hair with her left hand, her wrist gracefully arching. He wasn't annoyed to see that she was laughing at him. It was friendly laughter, and in hell there would be no friendly laughter. "Judy has paper," he said, "for parcels." "Well, if that's all a girl needs nowadays . . ." She waved him into the wide hallway, over grey stone flags and furry rugs, through a door above which long brown antlers were fixed in the wall. His eyes were on the tapering antlers, and he didn't see Mr. Fiddis until he was over the threshold and into the room. Her voice behind him said: "Bernard, a young man wants paper for parcels."

Mr. Fiddis was stretched to his full length on a couch to one side of the wide fireplace. He was dressed as Dinny Campbell had never seen him, or any other man, dressed. In the town, in his office, about the court-house when sessions or assizes were being held, Mr. Fiddis's big body was always smoothly cased in dark cloth, sometimes lightened with a thin pin-stripe; trousers sharply creased, shoes brightly shining, coat always buttoned as it should be buttoned. But here resting above the river, the long legs, the thighs going slightly to superfluous flesh, were covered in loose battered corduroys of a faded green; the shoulders fitted with effort into a white jacket that refused to button across the wide chest; and a red shirt, open as far as it could open, displayed a triangle of white flesh bristling with dark hairs.

He was barefooted. He put his bare feet down slowly on the carpet like a man testing the temperature of a warm, scented bath. His face was different, more friendly, without the rimless glasses that he wore in the town. He ran his left hand backwards from his bald temples, smoothing his hair into place.

"Hallo Dinny," he said. "What do you want to parcel?"

"It's a sword."

"A sword! You're original anyway."

"It's a sword Chris Collins and myself found in the river."

"Maybe it's a swordfish," ventured Mrs. Graham.

"We didn't want to let the police see it."

"Quite right too. Never show anything to the police. That's the advice I always give my clients."

He stood up and stretched himself, his large body, his long arms, right to the square tips of his fingers. He said: "Alice, you know where Judy keeps the paper. Follow us when you get enough to sheathe a sword. Dinny will lead me to it."

Dinny led him to the corner behind the laurel where Chris Collins sheltered with the sword. Mr. Fiddis walked on the smoothly cut grass, protecting his feet from the gravel of the avenue. He drew the sword carefully from its sodden scabbard, held it up in the air, turned his wrist so that the blade, quickly turning, shone in the sun.

"It's a great find," he said. "The rust hasn't got at it yet." He told them how to polish it back to its original brightness, how to repair the scabbard, how to restore the hilt so as not to damage the intricate metal work. He told them the age of the sword and the country of its origin.

"Gee," Chris said, "you know a lot about swords."

"I wish I knew as much," said Dinny.

"You'll learn it all," said Mr. Fiddis, "as you grow older. You'll learn about swords and the people who make them and the people who use them and the people who are afraid of them and the people who are wise enough to have nothing to do with them."

Alice Graham came down the avenue carrying a bundle of newspapers and a handful of twine.

"No brown paper," she said. "Judy must have it under lock and key."

He said: "Judy has her soul under lock and key."

He knelt down on the grass and spread the sheets of newspaper. He read out a headline: "Jury Disagree in Maxwell Trial." "Most appropriate," he said. "The story of a murder in which to wrap the instrument of death." He wrapped the sword in newspaper, making a long, neat parcel, tying it securely with twine. "The symbol of war," he said, "to be carried by two boys through a peaceful town." The two boys and the tall dark woman watched and listened. He handed the parcel to Chris Collins. "Some day," he said, "when we all have time you must come and see my collection of swords."

Standing with Alice Graham he watched the two boys walking away down the avenue. They were proud. They were grateful.

"How the sword got into the river," she said, "is another question."

"Easy to answer. It's from my collection. You remember the burglary, when I was on holidays."

"The same fellow that robbed the boxes in the church."

"The very same. The only son of a good family, poor fellow. He didn't get much here. Some loose cash and a few ornaments and that sword. Apparently he didn't like the sword."

"And you let those boys keep it?"

"I give it to them. As a gift to youth. They'll never know they had a benefactor. The young never do."

"You're a fool."

He put his arm around her waist, teasingly pressed her ribs. "Alice, from Caledonia stern and wild.

Would you ruin all the joy of their discovery?"

"You're a fool."

But going up the steps to the door she caught his right hand and pulled his right arm more tightly around her waist.

V

Jim Collins was upstairs in his bedroom at the back of the house when he heard the postman battering at the front door. He bundled his blue-and-white jersey, his knickers, boots, shin guards, and a towel into an old battered brown bag that had belonged to his uncle Harry who, for six years of his life, had been a commercial traveller. Jim was proud of the brown bag. It was a handy thing to have, and, like a head of black hair well-oiled and parted up the middle, it made one really look like a footballer. Sitting on the edge of his bed and squaring himself before the small mirror, with comb in one hand and brush in the other, he assured himself that the parting was exactly as it should be. Then he rested himself, his feet on the window-sill, and looked out of the window at the weather.

It was a grand day for a game: no wind, no glaring sunshine, the pitch would be as smooth as a billiard-table and as dry as a bone. That pitch, too, with the river looping all around it, needed dry weather. After a rainy week a fellow would need a life-belt there, and the ball would stick fast in the mud defying the force of the strongest and most accurate kicks. The game began at four o'clock. His mother was opening the door for the postman and the afternoon post came at three o'clock. He could walk to the field in fifteen minutes, and, allowing for fifteen minutes in the pavilion, he had a whole half-hour for relaxation, easing the muscles, steadying the nerves. The soldiers had a tough team this year.

He looked out, across the backyard and a patch of brown wasteground spotted with sparse grass, at the grey gable-end of a row of houses built at right-angles to the row in which he lived. On the smooth concrete of the gable-wall a small, broad-shouldered youth with unkempt dark hair was drawing something with soft black charcoal. A tall, thin youth with stooping-shoulders was holding an opened magazine before the artist, and what the eyes saw in the magazine was with quick, careful touches being transferred to the hard wall. Jim watched the drawing take shape: a girl in a bathing-suit, seated on the edge of a rock, her right leg extended in a sweet ripple of gracefulness, her left leg bent upwards and her hands locked around her knees, one short curve of her breasts visible above her straight arms. She had no head yet but, boy, Jim reflected, she looked the hot potatoes, the genuine article.

He knew a wee girl could look like that.

The artist stood back from the wall and surveyed his headless handiwork. That Joe Keenan fellow could draw as nobody else in the town could draw, but buried down there in a hole of a house in Crawford's Alley he'd never make anything out of his talent. Raphael himself wouldn't have made much of a job of life if he'd started it in Crawford's Alley, or in the constant company of a rascal like the Bear Mullan. Look now at the Bear pointing at the figure of the girl and saying something to Joe Keenan. Jim couldn't hear what the Bear said, but he could make a fair guess, and the sight of Joe and the Bear slapping each other on the back and roaring with laughter that was not innocent laughter filled him with a sadness that he was not subtle enough to understand. He liked Joe Keenan. The way he could draw. The way he could play the mouth-organ, squeezing fine music out of thin tin reeds.

His mother's voice was calling up the stairs, breaking in on his sadness, disturbing the poise of curving bodies drawn by a skillful hand, disturbing the rhythm of silver melodies played in tune: "There's an urgent letter here for Jock the lodger."

He took up his bag, descended the straight steep stairway into the narrow hall. He said: "It'll be soon enough when he comes home for his tea."

"He won't be home for his tea. He's going out to the lake to the swimming club."

"Send Chris down with it then. The match starts at four."

He opened a door and looked from the hallway into the kitchen. His mother was standing by the table, her sleeves rolled up on her strong stout arms, her fat good-natured face lined a little with long years of work and worry. His sister Anne was sitting where she always sat in a high chair between the range and the window, her crippled right leg extended and rested on a cushioned stool. He had a vague feeling that Anne in her chair was a bitter parody on the curving grace that Joe Keenan had transferred from the coloured magazine to the grey wall. But when Anne spoke to him he was suddenly ashamed of that feeling.

"Chris has gone out," she said gently. "Dinny Campbell called for him and they went out for a walk."

"The bloody wee pipit," he said. "Is he ever in the house? Himself and Dinny Campbell."

"He's in as often as you are," Anne said, "and he's doing less harm when he's out."

"And that's no language to be using in your own home," his mother said.

He laughed at them, his body in the hall, his head and shoulders in the kitchen. He said: "Amn't I a man? Won't I soon be doing my last exam? Won't I have a job?" He took the letter his mother gave him, and read out the name on the envelope: "Graham King, Esquire." He said: "It's a hell of a name for Jock the butcher. I suppose he's some connection of Mrs. Graham of the hotel."

"If he was," his mother called after him, "he wouldn't be long lodging in this house."

Jim edged his way between the wall and the hall-stand. The hall was narrow and the large hallstand was almost always bulging with coats. He walked through a gridiron pattern of thin streets, shrill with playing children and walled by small houses, to come out on Devlin Street at the tree-shaded Methodist meeting-house. Fifty yards along Devlin Street he turned down a laneway, turned again between high stone pillars with white iron gates swinging open, crossed a wide yard where three heavy lorries were parked, went through a doorway into a huge building of corrugated iron. Six aproned men were sitting on benches plucking fowls. The floor was soft with feathers, the air unpleasantly tainted with the smell of singed feathers. A seventh man was standing up and putting on a tattered navy jacket and a red muffler that filled the place of collar and tie; a small man with a face never completely shaven, always coloured with a stubble of dark hair. He fitted a greasy cap on to his head, saw Jim approaching carefully around dark bundles of feathers, and shouted hallo. He said: "All fit for the game, Jim?"

The six pluckers raised their heads and nodded simultaneously.

"Fit as a fiddle, Brass," Jim said.

"Your team has the best trainer in the town," said one of the pluckers. Somewhere under dark stubble Brass MacManus's face smiled at the compliment. "I'm maybe not the best," he said, "but I've the most experience. I've been at the soccer, playing and training and doing coupons, since I was that high." He indicated with his hand a point about eighteen inches above the feather-covered floor. "In nineteen ten as anybody in the town will tell you I sold me mother's dresser and four chairs out of the house

25

to buy goalposts for the Wanderers."

"It's a well-known story," said one of the pluckers.

"The Wanderers were a great team," said another plucker. Brass and Jim went up a high, steep, wooden staircase to the upper floor of the building. The six pluckers wished them luck. They walked between rows of white packing cases and their nostrils were filled with the fresh smell of clean wood; they passed three men attentively industrious around an egg-testing machine, and two men in white coats carrying sides of beef into a cold storage room, and a chugging machine attended by two men making sausages, and into the butcher's shop walled with cool clean tiles, where Jim gave the letter to Jock who said thanks laddie, and, without looking at the letter, went on weighing out a parcel of meat for a thin woman in a puce coat.

In Devlin Street they shook the sawdust of the shop off their feet. They passed the court-house and went down the steep slope of Tower Street. The nails in the boots that Brass wore rattled on the pavement. They went through a narrow street where children played around dishwatery doorsteps, over a red metal bridge spanning the river escaping with a glad rush of broken water from the shadows of the houses, along by the high grey wall of the barracks and through a gateway where a sentry nodded a friendly nod, across a wide square of blue gravel and past four ornamental guns and into the dressing-rooms. And in fifteen minutes Brass, small and shabby and muffled in red, was leading his eleven blue-and-white jerseyed men across the grass, giving them the final words of advice and encouragement, running towards the touchline and the shouting crowd when the referee blew his whistle and the game was on, cupping his hands to his hirsute mouth to shout: "Keep it on the carpet, Jim, on the carpet all the time." He smiled with gratification when Jim raced away with the ball at his toe, and somebody in the crowd said: "God, Brass, that Collins lad will make a name for himself yet."

VI

Ten yards along the touchline Dympna Campbell was watching Jim Collins and listening to the voice of Brass MacManus shouting encouragement.

26

She said: "May, Jim Collins is the best footballer in the town."

"If it's a footballer you want," May said.

"He wouldn't be playing football all the time."

"He wouldn't need to be."

Around them the shouting of the people grew louder, died away suddenly into a few isolated voices calling abuse or encouragement, rose again suddenly like the advance of a roaring wave. Dympna stood on her tiptoes, swayed right and left, through gaps in the crowd catching glimpses of green field and coloured running figures. She joined her voice to the general shouting. In a lull in that shouting she laughed and said: "If Aunt Aggie only knew the choir practice we were at."

"If she finds out there'll be murder. I wouldn't mind if I was enjoying it."

"There's no sport in your blood, May."

"Not this kind of sport. Backstreet boys playing football with army recruits. If Aunt Aggie only knew."

"She won't know," Dympna said, and once again her feet were dancing and her black hair was dancing and her small body was swaying right and left following the movement of the game.

May sighed patiently and stood back a little from the excited crowd. She looked up at the grey walls of the barracks high on the hill, around at the wide levels of fresh grass, at the tall trees on the sloping ground beyond the wide loop of the river. God Almighty knew that Dympna thought of the daftest excuses for covering up her meetings with Jim Collins: choir practice, and a half circle of girls standing around a nun and a harmonium in a convent room and singing hymns, and here instead were hundreds of people shouting and cheering and yelling curses that would make Aunt Aggie give birth to kittens. Dympna had daft excuses and peculiarly low tastes. She knew people in parts of the town where the Campbell girls were never even supposed to go.

Even the whistle of the corner-boys, greasy backs against the greasy wall at the junction of Tower Street and Silver Lane, was a friendly inoffensive whistle when you were walking in Dympna's company. Normally, May Campbell was self-possessed in public places, never painfully conscious of her body as something to be carried about like an awkward parcel. But the low whistles and the clicking tongues at the corner of Silver Lane could make a girl realize very vividly every inch of the length of her legs, the lifelessness of her arms, could even make her feel intensely all the minor discomforts of crumpled underclothes. Walking with Dympna there was none of that awkwardness: a shrill whistle, a catcall, an answering wave of the hand from Dympna, a half-shaven youth shouting: "Dympna, give us a knock-down to the sister," another youth making almost inoffensive references to Joan Crawford. Dympna was popular. The roughs knew her as the girl that Jim Collins walked with and Jim Collins was the hero that the roughs worshipped; and, for a moment, May was gratified that the Campbell sisters were respected even at the corner of Silver Lane.

Only for a moment. For what Silver Lane thought, couldn't matter much to the rich world, the clever world, the strong world, the world where May belonged, even if her young sister was fool enough to run after the son of a private soldier. Going with a boy, any boy—provided he didn't stink—was one thing. Falling for a backstreet boy, cheering him at football matches, waiting for him when the match was over, was another. May disapproved, but she kept Dympna's secrets because Dympna loyally kept May's secrets. Sisters must stand together, women must stand together, and standing together or walking together, going over green grass or hard pavements, May knew and was glad to know that Dympna and herself were worth looking at or whistling after, were different enough from ordinary girls to be able to afford their own rules and regulations.

The match ended, the shrill final whistle drowned in universal shouting, the coloured players lost somewhere in black crowds of running, congratulating spectators. May and Dympna moved away from the crowds, along a green path by the side of the river, over a strong wooden stile, under a long archway of beech trees where the perpetual wind-whispering was already hardening in the drying, withering leaves. Beyond the beech trees the river widened and deepened, to spill with the laziness of low water over a long weir. A green-painted tin hut stood beside the water, a battered diving-board, end covered with ragged matting, went out over the shiny surface. May sat down on a wooden bench, sheltered by the green hut from the cool autumn air that moved like a very gentle wind away from the falling water. She said: "Will he be long?"

"Six or seven minutes," Dympna said. She walked, carefully

balancing, to the end of the diving-board, set it swaying by raising and lowering her heels.

"Fall in, do," May said.

"No fear. Aunt Aggie would say it was a wet choir practice."

"You'd look lovely going through the town like a drowned rat. You and your athlete."

"I'd look lovely anyway."

Dympna laughed down at her own reflection, moving gently in the still water. She liked, with a careless, good-humoured liking, her own plump figure, her dark hair and dark eyes and soft, laughing face. She liked, with a more active positive liking, her blue costume, her white blouse. Clothes were things you could be sure about. They looked well or they didn't look well, they suited you or they didn't suit you. But unless you were, like May, a raving beauty, tall and slim and slightly blonde, with oval face and perfect eyebrows and lips made as if drawn with a careful pencil, and everything that the magazines said, then you couldn't be sure about your own body, not even when you were looking at it in a long mirror, with feelings that had in them a little pride and a little shame and a great deal of wonder. Anyway, Dympna supposed, it didn't matter much what you thought of yourself provided you could find somebody else to think favourably of you. Somebody else who had a strong, active body, a friendly laughing face, polished hair parted up the middle, a quick firm step as he came down the walk under the beech trees with Brass MacManus clumping hobnailed by his side.

"Tell me your company," May said. "Am I to walk with the bearded boy?"

"It's only Brass MacManus."

"Only."

Jim came heartily forward. Brass lingered shyly in the background until Dympna said: "Congrats, Brass. You've a great team."

"Thanks to Jim, Miss Campbell. He's a hero."

"This is my sister, Brass."

"Pleased to meet you, Miss Campbell." His cap was in his hand. He moved two steps forward, then halted again. Jim said: "Brass says his mother has a new photograph we oughta see."

"It's the first one was ever took of a team in this town," Brass said. "My father, God rest him, was the inside right."

"I'd love to see it," Dympna said.

May said nothing. She was cold with carefully concealed rage. Going anywhere with Dympna always left you in a fix like this: to be seen in public with that wee bearded man, to be seen entering the shack he lived in, and the feathery smell of him from McCanny's plucking yard. Suppose—God forbid—that Mr. Fiddis drove down the road in his car and saw Dympna and herself walking with a dirty little man who plucked fowl for a living, and a boy who played football and carried his boots and togs in a battered bag that had obviously seen better days. She could see the smile on Fiddis's face, the fatherly, understanding, half-contemptuous smile saying more plainly than words that he knew that boys would be boys and girls would be girls. May was fed up to the teeth with boys being boys and girls being girls, with Aunt Aggie, with a town where you couldn't cross the street without being seen and heard and noted.

She couldn't desert Dympna because Dympna had never deserted her, and, Aunt Aggie being Aunt Aggie, it was better to go out with your sister and come back with your sister. Hand-in-hand with Dympna she walked along the river path. Brass and Jim followed. She couldn't let Dympna walk with Jim because no amount of sisterly loyalty could have made her walk with Brass. The house, fortunately was outside the town. They wouldn't have to walk through the streets, and the path along the river was deserted going quietly under withering trees and beside the quiet water, and waiting quietly for night and autumn and the cold death that would follow autumn. Up and down over another stile and they were on a white by-road going away from the river, curving around a water-logged, abandoned quarry to meet the main road where cars and carts and lorries were going, too far away—May hoped—for any civilized man who had seen the world to look out from his passing car and recognize the two girls entering the white cottage on the hill beside the quarry.

The cottage was white on the outside but very dark within. A little of the evening light filtered through one small window into a cluttered kitchen where a faint spark of fire struggled in a high grate, illuminating only the two dusty hobs, showing vaguely the outlines of a tall woman sitting on a low chair. Her hands on her knees, she gently rocked her body backwards and forwards, softly talking to herself, not noticing that she was no longer alone. They listened for a moment to her raucous sing-song. It was like hearing a voice from another world, or overhearing a fragment of a sentence spoken in the secrecy of the confessional. "When he was in it," she said, "we wanted for nothing. As good a man as ever drew breath."

In a whisper by the low doorway Brass explained to May: "Now and again the mother doesn't be properly at herself. Thinking of the father, God rest him, that was killed outright in an accident."

"The class of him isn't going nowadays," the old woman was saying. "Bloody murderers, no less."

"She's thinking of old Maxwell, the villain," Brass whispered. He went towards the fire, very quietly for a man walking in hobnailed boots. He put his hand on her shoulder and shook her gently as if he was waking a child from a gentle sleep. "Visitors, ma," he said. "Here's Jim Collins and Miss Campbell and her sister come all the way to see the new photograph."

"They're heartily welcome," she said.

When she stood up, her head and shoulders were lost in a shadowy place beyond the dominion of red light from the fire or grey light from the window. Her handshake was strong, almost fierce, the palm of her hand like hard leather. She fumbled somewhere on an invisible mantelpiece, scraped with a match, lighted a long candle, and led her visitors around the kitchen from photograph to photograph, footballer to footballer, team of footballers to team of footballers. She pointed with a long yellow finger. The circle of light from the candle showed her straggling, grey hair, her long, strong-boned face, her bloodshot eyes that softened and brightened when she paused before one particular photograph. She said: "There's Francie, and Joe, and Jimmy and Harry and Billy Arthur." They stared back at her in the candlelight: tall whiskered men wearing skullcaps, arms folded on broad chests, long legs slim and muscular in tight old-fashioned togs. Her voice softened. She said: "They were young when I was young. The fellows nowadays aren't fit to wipe their boots."

"That one is my father," Brass said, proudly pointing. She carried the candle back to the mantelpiece. "He died sudden," she said. "They carried him in at the door and the priest held me and wouldn't let me out to see what was wrong. We had a big house then in a street."

The three young people had nothing to say. She took a small bellows out of the shadows and blew the fire to brightness. She said:

"Fill the kettle, Brass boy, till I make the girls a sup. Set chairs there Jim Collins, and tell me about the match."

Afterwards, Brass walked with them down the tarred road as far as the railway bridge. They looked down the slope towards the town and talked about the vanishing summer.

"In the summers when I was younger," Brass said, "I used to go on the road with the melodeon. It wasn't bad at all, except that some of the lodging houses were very dirty."

"Cooking over candles," Jim said, "like MacSorley's house where the yellow Indian pedlars lodge."

"I never saw that done. But I saw myself hammering my trousers between two bricks when I got up in the morning." He pointed down the slope, the road and the railway going together to vanish in a huddle of humpy roofs topped by a few spires, and blue in the distance the long, lonely curves of the hills. "Saving your presence, ladies," he said, "the trousers could have hopped on their own from here to the Gortin mountains." His queer slow laughter followed them down the road. He stood for several minutes on the bridge waving his hand. Jim and Dympna waved in reply.

"Go back, Dympna," May said, "and give him a nice kiss."

"May, you're a cat."

"It was nice of him to tell us all about the fleas."

Dympna laughed. She stood in the middle of the road and folded her arms on her stomach and bent down in laughter.

"All I can say is the two of you have queer friends."

"Poor Brass," Dympna said.

"He means no harm," Jim said.

In Devlin Street they saw Chris Collins walking with Dinny Campbell, Chris carrying in his arms something long and carefully wrapped in newspaper. Jim called across the width of the street and Chris and Dinny, calling in reply, quickened their pace and went on with their parcel.

The shadows were thickening around the pillars of the courthouse. From a shadowy covered entry that opened off the Diamond came the sound of a mouthorgan quickly playing, feet shuffling on gravelly ground, two voices tunelessly singing. Where the entry opened out into a wide yard Joe Keenan sat tailorsquatting on an empty packing-case, his shoulders hunched, the mouth-organ almost completely hidden between his caressing lips and his soft, long-fingered hands. Around the packing-case Gerry Campbell and the Bear Mullan circled in an imitation of an Indian war dance, knees rising high, hands waving in the air, singing and shouting and chanting and laughing as they circled.

"That fool, Gerry," May said, watching his fair curls rising and falling as he danced.

"All the fun of the fair," Dympna said. "It's good playing, too."

"The best," Jim said. "But if he was my brother, I'd ask him to choose a better dancing partner."

"You've no room to talk, Jim Collins," May said, "you and your beardy men and mad women."

She walked on across the Diamond, leaving Dympna talking to Jim. They looked after her slim body, her hips slightly swaying, her head erect, her hair falling down on her shoulders. She went in by the front door, wondering why it lay so carelessly open to the street. Her father met her on the stairs, his face almost white with shocked seriousness, blocking her way upwards to the retirement of her bedroom, to escape from the foolishness of Dympna and Jim Collins, from the town, from the censoring presence of Aunt Aggie.

Her father said: "Did you meet the messenger?"

"What messenger?"

She had never seen his face so white, so nearly drained dry of the blood that reddened his cheeks in a false appearance of strength. He wiped his forehead slowly. He was perspiring. He said: "I ran a messenger to the convent for you and Dympna."

"Why?" She was suddenly chilled.

"Chris and Gerry are out, God knows where. Nobody here to do anything."

"What is it?"

"Your aunt's not so well. She had a stroke. The way her mother died. The doctor's in now. Go and see. He might be needing things."

She squeezed past him where he stood helplessly on the stairs. He was thinking of deaths that had been, of deaths that would yet be. She went slowly up the stairs, taking off her coat as she went, draping it over the banisters opposite the door of her aunt's bedroom. She needed time to think, to discover what this meant. She stared at the blank wood of the bedroom door. It didn't mean death except for Aunt Aggie. Her hand was poised to knock. Beyond the doorway there was a faint, whispering sigh, the murmur of a consoling voice. And Aunt Aggie was old and the old must die. She tapped the door gently, then slowly turned the knob.

VII

Big Pat Rafferty knew that when he had driven the trap to the head of Conn's Brae and when he was pulling on the reins to steady the mare for the descent, his father would brush his long whiskers upwards with both hands and commence talking about the uselessness of the county council and the menace a flooding river was to lowland farms. The same thing happened every Sunday morning. It was three miles from Rafferty's house to the church and one mile to Rafferty's house from the head of the brae. It was a steep brae. The sandy, rain-torn road went down steeply between high hedges to wind across a belt of bog land, a black deep lake to the left hand and a black deep lake to the right. Beyond the bog the road rose steeply, hid itself for a while in a rough wood that covered the far slope, then went on straight across flat farmland, rising gently to the ridge of the horizon. On a clear day from the top of the brae you could see, delicately blue in the distance, the mountains away on the edge of the ocean. On any sort of a day you could see the river, sometimes twisting lazily through placid farms, sometimes spreading into sheets of dangerous shining water, covering the low meadows, lapping greedily to the doors of the less fortunately-placed houses.

For the last forty years of his life, Pat thought, his old man must never have seen those blue distant mountains. His eyes were held by the twisting river, by the uprooted trees and gravel from the brown hills that clogged its course sending floodwater seeping through the meadows after every heavy rainfall. His old man could talk for hours about that river. Every Sunday morning he talked about it from the head of the brae until the trap was past the stable and the orchard and halted on the street before the house. Going between the two lakes Pat's eyes were on the shadowy corner by the clump of bog birch where he had night-lines set for pike. His father was saying in the loud voice he used when heading deputations to the county council: "There'll be no farming in this backside of a country until the land is properly drained. In England

34

the farmers have pipes under every field, under every bloody field. Remember that, Pat. You'll be an educated farmer. And by God this country needs educated farmers." His mother listened patiently, a smile on her thin quiet face. For so many years she had seen neither the mountains nor the river, nor the lakes nor the wood nor the flat fields, except in so far as they backgrounded the growing and developing of her one strong son.

In Drumard Wood the hazel nuts were showing in darkening clusters, the unfallen leaves moved crisply on the branches over-head, the fallen leaves crackled under the turning wheels. His father said: "From the hills to the junction with the big river, all along the catchment basin, one half-penny on the rates would clean the river. And by God there isn't enough organization in the country to get that done. Is it much wonder the Irish are where they are?"

Eating his dinner at the bone-white table in the wide, flagged kitchen the old man retold the story of his latest encounter with the well-dressed, town-bred, sparrow-fart of a county council secretary. He mimicked the placating, deprecatory gesture of smooth shamefully-soft hands. He rounded his vowels and shrilled his voice imitating an accent that the man, he said, must have learned off a gramophone or at the talkie pictures." "Nothing can be done, Mr. Rafferty. Nothing whatsoever. We must retrench." And I said, "Retrench my arse. When half the farmers along the river are drowned you'll have to raise the rates to pay their burial expenses." And he said, "Nobody has been drowned yet, Mr. Rafferty." Through the window Pat saw the orchard trees heavy with ripe apples. The old man turned to the hearth to redden his pipe. "And I said, 'When the next war comes you won't be retrenching, and you'll be calling on the farmer to help you.' And he said, 'There won't be another war. Peace has come to stay.' 'Oh, has it by God?' says I. 'And so has the diarrhoea.'"

Pat was glad when his father and mother had driven off visiting, when the servant man had cycled off to a football match, when he was free to sit down lazily and read, his time his own until the cattle, impatient for the milking, lowed at the gate beyond the orchard. His old man was right about the river but, holy God, you couldn't have the river and English drainage and the educated farmer for breakfast, dinner, tea and supper. His father was a progressive. His father was a proverb among the local farmers who admired him and laughed at him and called him, when he wasn't listening, old man river. Pat was not affected by his father's enthusiasms. Maybe it was laziness. Maybe it was just a difference in temperament, a liking for listening to songs, for reading books that had nothing to do with drainage or practical farming, for walking in the orchard under the fragrant apples, for fishing by the black lakes in the quietness of the bog.

He sat in the kitchen, his back to the deep window, opened the book that the English teacher in the school had loaned him, and began to read. He read:

> Coming, one dark February night, to the Osharsk square, I saw a frisky fox-tail of fire peep out of a garret window and shake itself in the air, speckling the night with large fluttering sparks that fell to earth slowly and unwillingly. The beauty of the fire excited me. It was as though some red beast had sprung suddenly out of the moist, warm darkness into the window under the roof, had arched its back and was gnawing furiously at something; one could hear a dry crackling—as a bird's bones crack between one's teeth.

Where that fellow came from, Pat thought, apparently they ate the turkey bones and all, the way the rhyme said the Donegal people did with the skins of small potatoes. They were also apparently fascinated by fires, not fires like the gold-red aromatic pyramid that glowed quietly on the hearth before his eyes, but fires that roared and crackled out of control, and reddened the night sky, and embraced frail wooden houses and frail human lives in one general ruin. Queer stuff, but then the English teacher had a lot of queer books in his possession, and was very decent about loaning them to fellows that might take some sort of an intelligent interest in them. He would say:

"Go out to the cloakroom, to the pocket of my coat, and you'll find the book I promised you. But leave my cigarettes alone." He could be funny, too, even in attempting to reclaim books from bad borrowers: his elbows on his desk, a quiet whistle coming at intervals between his teeth, an inquiring stare in the eyes behind his rimless glasses. He would say: "Let down the bedroom window, you, and bring me back my book," or, "When's the next mission in your parish? Do you think it'll have much effect on the morals of the parishioners?"

A decent spud. Pat liked him; liked him well enough to see him even when he wasn't there, to see his face somewhere in the radiant pile of burning sods, to feel the strong grip of his hand on your bicep as he drew you aside to talk confidentially about something, to hear his voice: "Now here's a book, Pat, by a Russian that died recently. The Russians are queer specimens. I was there once before the Bolshies closed the door against the world. This fellow's not as long-winded as some of them. Read this stuff about fires, and maybe you'll see what your father means by trying to have the river drained. Fire and water, you know, and earth and air. The elemental things, and man fighting them, and twisting them to his own purposes." Then the strong fingers would squeeze your arm, a final squeeze, and the slow heavy step would go away from you along the corridor, slow and heavy and decided like the step coming now across the cobbled street towards the door of the house.

Pat closed the book, put it on the table, and walked quickly to the door. It would be a wonderful thing and a terrible thing if thinking hard enough about anybody could make and shape them out of the empty air. He stooped his head through the doorway and walked out into the sunshine. The big man coming towards him across the street wasn't, naturally, the man who taught him English and loaned him books. The slow-stepping feet were heavy in coarse, hobnailed boots, the tall, spare body was dressed in hard, grey cloth like the cloth the paupers wore in the poorhouse, the long face had grown thin and bony and hollow-jawed since Pat had seen it last. Grey stubble showed on the chin, the grey hair was clipped close, the watery blue eyes stared at you and saw you, stared through you and saw something else.

Pat walked towards him across the street. The man carried his cap in his left hand, a crooked blackthorn in his right. His yellow collarless neck was scrawny with sinews. He moved the blackthorn to his left hand and shook hands with Pat. "I didn't know you were home yet, John," Big Pat said.

"I'm home all right."

"You're welcome."

"Tisn't many would say it. But you're your father's son, even though you'll never make as much noise in the world."

They walked towards the door of the house. "You're your uncle's nephew, too. I owe a lot to your family, Pat. "Twas the hard talking of your uncle confused them."

Stooping again as he led the way over the threshold Pat felt suddenly as if a cold wind had blown from some hidden, mysterious place without sunshine or ripe red apples. "Sit down, John, and rest yourself," he said. "They're all away."

"You're housekeeping, so."

"I'm housekeeping. You'll drink a sup of tea?"

"I'd be glad of it, Pat boy. I'm housekeeping myself these days. I'm not much of a hand at it, for bye that it's lonesome."

The watery blue eyes were looking into and beyond the red pyramid on the hearth. The two white enamelled buckets in the sink were empty of spring water. Pat said: "I'll walk to the well, John. I won't be a minute."

"I'm a trouble to you."

"No trouble. I'd have to go anyway. Sit and rest yourself."

"And you in the middle of your books. They say the learning is a great cure for loneliness."

Pat crossed the cobbled street, an empty bucket swinging in each hand. The way to the well went round the haggard, across a narrow meadow by a footpath. Above the well was a high stone wall, edging the road that was there on a higher level than the meadow. Six stone steps went down to the shadowy, blue water. He filled the white buckets, watching as he did so the frisking of a small trout that he had captured by tickling in the burn that joined the river at the black stones. Maybe it wasn't right to imprison in a quiet well a creature that was accustomed to the quick movement of a stream. Still it looked happy and healthy. It was lucky to have a living trout in the well.

He came up the six steps, carrying the heavy buckets so full that the cool water lipped over the enamelled rims, splashing his big boots and the legs of his blue serge trousers. He steadied the buckets on the grass, looked towards the haggard and the long, thatched roof of the house bright yellow against the darkening leaves in the surrounding orchard. He thought about the gaunt man sitting quietly by the hearth, awaiting his return, stood thinking until a girl's voice spoke to him from the road.

"If the water's good," she said, "we're thirsty."

He said: "It's as good as water ever is."

He turned slowly and looked up at the high wall.

The two girls were standing on the road looking down at him, the small dark-headed girl with the friendly laughing face, the tall girl with a look that was mostly impudence but had in it also a little of invitation. He knew who they were. He had seen the tall girl one Saturday at a matinee in the picture house, and once or twice passing up and down the footpath outside the gramophone shop. He knew, too, that she had seen him. She wasn't unlike her brother: the same soft oval face, the same well-shaped mouth a little awry with something that might be tenderness or might be contempt. Her hair was more fair than her brother's hair.

He said: "You're a long way from home."

She said: "Is this where you live?" If she had met him by an igloo in the Arctic she might have spoken in the same way.

"It is," he said. "It's a quiet place." He couldn't think of anything better to say. He looked down at his big boots, wet with the splashing water and the damp of the autumn grass. His hands felt as big as his boots looked.

The little, dark-headed girl came to his rescue. She said: "We're cycling. And we're thirsty."

He stooped and picked up the buckets. He said: "It's good water, but water's not much of a drink. Come over to the house and I'll make tea."

The tall girl said: "Can you make tea?" It sounded as if she had asked him could he read or write or wash his face or button his own trousers. He said: "I can do more than make tea. There's a path down from the road through the little gate. Come on if you like."

He turned again towards the house. He knew they were following him but he didn't look around. They overtook him before he reached the haggard. Walking beside them he noticed that he was a good head taller than the tall girl. He said: "Mind your stockings in case the water splashes."

She looked at his strong hands closed firmly around the handles of the buckets. Thick black hairs grew on his wrists. "You're hospitable in your own peculiar way." she said. "We're giving you trouble."

"I was making tea anyway. I was housekeeping and a visitor dropped in."

"A distinguished visitor?"

"He's a man that they say murdered his wife. I suppose that's a distinction."

Dympna said: "Old Maxwell the murderer. Well, the people you meet when you travel."

Old Maxwell was sitting where Pat had left him, his hands locked across the handle of his blackthorn, his eyes on the red fire. He said: "The kitchen in this house was always a comfortable kitchen. The woman that's gone was always a great admirer of the cosiness of this place, on high ground, too, above the floods."

"I've brought home two visitors, John," Big Pat said. The old man stood up awkwardly when he saw the girls. He said: "Young ladies, no less. Maybe I'm in the way."

"Sit down, John. The young ladies will lay the table for the tea. They knew I wouldn't make much of a fist of it."

The gaunt face suddenly softened in laughter. He sat down again. It was as if a skeleton had suddenly come alive. He said through his laughter: "Good for you, Pat boy. You're your father's son. A man needs a woman in the house. The woman that's gone always said that your father had a joke the worst day ever he was."

Pat filled the kettle and swung it on to the black crane. He showed May and Dympna where the delf was kept. He said: "Here we are, John, two men with two women in the house." He stood to his full height, his back to the fire, old Maxwell seated to his left hand, the two girls seated together on the form by the window, waiting for the kettle to boil.

"By the cut of your clothes," the old man said, "I'd say you're from the town."

"We are," May answered coolly. Pat admired her coolness. Dympna looked at old Maxwell out of dark troubled eyes.

"Do you come this road often?"

"We were never here before."

"Pedalling bicycles you are?"

"We are."

The old man sighed. "It's good to be young. And well-favoured. And the wide world before you."

Dympna looked through the window. "The apples are lovely," she said.

"I'll shake the tree for you," Pat said.

He walked towards the door. Dympna rose, her eyes on the old man. "Don't bother, please," she said. "We can get them when we're all going out together."

May smiled. "Go on out, too, Dympna. I'll wait and wet the tea."

When Pat and Dympna came back from the orchard May was standing by the table pouring out the tea, and the old man was laughing loudly at something she had said. Sitting at the table, his watery blue eyes looked at her with genuine approbation. Once he tapped her shoulder with his right hand and said: "You're a sonsy saucy girl."

Pat walked with the two girls to the place where they had left their bicycles. He said: "You've captured his heart."

"Some capture."

"I was frightened out of my skin," Dympna said. "Did he really hang his wife?"

"The jury acquitted him," May said.

"She was found hanged, anyway," Pat said.

"If we followed this road where would it bring us?" Dympna asked.

"Down to the stepping-stones where we cross the river."

"Some day you'll show us the stepping-stones."

"We'll see you in the town," May said. "Don't you go to the pictures?"

"Next Tuesday night I could stay late in the town."

"I'm going next Tuesday night myself."

He looked after them until they turned the first corner, then walked back slowly to the house. Old Maxwell had gone, so he reopened his book and sat down again by the fire. The smell of her faintly-perfumed body was still in the corner above the table where she had sat. He moved across to the side of the kitchen where Maxwell had rested. He remembered her lovely, impudent face, the something that vaguely invited, the something in the shape of her mouth that seemed always about to harden into contempt for the whole world. He remembered her courage. He read at random:

> The ordinary murderer is a hopelessly dull and obtuse creature, half man, half beast, incapable of realizing the significance of his crime.

He snapped the book shut and threw it on the table. How the hell had anybody, Russian or Irishman, the neck to say what the ordinary murderer was, or the ordinary man, or the ordinary woman? He walked out of the house, around to the high field behind the orchard. Across the fields, and the hump of Drumard Wood, and the low bog, he could see near the top of the brae two figures, shrunk by distance, wheeling their bicycles up the dusty slope. He said to himself: "Sunday and Monday, and then Tuesday."

3

Rehearsal

I

TWO weeks after Aunt Aggie's stroke the town knew that Alice Graham and May Campbell were as thick as thieves. Somebody had seen them one day walking arm-in-arm along the Gortland road, the elder woman talking, the young one listening and occasionally laughing as no motherless girl whose aunt was next-door to death should laugh. Somebody else had seen May Campbell on several occasions entering and leaving Graham's hotel; and one night, somebody who had occasion to bring a message to Alice Graham found her in her own private sitting-room with Fiddis the solicitor and May Campbell, and two glasses of whisky and one glass of pale sherry on the table between them.

Aunt Aggie didn't hear the rumours. Aunt Aggie didn't seem to hear anything any more, didn't say anything, didn't move in bed except when two people assisted her. But she saw everything within the limits of her half-darkened room: her eyes following you as you moved about the room, her movement and her words and her whole life concentrated into those curious swivelling eyes. May felt uneasily that Aunt Aggie, paralysed and half way to death, could read her thoughts as Aunt Aggie, in her health and in control of her household, never could. She was always uneasy in that room, glad to escape from it, from the house, to go cycling in the country with Dympna, or to the pictures with Big Pat Rafferty, or across the street to Alice Graham's place where the alien taste of wine would be sweet and exciting, and where Alice Graham's crowded years would come tumbling tumultuously through her conversation,

43

sometimes sweet and exciting, sometimes edged with mysterious bitterness.

Slipping quietly out of that room, down the stairs silently to the door, was like escaping from a confessional, where eyes watched you through a grille, where no word was spoken but where every sin was known. Sometimes her father would be on the stairs, or standing meditatively in the doorway looking out across the wide street.

"Off again, May?"

"Yes, Father. Dympna is with Aunt Aggie. And the nurse will be back in an hour's time."

"I don't blame you, girl. You've a big responsibility now for a young woman of your age." He was overwhelmed by the disaster that had overtaken his sister. He was a little frightened by the change that had come so suddenly in the ways of his eldest child: life withering away in one woman, life crying out like a challenge in another woman. His face had never returned fully to its contented and prosperous floridity. He was a bewildered man.

"I doubt if she's the right company for you all the same, girl."

"She's good fun and she's good-natured."

"She's a woman that for her own good reasons your Aunt Aggie would never allow across this threshold."

"She's a friend of Mr. Fiddis. And surely he knows the difference between good and bad."

"Oh, Fiddis knows the difference right enough."

And he would laugh feebly, remembering how death had taken from him a young woman like this woman, and knowing that no man, strong or weak, can save a woman from death or from life.

Across the street, in and out through the traffic—the cars, the slow carts, the green buses crowded in the afternoon with country children going home from school—through the maze of mowing machines and wheel-barrows outside the town's biggest hardware store, along the footpath to the door of Graham's hotel, was a journey from one world to another world. Alice Graham was different. Alice Graham knew things that the town didn't know. Alice Graham could tell a girl things, about girls, about men, about ways of life in places where there were more streets and houses, more people, more fun. Stretched in a deep, easy chair by the bright fire in her own room Alice Graham looked a lot younger than she really was, her figure almost as good as May's figure, drink and the heat of the fire flushing all the hardness of gathering age out of her face, her skirt slipping upwards to display soft underwear and a stockinged thigh that men might still find worth looking at.

Alice Graham's greeting made you feel that you were really welcome: never too busy to stop for a moment, never so relaxed in warmth and drink as not to be able to stand erect, her arms extended, her tongue babbling words: "Darling, you look lovely. Your skin, child, how do you do it? If I only had that complexion for twenty-four hours the streets of even this town would be littered with dead men." The thin sensitive fingers would touch May's cheek lightly, so lightly and only for a moment, but still in that moment something passed from woman to woman, setting May's heart dancing a jig, depriving her limbs of weight and substance, heating her face with the slow flowing and gathering of blood. "What you want, May, is just this perfume. It's French. A little behind the ears, and they'll eat out of your hand." And a small, square bottle of green liquid would be inspected and sniffed and talked about and held up to the light in which it brightened as if alive with a burning secret.

Outside the window the traffic of the town moved up and down the street. In the cosy room the two women talked about the town. "For most women a town like this is heaven. For the good little girls who say their prayers and the good little wives who love their husbands."

The town, showing its life in the movement of the street, was the only town May knew. She felt her disadvantage. She said slowly and half-willingly: "I suppose when you're married you might as well love your husband. It's the easiest thing to do."

"The easiest thing to do with a tasty meal is eat it. But you'll get hungry again and you can't eat the same meal twice."

The moving traffic was only fifteen feet away: a red-leaded farm cart, a green bus, a crimson petrol-lorry, the people walking up and down the pavement or lazily crossing the street. But the things that Alice Graham said were in another world of roaring traffic and high hotels.

"I doubt if there's a man in this town would be worth a thimbleful of French perfume. Anyway they'd all call it scent."

"Oh, Mrs. Graham. They're not as bad as that."

May was tossing her long hair, shaking her head in delighted laughter. Alice Graham could be so comically serious about some things.

"Call me Alice, darling. Alice is the permanent part of me. Graham is the thing that changes." And then after a pause, and a sip of whisky, balanced by May's sip of pale sherry: "Except Bernard Fiddis. Now there's a man in a million."

The talk always returned to Bernard Fiddis, as the talk of two gossiping girls might return to the man that one of them or both of them loved. But May knew that what she felt for Bernard Fiddis was not love, because it was not love as the books described it. She couldn't imagine, either, the tall, dark self-possession of Alice Graham descending to love according to the books. They talked about Bernard Fiddis because he was more interesting than anything or anybody else in the town: his travels, the way he talked, his quiet, good manners, his long-fingered hands, the house he lived in, his long cream-coloured motor car. He was what every man, young and old, should be.

"He'd make a grand husband for a girl like you."

"He's old enough to be my father."

"He's not so old. Anyway, what do you want? A young fellow with no money and no experience? Six months ecstasy and misery for the rest of your life."

"Couldn't I leave him after six months?"

"Not here you can't. Not without hurting yourself. That's one thing I've learned about your country. Holy deadlock comes to stay. Or everybody wants to know the reason why."

The people going up the street to the church for the October devotions in honour of the Holy Rosary would, May thought, want to know the reason why. If she went to the pictures with Pat Rafferty some rattling tongue would carry the story back to her father, if she sat in the car with Mr. Fiddis, if she walked down the street arm-in-arm with Alice Graham. The talking town would approve of Pat Rafferty: a decent boy and a lovely girl together the way God meant them to be together. The talking town would dismiss Mr. Fiddis as a friend of her father, a solid and respectable citizen. But the talking town would never tolerate her friendship for Alice Graham: God save us, she's no company for a motherless girl, the painted face of her, the husbands she put through her dirty fingers over in the big cities of Britain.

Walking along the street and out the Gortland road with Alice Graham was like spitting a challenge in the face of the town. May loved it. Aunt Aggie was dead, or as good as dead, and she was her own mistress, and, anyway, she liked the Gortland road. You went down Tower Street, past the corner of Silver Lane where nobody whistled after you because the company of Alice Graham made you a woman, up the steep hill by the grey-walled, military barracks, down another hill with a view along the green river valley going out towards one solitary, round, blue mountain. Then you were walking on a wide flat road lined with shiny beech trees, and you knew the year was changing because every day brought more and more leaves to the damp ground, and one day the branches were creaking nakedly in a cold wind and you knew it was winter.

That was the day they met Pat Rafferty cycling strongly home against the cold wind. The blue suit that covered his big body could have been tidier. He wore a cap and a muffler and no gloves.

"You might have told us you were in the town," May said. Since he had stopped going to school he came to the town only once a week to go to the pictures. Sitting in the cinema with Pat's strength in the seat beside you was a comforting experience. May would have liked it more often than once a week.

"I was round at your house," he said. "I was talking to Gerry. I only came in to do a message for the old man."

"Your hands will be frozen without gloves," Alice Graham said. He opened and closed his strong fingers, looking at his hands as if they didn't belong to him. "I never wear gloves," he said. "I never feel the cold." He closed his right hand over the small, black-gloved hand that Alice Graham had rested on the handlebar of his bicycle. He pressed suddenly, laughing quietly in the back of his throat, and Alice screamed in mock panic and mock pain, and then laughed with him, a shrill, breathless laugh. "You've a grip like a vice," she said.

"The dramatic society starts its rehearsals next Monday," May said. "I suppose you'll be there." She was annoyed at that silly hand-pressing, and annoyed with her own annoyance.

"I will. But I'll see you before that."

"You might."

He threw his long leg over the saddle of the bicycle. He was no longer laughing as he had been laughing when he pressed Alice Graham's hand. "I'll try," he said, "next Saturday."

Watching him cycling away down the road under the bare beeches May was no longer annoyed. She was proud. Any woman could make a man laugh. Alice Graham was silent. "Would he do for six months?" May asked.

"He might do for twelve." The words were jocose, but the face was serious. "He might do for twelve years if the naked light was kept away from the gun-powder. He's full of gunpowder."

That was the day, too, that Mr. Fiddis overtook them when they had turned about and were walking back towards the town. He pulled up behind them, hooting the horn of his car so loudly that they jumped sideways to the safety of the gravelled footpath. He smiled at them through the wide windscreen and over the long bonnet of the car. He said: "Jump in, and take the weight off your legs."

Alice Graham said: "I'm not sure that we should. By all appearances your reckless youth is returning to you."

"It never deserted me," he said. "It's always deep down in my heart. Jump in all the same."

He drove them back to the town. May sat beside him in the front of the car. His hands were very firm on the wheel; there was a vague smell of good shaving soap or good hair oil or something, a pleasant manly perfume, as different from the smell of the green Paris perfume as man was different from woman or day from night. Alice Graham sat in the back, wrapping the heavy rug around her knees, complaining bitterly of the wintry cold.

"We're growing old, Alice," he said. "We haven't the warmth of youth. Like May here."

He rested his left hand on May's right leg, a little above the knee, as if indicating where warmth was to be found. The heel of his hand rested on the little ridge that was the top of her stocking. He took his hand away, then replaced it gently. May didn't move. She was looking at his hand: a large hand like Pat Rafferty's hand, as strong maybe, but not as hard or as hairy. Alice Graham stopped talking about the cold. She asked Fiddis where he was coming from.

He was coming from assizes in another town. He described the assizes. He commented on the eccentricities of the judge. He mentioned some of the peculiar cases: the farmer whose servant girl

48

had prosecuted him for the maintenance of an innocent and unwanted third party, the young man who had broken into the widow's house with crudely amorous intentions. His talk could turn corners skilfully, avoiding abominations, making crudities comic. He was entertaining, *risqué* enough to add spice and a little breathless speculation to that entertainment, but delicately careful to avoid giving offence. From his lips the story of the dark, twisted passions of quiet country places was as light as froth and as funny as a jig. He was a wonderful man.

He drew up outside Graham's hotel, resisted all invitations to come in for a minute, delayed for a while to finish the story he was telling. The fingers of his left hand gently stroked the smooth stocking on May's right knee. When the story was ended he drove on down the street, and May and Alice stood chatting on the pavement while the watching town passed up and down.

II

He drove home over the stone bridge. The river was rough and brown with winter rain, falling on high moorland, seeping down through sodden brown soil. The wheels of the car scattered gravel on the smooth grass that edged the drive. The smell of green Parisian perfume lingered about the seat. The feel of smooth silk, covering flesh and bone, irritated his hand, and he looked vacantly at his palm as if he expected to see a mark there. He garaged the car and walked towards the house. On the steep slope above the river the bare trees gossiped bitterly in the cold wind.

He took off his overcoat, massaged warmth back into his hands, rubbing away the cold, rubbing away the sweet feeling of silk, the mark that no eyes could see. Half way up the stairs Judy dramatically raised her right hand, attracting his attention, signalling for silence. "There's a deputation," she said, "stewing for the last hour at the fire in the dining-room."

"What deputation?"

"There's Jack MacGowan and a sleeky-haired boy called Collins on behalf of the dramatic society. One of the Collinses of the hill, and God knows they're not much."

He took his wallet out of his inside pocket and walked towards the door of the dining-room. Every year he came second on the subscription list in aid of the dramatic society. The arts must be encouraged. The monsignor came first, but then for the monsignor it was a good investment because the profits at the end of every season—a season meant two much-rehearsed plays—went to the church building fund or, sometimes, to the foreign missions. He closed the dining-room door behind him. Firelight shone back from polished mahogany and the night gathered sulkily in the corners of the room. He switched on the light, and reached his subscription to Jack MacGowan.

"The winter's with us," Jack MacGowan said, recording the amount of the subscription in a small, red notebook. He was tall and darkly serious and hollow-jawed. He looked at the world through heavy, horn-rimmed spectacles, obviously wondering always how much of the world was real and how much merely play-acting. Jim Collins stood uneasily behind him, his back to the blazing fire.

"The winter," said Fiddis, "is the time for rehearsals. What's your first play this season?"

Jack MacGowan said poisonously: "A good Irish Catholic play. We had to please the monsignor."

"What about The Plough and the Stars?" Fiddis asked taking a whiskey bottle and three glasses out of the sideboard.

"We went to see him about that. The whole bloody committee, and myself in the lead. Sitting like stiff statues on the hard chairs in that cold parlour where he sees his visitors. By the way, Mr. Fiddis, Jim doesn't touch the hard tack. He's in training for football, anyway."

"An athletic actor," said Fiddis. Gently he squirted soda from the siphon.

"I'm the stage manager," Jim said. "I couldn't act to save my life."

Fiddis laughed. He wiped a drop of spilt soda water from the polished table. He raised his glass: "Here's hoping you never have to act to save your life. Judy will have tea for us in a few minutes." He touched his glass to MacGowan's glass. He said: "To the sock and the buskin."

Jack MacGowan sipped his whisky. He said: "God help the arts in a town like this, and save them from the monsignor and his likes. We sat in that room, Mr. Fiddis, until our hips were blistered, and our faces and hands blue, and our teeth chattering. In he comes, warm and content, with the subscription that he'll get back pressed down and flowing over."

MacGowan was seeing the cold room as a stage. The monsignor was making a smiling, round-cheeked, cherry-faced appearance, presenting his subscription, discussing the society's prospects, smiling and smiling and smiling and being a philistine.

"Says he at last 'What plays have you in your mind?' Not one of them spoke. Leaving it all to me. And that barbarian the manager of the school I teach in, and could turn me out in the morning if he took the notion. Says I, at last, *The Plough and the Stars, Monsignor.*' And he looked at the floor for two full minutes and says: 'That's by O'Casey, isn't it?' And when nobody answered says he: 'The dog. If he wrote the thirty days prayer it would be a sin to say it.'"

Fiddis was laughing, filling out two more glasses. Judy was rattling into the room a loaded tea-trolley.

"I ask you," MacGowan said, "what can you do with a man like that?"

"Nothing, Jack, nothing," Fiddis said.

"What kills me about it is that we have some good new talent. A young lad called Rafferty. The eldest of the Campbell girls. That girl has what it takes, looks and everything. She's as much at home on the stage as if she grew there. It'll all be lost now in some twaddle about Irish Ireland and the three wise kings."

Judy was closing the door behind her. Fiddis was pouring tea into three fragile cups. He said: "Even a footballer can drink tea." But he was thinking of the young girl who had what it takes, looks and everything; and the gentle steam rising from the amber tea might have been the green, tormenting odour of perfume, and his left hand was once again restless with the feel of the texture of thin, tight silk.

He passed the cups around. He said: "The monsignor means well, Jack. You mustn't be too hard on him. He's thinking of the morals of his parish."

"If he is, he should know there's worse goes on in his parish than Sean O'Casey ever put on the stage, from oul fellows executing their wives to young girls having infants that can't be logically accounted for."

"There's very little that somebody hasn't put on the stage at some time or other since Sophocles."

Jack crunched a biscuit between his teeth, rested his teacup on the tiled hearth, raised his right hand slowly to emphasize his argument: "What's wrong with the monsignor is he can't mind his own business. He must always be interfering."

"He doesn't interfere in football," said Jim Collins.

"He doesn't half. Tell me who prevented the match between the Rovers and the ladies soccer team from a Glasgow factory, on the grounds that it was immodest?"

Jim was silent. Fiddis said: "Can't say I blame him. No ladies play soccer."

"There's a ladies pipe band in Dublin," Jack said, "and as far as modesty goes I don't see much difference between playing soccer and playing the bagpipes."

"The sound is different," Fiddis said smiling. He neither agreed nor disagreed with poor dramatic Jack. But he found him diverting, as play-actors and small-town revolutionaries were meant by God to be diverting.

"He interferes in politics," Jack said. "You know that better than I do, Mr. Fiddis. That's your own particular province. You know he'll be up to the neck in everything that goes on at the next by-election."

"His interference will help us to win the by-election." Fiddis was himself again, felt as he had felt months ago before memories of her face, her tall, strong, young body her hair rolling over her shoulder, had commenced following him about as a beautiful, evil spirit might follow a doomed man. He was a little apart from but still in complete control of the conversation. He was seeing politics and play-acting as two equally comic manifestations of life, completely different from the weak, burning moments of desire when you were actor and author and audience and candidate and electorate, all rolled together in one hopeless confusion.

The mood lasted until he had left the deputation to the door, listened to the crunch of their feet going away down the avenue. It followed him up to his study, stayed with him until he had plugged in the electric fire, opened his desk and sat down to write. He shaped the letters slowly and carefully, as he had shaped his words in the argument with Jack MacGowan. He wrote:

52

The politicians and the play-actors and the priests of this town are each in their own ways and in their own degrees irresistibly comic. Jack MacGowan is a zealous young man, a school-teacher half-educated. Living in Marseilles he would be a Communist, and would also be, in a discreet and honourable way, unfaithful to his wife. Living in Ireland he's as pure as an angel, hasn't got a wife to be unfaithful to, is—in politics—only a voice on the wind, lives for amateur dramatics, makes a hobgoblin and a bogy out of the poor, gentle, holy, old monsignor, thrills himself periodically by imagining that he has discovered the makings of a great actor or actress.

He stopped writing suddenly. He might have known that every subject would lead back to the same subject. Begin, with great superiority and detachment, to analyse poor Jack MacGowan, and the relentless circle in which all thought moved brought you bitterly around to the admiration in Jack's voice saying: "That girl has what it takes, looks and everything." Looks and everything, heaven and hell, a voice like music, long hair falling down, the sweet, soft skin, the shapely knee and thigh covered in smooth silk that marked the hand as a burning iron might leave for ever a brand. He closed his book wearily. Superiority and detachment were fragile bubbles. He went out of the house and across the gravel to the garage. The cold air was alive in the place. Far below was the continuous roar of the swollen river; all around him the bitter complaint of the naked trees, the voices of the damned, superiority and detachment and the hope of salvation gone utterly with the green leaves.

He sat in the driving-seat of the car. Hell was a cold place, not a burning place. Tormenting flames belonged to the living body, not to cold death. Hell was a cold place walled with damp concrete, smelling of damp, so that not even the smell of green perfume could survive. He reached his left hand, half fearfully, to the seat beside him felt only cold leather, smelt only damp concrete, heard only the roar of distant water, the bitter crying of the damned trees.

III

"I'd never make an actress," Dympna said, "not in a million years."

53

She leaned sideways, tossing her black hair out of her way, to whisper to Jim Collins. "What's more," she said, "it doesn't worry me, the way it worries May if she mispronounces a word, or if Jack MacGowan makes her raise her right hand when she thinks she should be raising her left."

Jim Collins laughed and when Jim laughed he laughed so as he could be heard. From the far end of the room, his back to the fire, a red book in his hand, his hair getting repeatedly into his eyes, Jack MacGowan looked frowningly towards the whisperer and the laugher.

He said: "I don't blame you, Jim. You're a good footballer. You're an efficient stage-manager. But you couldn't be expected to realize that learning to speak Shakespeare is the one and only way to learn to speak English. Even if the monsignor does compel us to do plays written by anonymous nuns about the life of Our Lord, we'll speak those plays as we would speak Shakespeare."

Everybody laughed. Everybody enjoyed Jack MacGowan. Jim Collins laughed. Everybody knew Jack meant no harm. Even May Campbell standing alone in the middle of the floor laughed.

"But I blame you, Dympna Campbell," Jack said. "Even if May Campbell is your sister, she'll be an actress some day, while you'll never do anything but whisper and create mischief. What chance, I ask you has William Shakespeare against you whispering and Jim Collins heehawing?"

Pat Rafferty said: "Poor old Bill has got the shakes," and a ripple of laughter ran around the walls of the room where the twenty members of the dramatic society sat on creaky chairs.

Jack MacGowan raised his hand for silence. "As you were," he said, and Harry Mahoney, the comic, clicked his heels with a click that seemed to fill the room with armed soldiers standing stiffly in line. Once again laughter went around the room like quick water, and Jack snapped the red book shut and said: "Jasus, Harry, give a fellow a chance. You're old enough to have sense."

A little more laughter, and then silence and May Campbell speaking slowly:

No Pandarus: I stalk about her door,
Like a strange soul upon the Stygian banks
Staying for waftage. O, be thou my Charon,

54

And give me swift transportation to those fields
Where I may wallow in the lily beds. . . .

Harry Mahoney whispered to Pat Rafferty: "What's it all about?"
"It's a fellow in love."
"He had it bad," Harry said, "the poor buck."

I am giddy; expectation whirls me round.
the imaginary relish is so sweet. . . .

"The fellow that talked like that," Harry whispered," was no
company for a clergyman's daughter."

Pat was silent. He sat stiffly, his feet solidly on the floor, the
palms of his hands flat on his knees, looking steadily at the girl who
stood reading in the middle of the room. The red dress she wore
brightened the place, made the dusty floor, the discoloured walls,
the battered fireplace perfect enough for a palace. Her body was a
flame, shaped and steady like a flame before a pagan altar, burning
up into that room from some secret place at the red centre of the
earth. He could see her profile, calm and delicately curving, the
white skin of her cheek, the mist of uncontrollable hairs half-hiding
her ear. Her voice was gentle, never rising much about a monotone,
never scorched into shrillness by the fire of poetic passion:

Even such a passion doth embrace my bosom:
My heart beats thicker than a feverous pulse. . . .

"Read beautifully, May," Jack MacGowan said. "A little bit near
the monotone, perhaps. But then think of Elizabethan music."

"We're thinking of it," Dympna whispered to Jim, and Jim,
holding his sides, restrained his laughter as Jack MacGowan, seized
with a sudden enthusiasm, went up and down the floor gesturing,
bending, crouching, smirking, and mouthing the words of Pandarus:

Come, come, what need you blush? shame's a baby.—Here
she is now: swear the oath now to her that you have sworn to
me.—What, are you gone again? you must be watched ere you
be made tame, must you?. . . Come draw this curtain, and let's
see your picture. Alas the day, how loth you are to offend
daylight! an' twere dark, you'd close sooner. . . .

Jack wasn't a bad actor. For a few moments the room was quiet, seeing, maybe, the first pimp bringing two lovers together in a legendary garden, the subtle snake wreathed round and round the tree, crabbed desire besieging the chaste and uncovered Susannah. Dympna broke the spell. Dympna, her chin on her hand, said with assumed solemnity: "I'm here to keep an eye on my sister," and Jim Collins relaxed into laughter, and the whole room was laughing, and it was nothing after all but Jack MacGowan acting the cod in a dusty room in Saint Joseph's parochial hall.

"With that class of talk," Harry Mahoney said, "you'd be the ruination of all the girls in the country."

Jack MacGowan was fixing his tie before the fly-marked mirror. He said: "The pubs'll be closed in half an hour, Harry." It was the fall of the curtain, the brief epilogue, the *ite missa est* of Jack MacGowan. Led by Harry Mahoney the dramatic society clattered down the rickety stairs, past the door of the room where one of the curates was playing poker with two publicans and an inspector of taxes, and out into the gaslit streets. The two young fellows who remained behind to lock up the room entertained themselves by fencing with two long swords, borrowed once from the military barracks to equip two Nubian eunuchs in a play about King Herod. The furious clashing of ancient and ornamental steel sounded down the stairway above the shuffling and clattering of departing feet.

"They'll do each other an injury," Harry Mahoney said.

"They'll break the bloody swords," Jack said, "and we'll have to pay the major for them. He borrowed them out of the military museum." But he didn't go back up the stairs to end the duel and to save the swords. Harry Mahoney said: "They won't need swords in the next war," and Jack and Harry raced across the street towards the lights of the nearest pub.

Pat Rafferty and Jim Collins stood at the corner of the street talking to the Campbell sisters. A cold wind coming from no defined point of the compass slithered around the corner, attracted maybe by the high spires of the church across the street. The door of the pub opened to admit Jack and Harry, and a burst of randy, warm singing crossed the street to perish in the cold wind under the stone spires.

"It's comfortable over there," Pat said. "I vote we go down to Joe's for a fish supper."

"You'll need it with eight miles to cycle," Jim said.

"The wind'll be on my back."

"If we went to Graham's hotel," May said, "we'd get a drink."

Dympna said: "I don't want a drink. And I wouldn't be got dead in Graham's hotel."

"You're mighty particular."

"I am."

"The wind," Pat said, "is getting colder." He put his arm around May's waist, brought her with him along the footpath. "I love Mrs. Graham," he said, "and by the look in her eyes I think she loves me. I also like my bottle, when it's good and the da isn't about to see me lowering it. But what a man needs on a night like this is sizzling fish, and chips soaked in vinegar, and scalding coffee."

"The delicate tastes you have," May said.

"Joe's is the warmest place in the town," Jim said.

"It should be," May said. "There hasn't been a breath of fresh air in it since Joe the Italian came to the town."

Crossing the Diamond the wind came at them directly from the north-east, swift and venomed and blowing low along the shivering earth. Arm-in-arm they battled against it, towards the white lights of Joe's fish-and-chip shop. "On a night like tonight," Pat said, "the poor world is destroyed with fresh air."

Joe's shop was warm and crowded, the air dense with steam and fragrant with the smell and crackling with the sound of frying. Behind the counter the great bulk of Joe moved slowly and smilingly, attended by the slimmer and speedier members of his brown-faced family, magic spirits in a magic misty cavern, speaking a soft, melodious language that was not the language of the people of the town. Pat found an empty snug. Jim battled his way to the counter, had from Joe the speedy service of a patron who is also a friend, carried the steaming cups and plates back to the snug. They ate and drank contentedly. The steam was a soft curtain, the noise was a strong wall, and the chill, wind-tortured world was somewhere beyond, enduring its own dark agony.

"Poor Aunt Aggie," Dympna said "always thought it was low to come here." May said: "She's low enough herself now."

"That's not a nice thing to say."

"So what, Miss Proper. Do you want her to get better? Do you want her up and about again telling the two of us when to blow our noses and change our vests?"

"You shouldn't mention vests before Pat Rafferty," Jim said. "He's an innocent boy."

From a tall bottle Pat squirted vinegar across the table at Jim. Dympna said: "She wasn't so bad. And she's suffering a lot now."

"It's a funny thing" Jim said "having an invalid in he house. Look at my sister Anne, now. She's as patient as a mouse. I don't know how she sticks it."

"She reads a lot," Pat said. "She's read more books than any girl I know. Good books, too."

"She reads all the books you bring her. She thinks the sun rises and sets on Pat Rafferty."

"It very nearly does," Dympna said, "he's so big and awkward."

Pat, silent for a moment, was roused by Dympna's words. His large hand closed around the long bottle of brown, bitter vinegar. Dympna said: "Now don't you squirt vinegar at me, Pat Rafferty, or I'll call Joe out of the smoke."

"Don't be childish," May said.

"We are corrected," Dympna said: "And that's the one that blames Aunt Aggie."

Pat and May were looking at each other across the table. He jerked vinegar carefully out over his own plate. He said: "It must be tough to be an invalid." He saw Aunt Aggie motionless on the bed that would be her deathbed, and Anne Collins always in the chair from which her quiet beauty would never rise to walk the world as beauty should. "Always there in the same place thinking the same thoughts," he said. Motionless people, chained like medieval prisoners to one place, always thinking the same thoughts. And then suddenly, for no reason that he could name, he remembered old Maxwell, and he knew that a man's body could be free and his mind chained to one thought, the prisoner in the dungeon, the young girl on her chair, the old woman on her bed: chained always to the same thought, a woman dead, or a woman alive, or a deed done or a word spoken and regretted through all eternity.

May was smiling at him across the table. Her white oval face came forwards out of some infinite darkness. It was now a laughing and impudent face, not a silent and discontented face. It was a challenging face.

"Big Pat, the sleeping beauty," Jim Collins said, slapping a hand on Pat's knee.

The surrounding noise was suddenly discordant. Her face was smiling at him, challenging him. The steaming air was dense enough to choke the lungs, and the cold wind outside would be a kind wind if only he could be out there with her, and her lips telling him her thoughts.

"I've a long way to go," he said.

"We'll walk a bit with you," Jim said.

The wind swept across the Diamond with increasing violence. A gas-lamp winked in the wind, then spluttered and went out. Somewhere a discarded tin can was blown, bumping and rattling, along the shivering ground.

"That wind will blow the waters down," Pat said.

"My old man will sleep in peace."

"Were the floods high?"

"They were rising. There were a few houses in danger."

A long car swept from Devlin Street into the Diamond, stalled for a moment encountering the full fury of the wind, then went on swiftly down the slope.

"That's old Fiddis," Dympna said.

"He's not so old," May said.

"He's old enough to have more sense than he has. The whole town talking about himself and Mrs.Graham."

"The whole town isn't doing anything of the sort. Except a few mangy gossips in the Children of Mary. Anyway it's all a lie."

"I wouldn't mind having his car," Jim said. "If I had I'd drive you home, Pat."

"It's easy having a car," Dympna said, "when you spend your life encouraging old farmers to prosecute each other."

"That's what you heard Tom Nixon, the grocer, saying," May said.

"It's the truth."

"If Tom Nixon would look after his shop and spend less time organizing practical jokes he might have a car, too."

"Peace," Jim Collins proclaimed. "My peace be with you." In the air, over the scarfed heads of the two sisters he signed elaborately with his right hand the sign of the cross. He stood as the monsignor stood every Sunday in the white marble pulpit. He said solemnly in a preacher's voice: "How good a thing it is to see two sisters who don't want to tear each other's eyes out." They laughed at him, leaning together, arm locked in arm, two lovely sisters, waiting in the lamplight while Pat Rafferty reclaimed his bicycle from the black shed at the back of a huckster shop on the edge of the town.

Pat wheeling his bicycle, they walked up the hill with the high grey wall of the military barracks to the right hand. On the top of the hill the town's last lamp burned steadily in the shelter of the wall. The wind came out roaring, a drunken giant staggering home to his cave, from the crippling confinement. of the streets; went roaring out over invisible, flat fields, through invisible, crying trees, forcing the swollen river more rapidly towards the delivery of the sea. The thin telephone wires sang like magic strings in a magic story.

They went down together into the darkness. Jim and Dympna were dropping behind, whispering contentedly to each other, dropping further and further behind until they and their contented whispering were lost in the wild night.

"Young love," May said, "is lovely to look at."

"The books are full of it."

"Don't ask me what I'm reading" she said. "I'm not reading a damned thing."

"You were reading tonight about young love."

"That idiot, Jack MacGowan. Did anybody ever feel like that?"

He leaned his bicycle against a gate. They sheltered from the wind behind a square, stone pillar. His arm was lightly around her waist. "Somebody must have," he said.

"Sometime. Somewhere," she said. "It's all very vague."

His left hand could feel the curve of her body, veiled beauty, beauty hidden in the cold darkness. Her body was a flower, growing out of the hidden warmth of the earth, sweetly smelling of lost summers and of summers yet to come. Somebody sometime, somewhere, had felt that way. Did she know how he felt?

"That's a lovely perfume," he said.

"It's French," she said.

He wanted to say: "It's you. You. You."

"Alice Graham gave it to me."

He said: "She's a rare one."

She was so close to him. His hand moving touched the soft curve of her left breast. She was so far away, a French perfume, as far away as France. He looked out over the gate into the dark fields, dark as despair. Her lips were so close to him. He thought that he could taste the perfume on his own lips, the taste of France, the taste of the whole gallant world bright with sunshine and on the other side of the fields of despair. There was no map to guide him across those fields to the gallant sunshine; no travellers tales except the one about Paddy the Irishman and the tin underwear of the innkeeper's daughter, or the one about the big boy and the donkey and the stiff stays worn by the schoolmistress, or a thousand stories that boys whispered, smelling like the steaming dohel, bawdy like the wind shouting behind him, driving him home.

"It's time for me to be going," he said; and then suddenly her hands were on his shoulders, and her body was close against his, and she was looking up into his face. He kissed her. Her lips clung to his, hurting him, hurting herself. His black hair fell down on her hair, and their mouths crushing together they laughed together. She said, panting for breath: "You need a haircut, Pat Rafferty. You're as strong as a bull."

He tasted blood on his lips. He said: "My hair maybe is like Samson's hair," and he kissed her again, crushing her body and then suddenly releasing her. She leaned panting against the sheltering pillar. She said: "I'd better go now. Before Dympna does any harm to Jim." But she made no attempt to move. He cupped his hands about her face. She said: "Not any more, Pat. Not here. It's too cold. Listen to the wind."

The wind was screaming through the dry, bare hedges, a bawdy wind, telling stories about what he said and she said, singing songs about British soldiers and Russian girls. The wind that blew for lovers was a blue, sun-shiny, spring wind. In the shelter of the pillar they listened to the wind. The smell of her perfume was all about his strong hands. They listened to the wind until they heard the footsteps and the laughter of Dympna and Jim coming after them along the road.

IV

The fair day filled the streets with cattle. From the stony slope of the fair green they overflowed one way into the narrow streets around Jim Collins's home; they overflowed the other way through a gap in a wall and past a smelly latrine into Devlin Street; they rubbed themselves against the doors of houses and endangered the windows of shops; crowded in the narrow streets or on the stony commons they bellowed their loneliness for soft green fields and dark, scented, cobwebbed byres; the steam of their breath and the steam of their dung filled the air with a fragrance alien to the bricks and the blocked, impatient traffic.

Bernard Fiddis driving from his home to his office steered his car carefully around a frightened red bullock, escaped from the herd, running in reckless terror through the traffic in the Diamond, pursued by a ragged, shouting drover.

Pat Rafferty cycling into the town to buy, if possible, a yearling bullock for his father knew the runaway bullock for one of the six that old Maxwell was trying to sell, knew the ragged, shouting drover for Brass MacManus.

Jim Collins, walking through the narrow, crowded streets on the way to his good new job in Waterson's office, stepped carefully to guard his polished shoes against splashes of liquid dung. A clerk of four weeks standing couldn't afford to go to his work with shoes that might have been worn by a farm labourer cleaning out a byre.

Brass MacManus guarding six red bullocks in a dung-spattered twist of Devlin Street waved hello to Jim Collins. He said: "I'm herding today for Maxwell the murderer. But sure I suppose his money's as good as the money of a decent man." Jim said: "Every bit, Brass. Money is money, all the world over."

Chris Collins and Dinny Campbell on their way home from school stood to talk with Brass MacManus. Dinny Campbell asked Brass MacManus how many cows had he sold. Brass said: "In that corner this morning there were six head. How many do you see now?" They looked and saw one small, red bullock, standing in slushy dung, abandoned and lonely, the last rose of summer, the last of the Texas rangers. Chris said: "He must be bucking mad that nobody bought him." Dinny said: "I could stand all day looking at a cow." Brass said: "You should be herding, then, and I should be going to school. You mightn't think it such fun if you were standing herding cattle for a man that vanished after his dinner and hasn't been seen since."

62

Jim Collins, busy in his glass-walled office, looked down into Waterson's shop and saw old Maxwell leaning drunkenly over the counter, gesticulating wildly, buying something from one of the assistants.

May Campbell pulled aside a curtain in Aunt Aggie's quiet, darkened room and looked out into the street. The shop-windows were bright, but the lame, red-faced lamplighter had not yet come to light the street lamps. The tall, thin man walking unsteadily along the pavement was the man she had met that day in Pat Rafferty's house.

Jim Collins walking briskly home from his work met Brass MacManus looking for old Maxwell. Brass said: "I've sold the last of his bloody bullocks, and I've more money for him than any one man should own."

"He was in Waterson's earlier on," Jim said, "and he wasn't looking too sober. I haven't seen him since, but big Pat's fixing the chain of his bicycle in Waterson's yard and he might know."

Big Pat and Brass MacManus searched the town for old Maxwell. They went from public house to public house. Their ears were confused with jagged fragments of different songs sung noisily in different pubs. They opened doors and closed doors on rooms of yellow light and drifting wreaths of grey smoke. They poked their heads into narrow snugs; and sometimes old fat women jocularly invited them to come in and drink, and sometimes a country fellow busy kissing a country girl would interrupt his embrace to ask them what the hell they wanted. They told nobody their business, because decent people didn't tell their business to the dregs of town and country getting drunk together on the night after the fair. They went up one side of the street and down the other side of the street. They found a tall, thin man lying on his mouth and nose in the shabby, deserted square called the Potato Market, and they turned him over so that he gazed upwards to the rising moon. The ground around him was greasy with half-digested porter, and the air around him smelt like a brewery. But he wasn't old Maxwell, and Brass said: "Thanks be to Christ, I don't want to have a corpse on my hands," and the man on the ground rolled over and was ill once again, and Pat said: "That fellow's still alive, anyway."

There were thirty public houses in the town and old Maxwell was in the twenty-ninth. It was a small public house belonging to Tom

Nixon, the grocer, but managed always by a thin bit of a barman, except on busy days when Tom, who was a teetotaller, condescended to help. The fair-day was a busy day, and Tom was there dressed in a long, white apron, his shirt sleeves rolled up, his bare elbows on the beer-odorous counter, his round, red face and shiny, bald head cradled between his pudgy hands, his little eyes twinkling with mockery at the world from behind a pair of small gold-rimmed spectacles. He was the town's practical joker, and the town was a joke and life was a joke. He was listening to old Maxwell, and old Maxwell was a joke, and everybody in the pub was listening to old Maxwell, and smiling or even laughing outright because Tom Nixon's twinkling eyes were telling everybody that murder was a joke, that Maxwell the murderer was a joke, that death was as funny as life and ruin ten times as comic as success.

Old Maxwell had the floor to himself. He stood a foot or two back from the counter, facing Tom Nixon, his back to the world, and the world was ten men sitting on a long bench along the wall. Now and again he reached forward to the counter, gripped a half-emptied pint tumbler, drank slowly, his Adam's apple jerking elastically on his lean throat. He had taken off his collar and tie and stuffed them into the pocket of his·long-tailed jacket, and a length of the sober, black, mourning tie straggled free from the lid of the pocket. He said: "They were round me in dozens, Mr.Nixon. Lawyers and lawyers clerks, and twelve jurymen sitting on their ass, and policemen as big as houses, and a bitter old pill of a judge."

"Twas a pity," Tom said, "that the twelve jurymen had only one ass between them," and the world on the bench at the wall laughed into its black porter.

Old Maxwell was a little more than half drunk, his eyes shining, his long, hollow jaws flushed, drunk enough to be foolish, not drunk enough to be easily offended. He said: "You're foolin', Mr. Nixon. But you're not foolin me." He drank from his tumbler.

He said: "Three judges and three juries couldn't fool me. All the questions that the police could put couldn't fool me."

A voice from the world said: "Guilty or not guilty," and the world laughed, but Tom Nixon didn't laugh because it wasn't his joke.

Pat Rafferty touched Maxwell's elbow. He said: "Time for the road, John."

A voice from the world said: "And the fun only commencing."

64

"Are you taking charge of him?" Tom Nixon asked.

"He's a neighbour," Big Pat said. "I wouldn't see a neighbour made a mockery of."

Tom Nixon took a cloth and fussily wiped the counter. He said: "It doesn't take much to make a mockery of a man when he makes a mockery of himself."

Pat's big elbows rested firmly on the counter. Tom Nixon wiped around them. Pat said: "It doesn't take much to belt the face off a wee, shiny bastard."

The world on the bench by the wall was nervously quiet. Big Pat was young and strong and known as the son of a tough father. Tom Nixon said: "Are you threatening me on my own premises?" With his hard lips Pat made a vulgar noise. He took the pint tumbler out of Maxwell's hand and poured its contents over the wiped counter. He said: "Keep wiping, Tom. It'll help you to mind your own business."

They steered old Maxwell carefully into the street. He walked along between them, docile, lost in thought, steadying himself by holding Brass with his left hand and Pat with his right hand. "His trap is in the yard behind Waterson's," Pat said. Brass led the bay horse from the stable into the dark yard, and Brass and Pat harnessed him into the trap, old Maxwell looking on in silence. "Hell to the bit of him," Brass said, "will ever be able to handle the horse himself. He's twice as drunk as he looks."

They helped him into the trap, settled him in a corner and wrapped a rug around his legs and feet. He muttered incoherently to himself, remembering something: the world laughing in Nixon's pub, the world sitting in judgment in a stuffy court-house. The horse trod the dark ground impatiently. "My bike, I suppose, will be safe here," Pat said. He drove the horse across the yard, hoof-clattering through the narrow, cobbled entry, into the street where the moon was brighter than the gas lamps. The pubs were closing. Singing crowds were gathered around the lighted windows.

"The old man," Pat said, "will think I've run away with his money." In the corner of the trap Maxwell was snoring gently, his head sinking forward, his mouth falling open. "I wouldn't mind only I couldn't get what he wanted from the fair. The sort of bullock my father wants was never calved or cut. It would have to be as big as an elephant, and able to fly like an aeroplane, and maybe able to give milk like a cow."

Brass laughed. "And maybe do a bull's business if the need arose. Your father is well known to be a hard man to satisfy."

They laughed together. Pat flicked the whip, urged the horse into a trot. They left the last houses behind them, and all around them were the fields whitened by the moonlight. Their laughter, the clopping of trotting hooves, aroused the old man. He came awake suddenly with a startled shout, snapped off half way as if somebody or something had choked it in his lean throat.

"What is it, Mr. Maxwell?" Brass asked.

He brought a hand from the shelter of the rug and wearily wiped his eyes. "It was nothing," he said. "It was a fool of a dream. There was wee Thomas Nixon sitting, putting the black cap on his head and laughing to split his sides."

"You'll need company," Brass said to Pat. "I might as well go the whole road with you."

"What about your mother?"

"She won't miss me. She has her fill of company in her own head or in the photographs. Anyway, I want my pay off this man when he sobers."

The horse spurted against the first slope of a hill, then slowed and steadied and pulled, harness leather creaking, up out of the shadows of high hedges up until they saw their road before them, and the glistening river winding away from them towards the north. The soft wind was mild with the promise of soft rain and dark, dripping days.

Old Maxwell said: "They were shouting guilty or not guilty but I was too cute to give them the true answer."

"Rest yourself, Mr. Maxwell," Brass said. "You've a journey before you."

He didn't seem to hear Brass. He leaned across and touched gently the hand with which Pat held the whip. His face was pale and his eyes dark with shadow, but it might have been the moonlight or the drink. "To your father's son, Pat Rafferty," he said, "I'd give the true answer."

"I didn't ask the questions, John. Forget about it."

"Nothing's over as easy as all that. Nothing's ever over when you keep it all to yourself."

"Shut him up, Pat, if you can," Brass whispered.

Halted by the long, white gates of a level crossing they waited

66

while a late train thundered past. The bay horse swerved away from the white gates, from the sudden noise and the flying line of lighted windows. Pat gave the reins to Brass and went to the horse's head, steadying with his strong hands, soothing with soft words, leading the frightened animal over the crossing as soon as the gates were opened, swapping a greeting with the crossing- keeper. Sitting straightly to his full height old Maxwell looked after the last vanishing light of the train.

"All the happy people," he said, "that went past this minute."

The moon was gone behind a cloud. They drove on into a shadowy country. "Happy and unhappy," Brass said. "It takes every kind to make a world."

"People in trains are always happy," Maxwell said.

"It must be good," Pat said, "to be an engine driver."

"I went in a train once," Maxwell said. "I went the whole way to Bundoran. Man, the sea-breakers there. The size of them and the roar of them. The noise of the train was nothing."

"I was there once," Brass said, "on a cheap excursion."

"We were happy that day. Laughing and talking all the time at jokes about the people that attended the wedding. A man in the train said to me: "You'll have two happy days," said he, "the day you marry her and the day you bury her." And she laughed, and I laughed. It was a great joke."

They passed a cross-roads. The moon was out again into freedom. A motor car went past towards the town. A dog barked from the barns beyond a white farmhouse.

"There was a third day," Maxwell said, "that the man knew nothing about. I'm sure he was a bachelor man like yourself, MacManus."

Brass said: "The football was always more in my line."

"It's all over now, John," Pat said. "Forget about it."

The old thin body was suddenly rigid; the two hands free of the rug were gesturing at Pat. "It's all over, is it? How do you know, Pat Rafferty a young cub that never touched a woman? You're the son of a knowledgeable man, but what do you know about a woman with a cruel heart and a wicked tongue? Oh, it's grand for a year or two. All laughing and fun, and you feeling always as if you were beginning a big dinner that would never come to an end."

Along a level stretch of road Pat whipped the horse. The old man's voice rose above the sudden rush of hooves. "If there was no child," he said, "maybe it was my fault, maybe it was her fault, maybe it was the Will of God. Maybe God saw what was coming and spared the innocent. I never abused her and surely she could have left me alone. Week after week, and year after year. As sweet as pie to the neighbours, so that they were looking at the two of us and saying that she was the long- suffering woman."

"They never were, John," Pat said. "They always knew the truth."

"Whisht, boy. It was said to my face before you were born. Didn't she go to the priest about me? About my cruelty. And, by the Cross of Christ, every word she spoke was a lie."

The horse, exhausted, had slackened his pace to an easy walk. The slope of a steep hill was against them, going up into shadowy places under high trees. Brass said soothingly: "We all know that, Mr. Maxwell. Rest yourself now."

"You all know nothing. You never heard her tongue the way I heard it. Year after year. Everything I did was wrong. You didn't see her face the day the devil came into her. Did you, MacManus, that never saw a woman barring your mother? Did you, Pat Rafferty that would run a mile from the sight of a cutty's pink shift?"

"That's enough, John," Pat said, "that's enough."

The old cracked voice was suddenly melodious with weird laughter. "Boys, but the young men today are easy huffed. When I was your age the mention of a shift wouldn't have troubled me. Maybe there's some wee girl that wouldn't let you see whether it was white or pink or blue."

"That's enough of that talk, John."

He leaned across the trap and patted Rafferty's knee. He said, quietly and humbly: "Don't be offended at an old man's joke. I won't make many more jokes."

They drove for a mile in almost complete silence. Pat and Brass breathed easily. Old Maxwell looked as if he was falling asleep: his body sunk backwards into the corner of the trap, his hands gone again into the warm shelter of he rug. They came to the head of the brae, and the high moon showed them the lakes like polished plates of steel, and beyond the lakes the dark shadow of Drumard Wood. Slowly the horse began the steep descent, Pat's hands firm upon the reins, sand crushing under the wheels, loose pebbles rolling away from the groping hooves. Old Maxwell was speaking slowly, as

68

slowly as the slow wheels turned or the careful hooves rose and fell. "You all know nothing," he said. "Nothing. Nothing. You never heard her tongue, taunting, from morning to night: kill me decent, John Maxwell, seeing you've reduced me to this already. Standing there in the byre, the halter in her hand, and the free end of it swinging. Why don't you, John Maxwell? Are you coward too? And the free end of the rope swinging ready for my hand, and the one cry she let, and the clatter she fell into the byre drain."

Holding with his left hand to the edge of the jolting trap, Brass crossed himself slowly with his right hand. The old man's head was sinking wearily on his chest, muffling his words in the high collar of his coat. "If I'd tied the rope to the round beam," he said, "and tumbled a stool on the floor, there wouldn't have been half the fuss." His head was suddenly erect, his voice defiant. "A man can't know everything" he said. "The smart man in the train didn't know so much."

They were on the level road between the lakes. Pat stood up in the trap, brought the whip down heavily on the brown back of the horse. The animal raced forward up the slope and towards Drumard Wood. Old Maxwell was huddled quietly in the corner of the trap. Pat saw, vividly in the moonlight, the stubbly face of Brass MacManus, the lips moving silently.

V

"If it was the right season," Chris Collins said, "we could have the unmerciful feed of green apples."

The leafless hedge between the road and the orchard was gapped and broken. Chris and Dinny scrambled up the wet, grassy bank and looked through the gapped hedge into the desolate orchard. The bare straggling branches were unpruned and blemished with spots of fungus. The leaves had fallen and rotted on the sodden unkempt grass.

"Last autumn," Chris said, "Hardhead O'Donnell filled one potato bag with red eaters and one with green cookers."

Dinny's round eyes widened with excitement and wonder. "Did nobody catch him?"

"Who'd catch him, for God's sake? Isn't the house as empty as a new coffin?"

They looked between the trees at the high, grey walls of the house, the windows without curtains, the chimneys without smoke, the grass growing from the long, sagging roof of the barn, the half-collapsed hay-shed.

"Nobody lived there since Andy Jim Orr died."

"Who was he?"

"Never heard of Andy Jim Orr? Well, for God's sake Dinny Campbell, do you know you're living?"

Dinny pushed Chris suddenly down the slope and into the orchard, followed him shouting, chased him in and out between the wet, slippy trunks of the trees. They halted, scuffling and laughing and panting, at the broken-down gate at the other end of the orchard. Dinny shouted: "Tell me who he was or I'll murder you."

Chris Collins was helpless with laughter. He said: "You couldn't murder a fly. Look behind you at Andy Jim's ghost."

Dinny looked over his shoulder. All around them the orchard was quiet. Beyond the thorny hedge a white goat with long horns and a long beard stood solemnly considering them. Dinny gasped. Chris laughed.

"Andy Jim Orr always had a breed of gentlemen goats with long horns about the place."

"How do you know? You're making it up."

"Brass MacManus laboured here when Andy Jim was living. And Brass told my brother. Told him all about Andy Jim. He was a Presbyterian, and rotten with money and the greatest miser ever lived. He built that big house and never lived in it. He worked from four in the morning till twelve at night, and never spent a penny. He never bought a big coat and on wet days he wore a sack around his shoulders. A big goat with long horns followed him like a dog at his heels, and ate with him off the same table."

They clambered over the broken, tottering gate.

"They say he hid his money in the house and his ghost comes back to count it every night at twelve o'clock."

They moved along a grass-grown pathway towards the house. From the far side of the hedge the white, horned goat, slowly chewing, solemnly watched them.

"He hired one day at the hiring fair a man from a place in County

Derry where the people talk the way they talk in Scotland."

"How do you know?" Dinny taunted. "you were never in Scotland."

"Me brother Jim told me."

"Your brother Jim was never in Scotland."

"Well Brass MacManus told him and Brass MacManus was in Scotland. Deny that if you can."

Dinny didn't deny it. Brass MacManus had surely been in Scotland. Brass MacManus had been in the British army. Brass MacManus had been everywhere. Dympna said that Brass MacManus had been a tramp on the roads.

"Anyway," Chris said, "Andy Jim and the wee Scotchy got drunk in the hiring fair."

"He wasn't a Scotchy."

"He talked like a Scotchy, and that's the same thing."

The house was before them, across a stretch of grass-grown gravel, tall and grey, bare empty windows. It hushed their argument. There was an awful silence about the house.

"At four o'clock the next morning," Chris said. His heart wasn't any longer in the story. He was watching the house.

"Come on away out of this," Dinny said. His soft, pudgy fists were tightly clenched. "And stop talking about Andy Jim."

"It's a funny story. It's not a ghost story. Anyway there's no such thing as ghosts. It's all a yarn."

He walked towards the house. Dinny slowly followed. Chris said loudly: "The wee Scotchy was sleeping in the barn. And at four in the morning he woke with something shaking him. And there was Andy Jim with the sack over his shoulders, and the gentleman goat eating the straw the Scotchy was sleeping on. "Get up for work," says Andy Jim. "Mon," says the wee Scotchy, "ha' ye no' gone to bed yet, yerself and the goat."

Chris laughed at his own story, not a very loud laugh. Dinny didn't laugh. He said: "It's not much of a joke." Chris couldn't disagree. It had sounded funny when Jim told it or when Brass MacManus told it, but somehow it was poor fun when you were standing at the bottom of the six steps that led up to the door of Andy Jim Orr's empty house, the house with the hidden money, the house with the wandering ghosts: the ghost of an old miser of a man with a sack over his shoulders and the ghost of a gentleman goat slowly chewing everlasting straw.

Two paces in the rear Dinny said: "You're only letting on you don't believe in ghosts."

Dark eyes in a brown face were dancing with defiance of ghosts, goats and devils: "I don't believe in ghosts. Anyway it's daytime." And in three jumps he was up the six steps, throwing his sinewy little body against the door, grabbing at the doorpost to steady himself as something suddenly snapped and the door, stiffly creaking slowly opened. They looked into the flagged hallway. It had a damp smell. In places the yellowing plaster had peeled off the walls, and the bricks shone with water. They looked across the hallway, through an open doorway and into a dark kitchen. "There's a funny smell," Dinny said, sniffing the air, edging nervously around Chris. The cold air was damp. They could hear in the kitchen water dripping slowly, drop after drop. "Divil the bit wonder," Chris said, "that Andy Jim Orr never lived in this place."

He led the way across the hall and into the dark kitchen. The one window was broken, but, outside, the tangled, withered weeds and the straggling shrubbery had made a dark curtain to shut out the light. They peered nervously around the shadowy room. It was completely empty, completely deserted, except for the fresh, yellow ashes and the charred, half-burned sods scattered on the hearth as if somebody had recklessly stamped out a fire with his feet. "Tramps," Chris said.

Sheltered from the cold, for one night with a roof over their homeless heads, crouching around a fire, cooking stolen food, the damp air savoury with the smell of that cooking, the kitchen was suddenly alive with tramps: all the tramps who came from nowhere, and begged or sang songs or sold shiny tins in the town, and passed on again into nowhere. There was Micky Alone, drunk as a lord every pension day, sitting speechless on a low window-sill in Devlin Street and giving you twopence for lighting his stump of a clay pipe; or the humpy man with the moustache who sang songs about the South Down Militia or about the great greyhound called Master MacGrath, or another song that ended up about hitting somebody on the kisser with a navvy's boot in our backyard last night; there was the little woman with the yellow face who sold white camphor from a bright blue tin and who chased you, screaming and roaring curses, if you called her Camphor Balls; or there was old MacCool with two tin cans tied with twine to the lapels of his coat. You could shut your eyes and the cold kitchen was full of them, no longer a cold kitchen but loud and smelly and warm, alive and cheerful and very faraway from the thought of an old crooked man with a sack round his shoulders, and the ghost of a chewing goat walking at his heels.

Chris began to sing. In the cold kitchen he sang:

Lord Lurgan stepped forward and said gentlemen
Is there any among you has money to spen'.

Dinny was laughing, and fear was gone. Dinny said: "Mickey Alone gave me twopence twice and the day I burned his nose with the match he gave me fourpence."

Going up the echoing stairs Chris sang loudly:

For your great English sportsmen I don't care a straw
Here's a thousand to one upon Master MacGrath.

They sang and laughed and shouted from room to empty room, until they entered a small room at the rear of the house, a room as free from damp as any room in that house could be, a cosy room with ashes in the small grate, and a teapot near the grate, chairs and a table, a gramophone, and a press securely locked. They were in the middle of the floor before they noticed these things. They had expected another empty room, and for one moment they were speechless with amazement.

Then Chris said: "A ghost wouldn't want a gramophone."

"There's somebody here," Dinny said.

"It's time we were going," Chris said.

They turned suddenly. The Bear Mullan was blocking the doorway and behind him were Joe Keenan and Gerry Campbell.

Dinny laughed with relief. It was great to see your own brother when you had expected to see a ghost or a goat or God knows what. Everybody knew the Bear Mullan was a bully; one day he beat a little boy about the face with a dead eel until the boy screamed himself into a fit. But Joe Keenan was all right. Joe Keenan played the french fiddle.

Dinny shouted: "Look what we found, Gerry."

Gerry said nothing. His pale face was more pale than usual. Joe Keenan said nothing. His black hair, bunching out over the collar of his coat, badly needed the barber. The Bear said: "Look what they found. Aren't they cute?" His thin sneering voice was the scrape of nails along dull brass.

He walked towards them. He was tall and thin, and stooped as if he could keep straight no longer and had started to grow in a different direction. His trousers were shabby and too short and too wide, the sleeves of his brown jacket were too short, his blue-and-white muffler swelled outwards under his pointy chin, his thin face, his little eyes set too close together. When he walked he turned in his toes and made quick little steps that jerked like a clock ticking.

He said: "How'd you get in?" They could smell the twopenny brilliantine off his hair. His forehead was greasy with brilliantine.

Chris said: "We walked in."

He struck Chris in the face, with his open hand, but so suddenly and with such force that Chris staggered back against the table. "I wasn't asking you, Cricket," he said. "I was asking the other one."

Gerry Campbell said: "The other one's my young brother." Joe Keenan said nothing. He leaned his back against the wall, put his hands into his pockets, and softly whistled a tune.

"If they just walked in," the Bear said, "then who broke the catch I had fixed on the inside of the door?"

Leaning against the table Chris said with a sob in his voice: "Who do you think you're hitting, you big bully; you wouldn't hit your match?"

"He can't find it," Joe Keenan said, and then continued whistling.

"The police could get you for breaking into places," the Bear said.

"It's not your house," Dinny said. "It belongs to Andy Jim Orr."

"Before he died I bought it of Andy Jim."

"Where'd you get the money?" Chris said, valiantly endeavouring to laugh. One side of his face was stiff. "Did you steal it?"

The Bear bit his thin lips. Very deliberately he struck Chris twice with his open hand, on the left cheek, on the right cheek, and Chris, a whirl of flying boots and hard little fists, leaped at him. Gerry Campbell and Joe Keenan grabbed Chris and held him. The Bear was panting from the fury of the attack that Chris had made. He said: "We'll tie them to the posts in the barn. We'll give them a lick of paint."

"Not to my brother, you wont," Gerry said. "Beat it, Dinny."

Dinny was frightened. He would have welcomed with laughter the ghost of Andy Jim. He moved slowly towards the door, halted with a great effort and said: "I won't go without Chris."

Joe Keenan released Chris, leaned against the table, took a mouth-organ from the pocket of his jacket and blew a sudden ripple of silver music. Then he said: "Take my advice, Bear."

"Who's boss, Joe Keenan, me or you?"

Joe slowly rippled his way up the scale. "We all take the risks," he said. "I'm not taking this one. Let them go friendly, and they'll keep quiet. Do what you want to do and the town'll be after us tomorrow."

"They won't talk if we let down their trousers and paint them."

"You just try," Chris said.

"Do you see what I mean?" Joe said. He drifted casually into the opening bars of a song about building a nest out in the west in a sky of heavenly blue.

"The last time that was done to a kid in this town," Gerry said, "the man that did it got a month in jail. And the judge was nearly giving him the cat. Maybe you want the cat?"

The Bear said something. Dinny had never heard the word before.

"Listen to me, Cricket Collins," Joe Keenan said. He wiped the mouth-organ and slipped it into his pocket. "You know your brother Jim's a pal of mine?" Chris nodded. He liked Joe Keenan. Jim said Joe Keenan could be an artist or a musician if he only had a chance.

"You wouldn't want to see me in a bloody awful fix."

"No Joe."

"Then say nothing to nobody about what you saw in this house. And don't come here any more."

Chris thought for a moment. "I will for you, Joe. I wouldn't for him." He pointed to the Bear, who had sat down sullenly on a chair close to the one dirty window. The Bear looked out of the window, and spat and said something else. It was another word Dinny had never heard before.

Joe Keenan turned to Dinny. "Dinny Campbell," he said, "if you don't want to get your brother in trouble, you'd better button up your lip, like this." He pulled his upper lip over his lower lip, twisted his fingers as if he were fastening a button. Dinny looked at him, and fear was suddenly gone, and he was giggling and laughing until he was ready to cry. "Mum's the word," said Joe Keenan. He led them down the stairs, across the cold, flagged floor of the hallway. He stood with them at the top of the steps, bending down between the two of them, pointing down the grass-grown cart-track that led, between leafless trees, back to the roadway. "Run," he said, "and forget you ever saw this place." They ran down the steps. They walked quickly towards the road. Standing in the shelter of the doorway Joe Keenan began to play his mouth-organ to the rhythm of their swiftly marching feet. He played the music of so we sang the chorus from Atlanta to the sea while we were marching through Georgia. Chris began to sing as they walked, kept singing even when they could no longer hear the sound of the music; and all along the wet, red-puddled by-road, twisting through fields that were sodden with winter, their feet were moving to the music that Joe Keenan had made, standing in the hallway of Andy Jim Orr's empty house.

"Joe Keenan is a good fellow," Dinny said.

Their shoulders bumped against each other as they walked. They had survived danger together.

Chris stopped singing. "I wonder what the secret is," he said.

Dinny whispered: "Maybe they found Andy Jim's buried treasure."

The red clay of the by-road ran out to mark the dark shining asphalt of the main road, like a river of fresh water fading into a black salt sea. The main road went up the long slope, and out of sight, and on towards Belfast; going the other way it went down the slope to the town, and in the distance they could see three spires, and bare trees down in the hollow and very faintly the distant, wintry mountains.

Dinny said: "Up that road tomorrow poor Aunt Aggie goes to hospital. Me da and May are going with her to Belfast. I wish I was going to Belfast." He looked up the road as if he could see Belfast in the distance.

"You're all right" Chris said. "You get to places. You were in Bundoran. I never was anywhere."

They walked down the road towards the town.

76

"If it's a bad secret," Chris said, "I'm sure it's the Bear Mullan's fault. Joe Keenan wouldn't do any harm to anybody."

"Neither would my brother Gerry."

"No," Chris said. He was thinking as hard as he could. He said: "I wonder what it is all the same. I'd like to give the Bear a broken mouth."

VI

May had her hair set in the new hairdresser's place, where all the fittings glittered with chromium, where coloured bottles shone in the soft pink light, where the air was delicately perfumed. It was a lovely place. The head girl there had been brought from Dublin to take control, and to show the three local girls how it was done. She was small and dainty, a mouthful to eat. She spoke so softly, complimenting May on her semi-blonde hair, showing her the exact sort of shampoo to use to preserve it as it was or to make it completely blonde. Her own hair was completely blonde and shone like satin. She admired May's new red costume, running a soft clothes brush down the back of that costume with a touch that was like a caress. May thought that she herself would like to be a hairdresser working with a girl like that in a place like that: soft pink lights, perfumed air, bottles all the colours of the rainbow. The new costume, the visit to the hairdresser, were in preparation for the journey to Belfast to deposit Aunt Aggie in hospital. It was an ill wind that didn't blow somebody good.

Aunt Aggie would go in the ambulance, escorted by trained attendants. May and her father would follow by car. May thanked God that she didn't have to travel in the ambulance, sitting holding Aunt Aggie's hand and consoling her. If you held her hand she probably wouldn't know it, and if you spoke consoling words she probably wouldn't hear them, and wouldn't anyway answer you because she couldn't talk coherently, couldn't do anything but look at you. That was bad enough in the shaded bedroom in which she lay; but bumping to Belfast over seventy miles of road, shut in an ambulance like a hen in a crate, it would have been horrible.

She sat in the front of the car beside her father. She stretched her feet forward as far as they would and leaned back and made herself comfortable. Drooping her eyelids two-thirds of the way down over her eyes she could follow the line of her figure from her breasts right down to her ankles. She was remembering the nice things the little hairdresser had said, a lovely little woman. The car hummed up the long slope out of the town, the ambulance a hundred yards ahead, and when the road was straight for a hundred yards you could look out through the windscreen and see the ambulance and think of Aunt Aggie. May didn't do that any oftener than she could help. She looked at herself. She looked at the countryside. On the mountains to the north there was a bright crust of snow. She looked at her father talking little and driving carefully, because the road was slippery and the surprisingly sudden frost of the previous night was crackling under the wheels of the car. She thought with joy of the day when she herself would own a car. She looked at her father muffled up like a mummy against the cold. Nowadays he was very careful of his health. He wasn't a very entertaining companion, driving with caution and never saying a word. She stretched herself in her seat and thought of big strong Pat Rafferty. She thought of Bernard Fiddis, and the pleasant entertaining way he could talk about everything, good, bad and indifferent. There wasn't much that man didn't know. Talking to him gave her the feeling that she used to get from reading magazines, borrowed at school, hidden from Aunt Aggie under the mattress of her bed.

She thought of everything, and then grew tired of silence. She said: "A penny for your thoughts, Daddy."

He inclined his head forward. He said: "I'm thinking of Aggie yonder in the ambulance."

She was sorry she had asked him. She might have known without asking.

"If I'm ever taken that way," he said, "stand by me like a good daughter."

Under the red skirt, in the pit of her stomach, she felt cold and hollow. She reached into the back seat for her overcoat. She said: "Don't be silly, Daddy. you shouldn't be thinking thoughts like that."

He wiped his lips nervously with the back of his left hand. "You never know," he said. "You never know. We're in God's hands."

After that, wrapping her coat around her shoulders, she was glad of silence, a silence that lasted all the way through the cold, quiet countryside; broken only when they passed through a town or a village and heard the sound of the movement of a life that was not their life, broken finally when they went down the long slope of a suburban road into the roar of the city. Where the traffic circled and circled around the monstrous city hall they lost sight of the ambulance. They drove to the hospital up a hilly, cobbled street. The noise of the city was shut out beyond a high wall and high iron gates, and a new silence that was not the silence of the countryside was around them: rubber-soled shoes walking in mute corridors, rows of white beds and patient silent bodies, the slow opening and closing of doors, whispering and nodding of heads, the smell of ether quietly soaking the air. May waited while her father whispered to doctors and nurses. She wondered would all the patients die if her father stopped whispering and did his talking at the top of his voice. She sighed with honest relief when the hospital was behind them and they were driving down again to the centre of the city. Her father sighed, too. He said wearily: "I hope they're able to do Aggie some good."

"I hope they are," she said.

He parked the car in a side street. He sat for a while leaning on the wheel, looking out vacantly through the windscreen. He wasn't looking at the street. There was nothing there to look at but a shabby, low-class cinema, and he wasn't a man to waste a glance on the grandest cinema ever built. He said: "When it gets to that stage it's nearly always fatal. She's a great loss. She stood to the four of you in the place of a mother."

May agreed without enthusiasm. She was cold and hungry. He said: "I'm afraid it's in us, too, in the Campbells." She could have cried with vexation: a new costume and a new hair-style to sit in the car in a side-street listening to her father ullagoning about Aunt Aggie. Aunt Aggie was safe in hospital, as safe as she would ever again be anywhere on this earth. She got out of the car. He followed her. He said: "I suppose you're hungry, daughter."

"I'm ravenous, Daddy," she said. She smiled at him with a great effort. "And you must be famished. You'll feel better when you've had something to eat, and something warming to drink." He shuffled at her side along the pavement. "Aunt Aggie is in good hands now," she said, "you needn't worry any more." He was proud of her: almost as tall as himself, and as straight as a steel rod. She walked so fast, her hard heels hammering, that he was puffed keeping up with her, and once in the cold wind he thought he was living two moments of his life at the same time, that he was walking also after another woman, the same quick steps, the same straight body, the same defiant, turbulent, puzzling ways.

They had lunch together in a small restaurant. She would have preferred a large hotel but her father wanted quietness, was almost apologetic for enforcing his wants against hers. "I'm poor company," he said, "for a young girl out for the day."

"Don't be silly, Daddy."

She studied him across the narrow table: the napkin tucked into his collar, his jaws steadily champing his food, a serious, old-fashioned, old man, but not a bad father to have, since one must have some sort of a father. The food was restoring the high colour to his long, curving cheeks. A light perspiration was breaking on his forehead and on the bald patch above his forehead.

"It's the truth all the same," he said. "You've had a big responsibility now ever since poor Aggie was taken bad. You want a bit of relaxation."

She was looking past him at a thin-faced, dark-headed, handsome man eating his lunch at the next table. He caught her eye and smiled hopefully. She couldn't afford to smile in answer, but a faint flicker of her eyelids said that she had noticed his smile. She leaned forward and listened to her father. "You should wait for the late train," he said, "and do a round of shopping." He was pushing towards her across the table four crisp banknotes. If one must have a father it was a good idea to have one who could afford to give you money. She said: "Thanks, Daddy, I think I will."

The man at the next table was still smiling. She liked the look of him, but then a stranger was a stranger, and her father was still with her. Travelling by train wouldn't be as comfortable as travelling by car, but it might be more exciting because you never knew your luck in meeting people on trains, the right sort of people, in first class carriages.

She left the restaurant, walking a little behind her father. The stranger smiled a last despairing smile, seeing so much that was desirable walking away for ever out of his life. Behind her father's back she considered it safe to answer his smile. Her skirt brushed the edge of the table as she walked past. It was a pity. Her father was an old dear, and very generous, but there was no use in denying that lunching with him could be dull, deadly dull.

Left to herself she wandered leisurely from shop to shop, forgetting the crowds that bustled around her, losing herself in the joy of handling and admiring expensive things. She didn't buy much. She wasn't going to burden herself with parcels. Having the power to buy was every bit as good as buying and was, also, far less trouble. Money was power. She fingered a small, glass, dressing-table ornament, and thought about Bernard Fiddis, for Bernard Fiddis and money and expensive ornaments chosen with taste seemed to belong in the same world. She went from shop to shop along a warm arcade, sheltered from the wind, sheltered from the roar of the street, a world on its own, a world of pleasant odours and little shops like glittering trinkets. The thought of Bernard Fiddis followed her from one small shop to the next, until in the end she was staring hard at every well-dressed man who passed, searching for a resemblance and then laughing at her own foolishness.

She stopped to look into the window of a bookshop, resting her eyes on a big red book about the writers of Russia, remembering Pat Rafferty who was still talking about a book, by some Russian, that one of the teachers had loaned him. Poor Pat, the bigness and foolishness of him, and the strength of him, the attractive overwhelming strength. It would be fun to buy the book and present it to Pat, and she opened the door of the little shop and stepped inside, and then stopped suddenly because Bernard Fiddis was standing with his back to the door, raising his left hand and carefully taking a book from one of the shelves on the far wall.

For one moment she felt panic, idiotic, unexplainable panic, the desire to retreat suddenly, closing the door softly behind her. He shouldn't be there. He couldn't be there. He had been in her thoughts and then suddenly he was there in the flesh, taking a book from a shelf, opening it and reading, his tweed overcoat unbuttoned and hanging loosely about him, his gloves and his white scarf protruding from one of the pockets, his brown hat tilted to the back of his head, the smoke of a cigarette making blue spirals around one of his ears. Behind her, the door, slowly closing on its springs, snapped shut, and she thought why couldn't he be there, why shouldn't he be there, didn't he as much right to be there as anybody else in the wide world who owned a motor car and lived within reasonable distance of

Belfast? So she walked across the shop and stood beside him, facing the shelves. He didn't look around, and didn't speak but he knew she was there, and she knew he knew she was there. He put the book back on the shelf. His hand was not as steady as it had been. She said: "Mr. Fiddis, what are you doing in Belfast?"

He wheeled suddenly, his face serious with surprise that almost looked genuine, and then smiling with genuine pleasure: "Why, May," he said, "hoping to see you, of course."

She accepted the remark as a joke, but she knew he didn't mean it as a joke; she didn't want him to mean it as a joke.

"Every time I come to Belfast," he said, "I come to his shop. It reminds me of the first and last time I ever felt embarrassed."

"I didn't think you could feel embarrassed."

"You'd be surprised."

The silence that followed was tense with embarrassment. She was conscious suddenly of how close she was standing to him and she would have moved away, even a few inches, but her feet seemed to be fastened firmly to the floor.

"It was once," he said, "I wanted to buy a book. Not a nice book. Not the sort of book a young man could ask for in any shop in our town." He was speaking slowly, like a man thinking of something else and trying hard to keep his thoughts concealed and imprisoned behind the fence that his words were building.

"A young man can't do much in our town," she said.

"Or a young woman," he said, and they laughed together and for a moment their embarrassment was gone.

"I came in here and whispered to the girl across the counter. She was a silly girl. She stood up straight and shouted the name of the book to the proprietor who was talking to a clergyman at the other end of the shop."

May walked with him to the counter and waited while he bought two books. "The proprietor shouted back: "We don't stock books of that nature," and the clergyman glared at me, and everybody in the shop turned to get a look at the young man who wanted the bad book."

May was laughing as they walked slowly along the arcade. "You must have been a rare young man," she said.

"Don't rub it in."

"I don't mean that," she said, and added hesitatingly: "Bernard."

82

He rested his hand on her arm as they crossed a narrow cobbled street, tightened his fingers and held her as a four-wheeled dray went rattling past. "This is Smithfield," he said. "The first book I ever bought I bought it here. It was a copy of *The Wealth of Nations*, and I've never read a line of it."

"I wouldn't blame you. It doesn't sound bright."

"It isn't. But there are bright books in Smithfield. Secondhand books. Secondhand everything." His gesturing hand comprehended the whole block of small shops, intersected by covered, musty alleyways. "Come on, and I'll show you," he said, "if you can spare the time."

"Time. I've all day. Until the late train goes."

"Come home with me," he said, "I'm driving."

"It's an idea," she said; and then they were going along one of the alleyways, dark and cluttered with goods, like a lane in a bazaar in some Eastern story of dark passion and darker hate. She was leaning on his arm, and they were walking like man and wife.

The town wasn't there to comment and criticize, and it didn't seem in the least peculiar to be walking with him, and leaning on his arm, and listening to his talk as he showed her the wonders of the market, even the corner with magazines that she never thought could be sold in public, or kept anywhere but under he mattress away from the eyes of Aunt Aggie and the disapproving world.

Very calmly she turned the pages of one of those magazines. He said: "You've got courage."

"There's little here," she said, "that a woman hasn't seen."

He laughed. "That's one way of looking at it," he said, and he looked away from the magazine and looked thoughtfully at her. She was a woman. She was a lovely woman. In there, in shadowy alleys and between dusty stalls, her loveliness was a challenge to darkness and cowardice and age and death.

"You're not like some young women I've met in my time."

"Have you met a lot?"

"A few. There was one in the university in Dublin with me. I brought her into the art gallery one day, and there bang facing us as we went in at the door was a picture some old villain of a Frenchman had painted in the eighteenth century." He smiled sadly, remembering that moment. "She was a nice girl. But she wasn't long out of a convent school in some part of Kerry. She turned and left me at the door, and never spoke to me again. It was a terrible picture."

She laughed at the woebegone face he assumed. "I was very hurt," he said. "God forgive that old Frenchman." And then squeezing her arm he said: "You're refreshingly different from that girl. From every girl. "

She was glad to hear him say that she was different, because he also was different from every other man she had ever met. Leaving Smithfield, leaning on his arm, her hand in his hand, she felt that those two stories of his youthful discomfitures had admitted her into some inner place in his life, some place shut even against Alice Graham. Dining with him in the biggest hotel in Belfast she felt that she was his best friend, she wanted to be his best friend, to laugh secretly with him at the silly joke that the world was. The waiters knew him. They whispered to him confidentially. They brought him exactly what he wanted. It was all so different from sitting with her father in a small restaurant and fighting against boredom by squeezing entertainment from every pair of wandering eyes. There was a lot to be said for Pat Rafferty. He was alive and he let you know it. But this was a world into which poor Pat hadn't the price of admission; a world of soft carpets, and orders obsequiously obeyed, and good food, and shining cutlery, and delicate glasses, and wine that was warmth and comfort and merriment without end.

She was laughing and chattily tipsy when they went to the pictures. She liked Eddie Cantor. He was a howl, dancing up and down a table, singing a song about building a little home with a carpet on the floor made of buttercups and clover. Bernard Fiddis's right hand was stroking her right hand. Eddie Cantor was being sold as a slave in the slave market in ancient Rome. Bernard Fiddis's left hand was resting on her right shoulder. She sat forward so that he could put his arm about her. Eddie Cantor was an unwilling food-taster in the palace of an unpopular and eminently poisonable Roman emperor. The crowd were roaring with laughter at Eddie Cantor. Bernard Fiddis's hand touched her left breast, and she winced, and then surrendered herself to the loud music, to the furious hilarity of an Eddie Cantor chariot race, to the soothing, hurting hand to the great laughter of all the people in the anonymous darkness—laughing at the comic antics of Eddie Cantor.

VII

Down in the hollow they saw a circle of lights, and that circle was made by the gas lamps of the town.

She said: "We could see the train from here. And I'd be home at the right time."

"You're the soul of discretion."

She was very proud of the approval in his voice. He drove the car slowly down the slope, turned left away from the road, drove for fifty yards along a narrow laneway, until they saw the high arch of a railway bridge before them. He looked at the clock on the dashboard as he turned off the engine. "Fortyfive minutes yet," he said, "and the train must pass right over our heads."

"You think of everything."

He thought of everything. He knew what to think. He knew what to say. He knew what to do. His hand was stroking the red skirt, and then she didn't care any more what his hand was doing, or what he was saying, or what the town in its circle of gas lamps was doing or thinking or saying. She was saying something herself, but when she tried to listen, her ears were booming with echoes, and she didn't know what the words were that were falling, one after the other, through her parted lips, and falling into bottomless emptiness; and the world was shaking with the thunder of the late train from Belfast roaring towards the station, and for one moment she thought she was on that train going out into space, in ever widening circles, out and out and out beyond the poor narrow limits of the world.

4

High Water

ONE afternoon the snow came suddenly out of a dark, low sky. The first flakes were wet like sleet and sharp like fine hail, and Joe Keenan looked up at the sky, tightened the collar of his jacket around his chin, said to Gerry Campbell and the Bear Mullan that it was going to rain cats and dogs. As a rule Joe Keenan was a good judge of the weather, but he was wrong this time for fifteen minutes later when the three of them were huddled against a high bare hedge, the rain grew white around them and the first crust of snow was on the ground. The red, sandy by-road shone through the thin covering of snow. The dark, slippery slates of the great house away on the far side of the road defied the whitening power of the snow, but the ridge tiles and the window-sills and the tops of the pillars at the gate were capped suddenly with snow that shone like white, precious fur. It was all so sudden and so quiet, the earth growing white under a dark sky; and the three of them leaned back against the thorny hedge, said little, and watched the snow thickening until it looked as if the air was choking with feathers blown from some plucking-yard in the high heaven.

They looked quietly at the great house across the road. The house looked back at them. They were a mile from the town and Gerry Campbell was the only one of the three who had an overcoat.

"We'll be here till Easter," Joe Keenan said.

Gerry said. "Funny we never get weather like this at Christmas."

"To hell with Christmas," the Bear said. "I'm perished."

Joe ran his lips up and down the mouth-organ, then coughed, wiped the mouth-organ carefully and put it into his pocket. "We'd be warmer walking," he said, "unless we get shelter in the house across the road. "

"Some hope," the Bear said.

They looked at the house and the house looked back at them, and for one moment it seemed as if the thin window above the front door winked at them through the darkness of the falling snow. It was a tall house, separated from the roadway by a low wall and a smooth lawn and across the lawn ran a line of monkey-puzzle trees.

"We could ask," Gerry said; and the house winked again, something white moving behind the dark glass of the high window. It was a girl wearing a white apron, and she was waving at them. They waved back at her, and stood in motionless surprise when she pulled down the window and leaned her head and shoulders out into the snow. Her shoulders were covered with dark cloth, but the little white cap on her head was like the cap of snow on the ridge tiles. She waved her right arm. She shouted: "Come in, out of the storm." Her voice was very shrill. She shouted again: "Run round the path to the back door and I'll let you in."

They hesitated. Joe Keenan dusted a wandering snowflake off his jacket with a cold hand. He said: "I've been asked to the party. Where's me Sunday suit?" He sang softly:

Hand me down me petticoat and hand me down me shawl.

"She's only the maid," Gerry said.

The Bear, in slow thought, sucked his lips. "There's nobody else in the house," he said, "or she wouldn't be shouting out of the upstairs window."

The girl excitedly was waving both arms. Her little apron was a white blob between the dark glass of the window and the dark cloth of her skirt. She called: "Come on, before you're frozen into snowmen," and then withdrew herself and closed the window with a bang. One final wink from the window and the white apron was gone. The wind blew over the bare hedge, tossing the snowflakes in wide drunken circles.

"She's gone to open the back door," Gerry said.

Joe Keenan sang:

And hand me down me hand-me-downs, for I'm off to Donegal,

and with a shout he was across the road and through the gate and running around the path to the back door, waving his arms at the falling snow like a swimmer conquering a strong sea, running so fast that he was in the kitchen and shaking the snow off his shoulders before Gerry and the Bear had turned the corner of the house.

She was a bony sort of a girl with shiny, protruding teeth and dark red hair curled in little rolls like sausages. Her legs were straight and thin, and, every time she moved, her hip bones and shoulder blades threatened to cut their way through her dark dress. She placed four chairs in a half circle before the range, huge and glistening and fitted with fifty contrivances, throwing out from its red heart a nourishing, radiant heat. "Take off your coat, Mr. Campbell," she said, "and sit down." Joe Keenan laughed. The Bear Mullan was already sitting down, his long legs stretched to the heat, his quick eyes occasionally glancing calculatingly around the kitchen. Gerry was embarrassed. The slight pink that always was in his cheeks deepened to a blush. He took off his coat and dropped it with assumed carelessness across the back of a chair. His good, brown suit exaggerated the straightness, the girlish slenderness of his body. He sat down on the chair between the girl and Joe Keenan. He said: "How well you know my name." The Bear yawned, lazily raising a foot to rest it on the polished range.

"I was in your house," she said, "and you never even knew it."

"You were not."

She laughed at his surprised denial. She was arch. "Not working," she said. "Visiting. Your Jinny's a friend of mine."

"She's not my Jinny."

Joe Keenan laughed again, combing his long, black hair back with a sweep of his fingers. "Gerry's sorry he missed you," he said.

"Jinny told me your house was a great house to work in."

"Did she?"

"I wish to God I could get a job in a house that had one decent-looking fellow in it."

Gerry's blush deepened. The Bear put his other foot on the range, tilting his chair backwards. Joe Keenan was genuinely amused. "Come to my house, Maisie," he said. "It's just exactly what you want."

"My name's not Maisie. My name's Jean."

He sighed. "You remind me of a girl I knew once, and her name was Maisie."

"This house is hell," she said. "They even lock up the grain of tea. I can't offer you boys a bite or a sup. Except apples. They don't count the apples. The pantry is full of green apples."

"Green apples are my delight," Joe Keenan said.

They followed her into the pantry. The cold air dripped with the smell of apples. They filled their pockets and followed her back to the kitchen. She bent over the range, carefully shovelling coal into the red depths. Her skirt was short, and bending over the range she showed them, in all innocence, an inch of pale thin thigh.

"I even have to go careful with the coal."

"Be careful with everything," Joe said, and the Bear sniggered. They munched apples. The warm air was drenched with the smell of apples.

"Old miserable people," she said, "that wouldn't give you the wind of their farts."

"I wouldn't want it," Joe said.

"It's all right to laugh," she said, "but nights sitting here on my own I could go across to the planting and put my arms around one of the trees."

"Cold sport," Joe Keenan said, "coortin' the trees. Sit down there on Gerry's knees and keep the heat in yourself."

She turned from the range, dusting her hands, giggling shrilly. Gerry had no time to protest. She was on his knees like a bird dropping suddenly on a nest. If he hadn't put his arm around her waist she would have gone backwards to the floor. The bones in her hips were cutting into him. She was the thinnest girl in the world. The Bear looked on, and said nothing. Joe Keenan leaned forward, modestly pulling down the dark skirt to cover the two bony knees. "Tempt me not," he said. His right hand rested gently on her right knee. He said: "Just a touch of housemaid's knee." That was something he had seen printed on one of the lurid postcards hanging in the window of the newsagent's shop: a fat, red-faced man dandling on his knee a blonde, smiling housemaid; her skirt was very short and her legs were very long, and one of the man's large hands greedily fondled one of her shapely knees. Joe Keenan had transferred the drawing and the inscription to the gable wall of a house on a hill in full view of trains entering the railway station. He was very proud of that drawing. He had done it in coloured chalks, and the rain never blew against that gable, and unless the house fell or somebody went to the trouble of scrubbing the wall, the drawing would be there for ever.

She was fondling Gerry's hair with her left hand, alternately ruffling and smoothing, running her fingers through it as if it were something precious like gold dust. Her voice was no longer shrill. She said: "Your hair isn't as fair as your sister's."

"She won't let him use her washing soda," the Bear said.

She ignored the Bear. She went on talking as if there was nobody in the kitchen but herself and Gerry Campbell. "Not the little dark sister. She's great sport. Always out for a reel. She's very nice to Jinny, too. Jinny would die for her."

"Jinny'll die when her time comes," Gerry said. He didn't know whether it would be more embarrassing to stand up suddenly and get rid of her, or to allow her to go on talking and sitting on his knee and slowly stroking his hair. He was glad the Bear couldn't see his face. He didn't mind Joe Keenan.

"Will she marry that Collins boy?"

"Not if I can help it."

"He's a nice boy. He hasn't much money. But many a girl in this town would be glad of him."

The Bear said: "The girls in this town aren't hard to please."

Once again she ignored the Bear. She said: "Your big sister's beautiful. She's like a film star. I wish to God I was like that."

"I wish to God you were," the Bear said. But she didn't seem to hear him. Her hard, thin back was a barrier between the Bear Mullan and the decent people that were worth talking to, and the beautiful people that were worth talking about. "Your sister'll never have any trouble finding boys."

"Not while I'm around," said Joe Keenan, sticking his thumbs in his waistcoat and waggling his lively fingers, and she laughed at Joe Keenan.

"She's found one already. She's the sort of a girl'll please herself. They're talking about her and that big Rafferty boy."

"They're talking about me and Greta Garbo," said Joe Keenan.

"Oh you," she said, "you're a card."

"I'm the pack," he said, "ace, king, queen and joker. "

"I know that Rafferty boy," she said. "I come from that part of the country. I know his father that's always lamenting about the

90

river. I know his uncle, too. It was his evidence, they say, that saved Maxwell from the rope."

"They're at it again," Joe said.

"At what?"

"Saying. They're always saying."

She said: "You're too smart." But she was laughing as if she didn't mind Joe Keenan being smart. "I saw them one night at the pictures," she said. "He had his arm around her and she had her head on his shoulder. It must be powerful to be in love."

The Bear stood up suddenly. He said: "Holy Christ!" He walked across the kitchen and looked out of the window. The snow had stopped. She looked at the Bear as if she was seeing him for the first time, and didn't like what she saw. She said: "What's wrong with him?"

"He was crossed in love," Joe said, picking some pocket fluff out of the teeth of his mouth-organ.

She was interested. She forgot about the Bear, stooped at the window and staring out at the white quiet world. "Can you play it?" she asked.

"Can I play it." He played a tune; quick, jigging, silver notes. She sang shrilly the words of the song that went lightly with the light tune: about building a nest in the west neath a sky of heavenly blue, and spending days discovering ways to say I love you. Her eyes shone with delight.

"I love music," she said. "There's a piano here and it would do your heart good to hear it."

"Joe plays the piano," Gerry said. The girl's pointy bones would have his thighs marked for life.

"I'll show it to you while they're out," she said, standing up, and Gerry also stood up quickly. She led the way out of the kitchen. The Bear asked: "Are they often out?"

"Often and often," she said, "thanks be to God. I find it lonely, but I'd rather be lonely than persecuted, any day of the week."

They crossed a wide hallway, warm with oaken furnishings and deep furry rugs. "From this out," the Bear said, "you'll have Gerry Campbell to keep you company." The Bear's little eyes went from object to object around the hallway, from object to object around the drawing-room into which she led them. Joe sat down reverently before the huge piano, his ragged and unkempt reflection looking back at him from its polished, gleaming depths. He had learned to finger out tunes on the battered piano in the billiard room at the bottom of the town. Reverently he touched the spotless keys and a ripple of notes ran around the room from object to object, following the path taken by the Bear's calculating eyes. Then with a quick jerk of his shoulder, he was into the middle of a tune. He played tunes about love, about marching through Georgia, about soldiers are we whose lives are pledged to Ireland. She swayed her thin body to the music. She stood close to Gerry and every time she swayed towards him her shoulder touched his shoulder. He was embarrassed, but he didn't move away. The Bear walked to the window and stood looking out at the white lawn, and the monkey-puzzles that were white on one side and green on the other. It was a wide window with a low sill.

It was powdery, sticky snow. It clogged their boots on the way back to the town. Joe Keenan said he wished to God he had a pair of snowshoes.

"You could have stayed all night," the Bear said, "playing music to that rickle of bones."

"You're jealous of Gerry."

"Who's jealous? If there wasn't another woman in the world …"

"The world's full of women," Joe said. "But not of them would risk their life with you."

There was an angry silence. Their feet made a little shuffling in the thin snow. "Mind you," Joe said, "there's not much doubt about that lassie being queer in the head. But she was decent enough to give us shelter."

"There's a lot of things in that house," the Bear said, "that could be taken without much trouble."

This time the silence was a meditative silence. The first houses of the town were in view far down the white road. The lamps were lit but the brightness of the fallen snow had prolonged the daylight.

"We've taken chances twice," Gerry said. "I've had enough."

"Soft," the Bear said.

"He's right," Joe said quickly. "We'll be in trouble yet."

"It's dead easy," the Bear said. "In Fiddis's house all we have to do is lock the old woman in her room. Ye promised to do that."

Joe and Gerry made no answer. The circle of radiance that the first lamp made on the snow was all around them. "In that house," the Bear said, "Gerry could keep the girl in the kitchen talking about love. No risk at all."

"Nothing doing," Gerry said.

"Soft," the Bear said again. "Your hair's not as fair as your sister's. You've a crush on skinny Lizzie."

They stopped and faced each other. Joe Keenan came quietly between them. "Fighting's no good," he said. "Fiddis's house will be the third and last."

The Bear tightened his muffler and spat sideways into the snow. A green bus passed, crowded with people, chains rattling round the wheels, going up towards the snow-choked valleys and the little stony hill-farms.

"Come on home," Joe said, "before we have an audience."

They went slowly and sullenly up the silent muffled street.

II

In the yard behind the house Chris Collins was hammering nails into wood. Pat Rafferty from where he sat could see Chris, the arm that held the hammer rising and falling, his light foxy hair cascading regularly over his eyes and being regularly brushed back with his right forearm. Jim Collins, sitting on the kitchen table with his back to the kitchen window, said that bloody fellow would hammer the house down.

"He's fixing the runner on a sleigh,"Pat said.

"The sleigh Jim and yourself broke last winter," Anne said. She sat where she always sat in her chair between the table and the corner where her books were stacked on two varnished shelves. Her right leg was stretched straight in front of her. Her right foot rested on a cushion on the shining steel fender.

"Maybe we should give him a hand," Pat said.

"The exercise will do him good."

"The size of you two," Anne said, "breaking the poor boy's sleigh and then refusing to help him to fix it."

"It's Sunday," Jim said. "I don't work on Sunday."

"You'll be working tonight at the play."

"Necessary servile labour," Jim said. "Every dramatic society needs a stage manager. And Sunday's the only night in the week that the people of this town would waste on a play."

"Nothing else to do on Sunday night," Pat said.

Anne flicked with her fingers the leaves of the book that Pat had brought her. She said: "I wish I could go," and the short silence that followed was the more intense because out in the yard Chris had ceased his hammering.

"You're missing nothing," Pat said. "Haven't you books? And the poor people who go to the play wouldn't know the difference between a book and a bullock."

"I'd like to see you acting," Anne said. "I'd like to see Dinny Campbell's sister acting. The one that everybody says is great."

"She's acting all the time," Pat said.

"She's good all right," Jim said, "but she knows it. Pat's good, too. You should see Pat in the robes of a high priest." He laughed at some secret joke. He crossed his legs tailor-wise on the table. "Hey, Pat, I'll be Jack MacGowan doing Herod, and you do your stuff as the high priest. We'll give Anne a special private performance."

Pat was on his feet, his brown-black eyes no longer sombre but shining with merriment. In the small kitchen his height was exaggerated to stooping, slow-moving monstrosity. Anne was laughing. She said: "You're a high priest all right."

Pat opened the door between the kitchen and the hallway. "This is the way of it, Anne," he said. "Herod's squatting there biting his nails." He pointed to Jim, who scowled fiercely and began gnashing his teeth and cracking his fingers. "He's just heard a few yarns about the arrival of the wise men. As well as that he has a pain in the belly." Jim groaned pitifully. "A Nubian eunuch stands beside the throne. The wee messenger boy outa Nixon's shop painted so as his own mother wouldn't know him. Here I come." He ran the hallway, and returned with slow and massive stateliness. "I'm Annas the high priest arriving with the whole low-down on the situation. Facts and figures and a general consensus of public opinion."

"Annas," bellowed Jim from the table, "step right in." Anne, her pale hands gripping the arms of her chair, was laughing helplessly.

"Ask the bloody eunuch to get me something to sit on," Pat said.

Jim bellowed: "Bring the clergyman a butter box."

Pat explained: "The seats in Herod's palace are made out of butter boxes covered with coloured paper. When the eunuch carries

94

me a seat he'll, sure as God, turn it upside down so that the whole hall'll be able to read: Shaneragh Creamery, fifty-two pounds."

Jim looked out of the window. He said: "Chris is gone."

"He's gone sleighing with Dinny Campbell on the big hill," Anne said.

"He tells you everything," Jim said. "It wouldn't be a bad idea, Pat, if we took the air ourselves."

"We've a hard night before us."

"Come back for tea," Anne said.

They left her, sitting in the corner where she always sat, quietly beginning to read the book that Pat had brought her.

"She's a martyr," Jim said.

"She'd love to see the play."

The little streets were uncannily quiet, snow piled around doorsteps, snow thick on the ground deadening the sound of footsteps. The playing children who generally made the air shrill had gone out to the sleighing on the big hill at the edge of the town. Jim and Pat turned their backs on the town and walked towards the open country.

"This blizzard," Jim said, "will do a lot of damage."

"In some places," Pat said. "It's not so bad out our way. The roads are clear. But it's very heavy in the mountains and that means floods when the thaw comes."

"Your old man will be good to listen to."

"He never stops these days. He met a returned Yank who set him off about the Tennessee Valley Authority."

"Sacred Heart," Jim said.

"My old man," said Pat, "is an American out of his environment. He wants to make the world turn the other way. Just for the fun of it."

"He's right all the same."

"I suppose so," Pat said, and he turned and looked back down the road at the town in the white, quiet hollow. Smoke rose from chimneys and stood still in the motionless air. The fury of the blizzard had passed on and left behind a white silence on the earth, a blue quietness in the sky. Here and there where the snow had thawed and slipped and fallen a roof glittered like black ebony. The spires of the churches stood up dark and slender, detached from the whiteness of the world. The ruins of the old tower were almost invisible, all the sins of the centuries covered in a coat of spotless snow.

They were looking back towards the part of the town where Jim lived, and they knew each other's thoughts.

"I wonder has she much of the book read by now," Jim said.

"I wonder does she like it."

"She'll like it because you brought it. Your visits and your books keep her alive."

"She's in her chair," Pat said, "the way we are in this town. She never sees the town and we never see the world."

"The town's good enough for me," Jim said. "The world can look after itself," and they walked on into the white country Pat with the countryman's long swinging, easy step, Jim with the quick accurate step that he was always proud to think of as a characteristic of the good footballer. Pat found himself envying Jim Collins: Jim wanted so little—the town, a moderately good job, a dance and ultimately a wedding with Dympna Campbell, a game of football. And the little that he asked was his with an automatic easiness. His quick step on the crisp snow was a happy step, definite, sure of itself, never too far away from the earth, a step inherited from generations of men trained to walk precisely on hard and unromantic barrack squares. Pat's own way of walking, and maybe his way of thinking, came from men who had meditatively walked in green fields, never quite contented with those fields, wanting to change them as his father did, or loving them and still wanting to leave them because other desires were stronger at times than the desire for the green fields: desire for the world or desire for a woman who had herself no place in green quietness.

The road turned a corner high about a level meadow, made more level than ever by the smooth snow. A path went straight across the meadow; the snow marked by a thin line, crushed and churned by passing feet. Beyond the meadow was the big hill, a white cone, glistening in the brief sunlight, dotted with black running figures, with loaded sleighs going down with direct, exhilarating speed. They could hear the shouts and the laughter, very thin and clear across the cool air.

"Chris is over there with Dinny Campbell," Jim said. "We'll go across to see what they're at."

"Dinny's a quiet lad," Pat said, and they went down the slope to the meadow.

"He's a different type from his brother."

"Gerry's all right. A bit weak, maybe. You can't deny he has two smashing sisters."

Jim laughed. "Poor Dympna," he said, "she's very worried about the old aunt. There isn't much hope for her, you know."

"Isn't she in hospital since before Christmas?"

"She's coming home again soon. The hospital can't help her."

"May went up with her to Belfast. But I didn't hear her talking much about the aunt since."

"I haven't seen much of May recently," Jim said.

"Neither have I."

The path grew narrow. They walked single file, Pat walking in the lead. "Except at rehearsals," Pat said. "And one night I was down with her in Graham's hotel. That Alice Graham is a hell of a woman."

"She's no company for May Campbell."

"That's what the town says, Jim."

"She divorced three husbands."

"She could divorce thirty, if every man in the town wasn't afraid to go near her. Except Fiddis."

"Fiddis can look after himself."

"I met him there," Pat said. "He's all right."

"I've nothing against him."

They stopped walking and talking suddenly. The meadow all around them, the conical hill above them, were quiet. The sound of laughing and shouting and sleigh-runners had ceased abruptly. The black figures were gathered together half-way up the slope of the hill. "There's something wrong," Jim said, running on across the meadow, climbing an iron gate, running the hill through the thick snow. Pat followed, running as hard as he could, but unable to run with the directed force that drove Jim across the snow-encumbered ground as if he were running in light shoes on a summery lawn; and when Pat, breathless with exertion, reached the crowd he saw little Dinny Campbell lying on the ground and Chris Collins kneeling by his side, and a few yards away Jim Collins and the Bear Mullan were facing each other. The crowd was very quiet. Pat elbowed his way through. A dozen voices coming to gabbling life tried to tell him what was wrong. He bent down over Dinny Campbell, and listened only to Chris Collins. Dinny was crying quietly with pain.

"He took the sleigh off us," Chris said. "And when we tried to stop him he ran it over Dinny's ankle." The ankle was bruised and bleeding, but not broken, Pat thought fingering it gently. Behind him he heard Jim Collins say: "What have you to say, Bear?"

The Bear said one word. It was expressive; and Jim Collins struck him a quick blow on the mouth. The Bear said: "I'll split you wide open, Collins."

"What with?"

"Anything. When I get a chance."

"You'll fight fair, Bear," Pat said. He still knelt, examining the wounded ankle. "You'll fight fair," he said, "unless you want my boot in the belly."

The Bear stood quietly, his long arms hanging by his sides. Pat told Chris to run down to the road and stop the first motor car that came along. "He won't fight at all if he has to fight fair," Jim Collins said, and turning around he walked towards Pat Rafferty, and the Bear, as if shot forwards by steel springs, leaped on him. The thin hard hands gripped Jim's throat. Two knees, as hard as mahogany, dug Jim suddenly in the small of the back, and, feet slipping in the snow, they fell heavily, the Bear on top, his thin mouth loose with words that came out like liquid out of a shattered sewer, his left hand gripping Jim's throat, his right hand groping in the pocket of his coat. Pat Rafferty advanced warily across the snow, placing his feet securely, watching his chance to disentangle the struggling arms and legs. The crowd of boys had closed in shouting with excitement. Pat turned for a moment to warn them away from Dinny Campbell, and turning again saw the quick white flash as the Bear's right hand pulled out of his pocket an open clasp knife. Pat kicked. It was a risk. He might have kicked anybody. He might have slipped and fallen and added his own long body to the tangle on the ground. But he was lucky and he didn't fall, his heavy boot cracked on the Bear's elbow, and the knife went up into the air spinning like a silver spoonbait, and the Bear was standing on his feet and nursing his elbow and saying again and again: "Rafferty, you bastard, you've broken my arm."

Pat listened for a few moments. His long, heavily-boned face was perfectly calm. Then he swung his long right arm and struck the Bear on the side of the head, a dull blow, and the Bear, cursing with pain and surprise, fell in the snow and lay still.

"That's enough Pat," Jim said. He nursed a wrist bleeding from a quick touch of the knife. "That's enough."

Pat didn't seem to hear him. He stood over the Bear Mullan and stirred him sharply with his boot, and when the Bear was half-way to his feet Pat struck him twice, slow heavy blows, a right arm and a left arm swinging down like flails; and the Bear ducked sideways and ran, sobbing and cursing, slithering in the snow down the slope of the hill, and a volley of snowballs followed him, making plopping noises and little white circles on the back of his coat, and once when he slipped and fell heavily the crowd cheered as crowds always cheer at the fall of a beaten tyrant.

Jim Collins was sitting on the snow, bandaging with his handkerchief his bleeding wrist. Pat was kneeling over Dinny Campbell feeling his ankle as gently as a mother might soothe a sick child. Jim was puzzled: under all that gentleness there was a calm iron anger, a terrible anger to see on a snowy Sunday when the whole world was as white as a row of little girls making their first communion.

"We'll take him on a sleigh to the road," Pat said. "He'll never be able to walk it."

Dinny had stopped crying. He said: "You must be the best boxer in the world."

They placed him sitting on a sleigh and went slowly and gently down the hill and across the meadow. Chris was coming to meet them, and a man walked behind Chris, and on the road beyond the meadow a car was waiting. There wasn't another car in the town like that long, yellow car. There wasn't another man in the town who could dress as Fiddis the solicitor could dress: a shiny motoring-coat with a warm, deep collar of fur, gloves that went up to his elbows. He bent down over the sleigh and examined the wounded ankle. He said: "He won't die this time, but all the same the quicker he's in a warm bed the better for himself." He helped Pat to carry the sleigh up the slope. He looked soft, but he was as strong as Pat and his feet never slipped in the snow. He wrapped Dinny in a rug and made him sip whisky out of a small silver flask. Dinny sat in the back between Chris and Jim Collins, and Pat sat in the front beside Fiddis, and they drove to Campbell's house.

"I'll run in first," Fiddis said, "in case we alarm the girls." A few words whispered to Jinny who opened the door, and he walked across the hall to the drawing-room where there was nobody to be alarmed except May, sitting, her face gently flushed with the heat, on a low stool before the fire. Her hair tumbled untidily down the back of her blue jumper. The placket of her skirt was half unfastened, and it was with an effort that he took his eyes away from the triangle of white cloth thus revealed. Lazily, half sleepily, crouching before the flame, her flesh had softened like a rich fruit ripening; and it might have been that, or it might have been because she had no longer the virginal hardness that was half fear and half ignorance that made him forget for a moment what his errand was. He was kneeling on the floor behind her, his lips finding through the silky fair hair the white sweetness of her skin. "There's nobody here except Jinny," she said. "It was lucky you came, Bernard." He remembered then. He told her about Dinny. He told her to listen to the shuffle of feet on the concrete outside the house for that meant that Jim Collins and Pat Rafferty were carrying Dinny towards the door.

She rose slowly. "Poor Dinny! I hope he hasn't harmed himself." She fastened her skirt properly; he counted aloud the tiny metallic sounds of the catches slipping into place. She smiled. She said: "In this house there's always something. You never have peace."

His hand rested for a moment on her shoulder. "After the play," he said. She nodded agreement. She went out before him, her feet moving quietly in soft slippers. He carried Dinny up to his bedroom, panting and puffing a little more than he needed to because a terrible elation threatened to crack his voice when he tried to speak, and he was remembering a phrase from some magazine story about an Elizabethan adventurer planting his sword in some rich newly-discovered land, and crying out in clear air never disturbed by a human voice: "All this fair country is mine. All this fair country is mine."

III

May was gone when Pat went heavily down the dusty stairs and knocked at the door of the ladies' dressing-room. The door was half open. He could hear the furiously intense hissing of the gas lamp.

100

He could see a section of the brightly lighted room, a pile of coloured clothes on the corner of a table, a cane chair lying on the floor with a peculiarly pathetic air of helplessness and injured innocence. He knocked again. The room was very quiet. On the ceiling above his head he could hear the bump of feet where Jim Collins and his men were setting the stage in order. The warm air was gritty with the smell of powder and grease paint. The room was empty. He satisfied himself by pushing the door wide open and looking in and looking all around, a little nervously in case he might discover some modest maiden cowering in an uncovered condition in a corner. The last scene of the play had needed a choir of angels, and the place had been lousy with modest maidens. But the room was completely empty; empty of maidens, empty of angels. On another table the long gowns of the angels were piled in a soft, white, shimmering heap, and if he had been in good humour it might have amused him to think of all the acres of angelic modesty that had been covered by that white cloth. But he wasn't in good humour.

He went very slowly back up the stairs. He had asked her to wait for him. She hadn't said yes and she hadn't said no. She had circled around the question, talking with him, laughing with him, liking him. He knew she liked him; and yet she was gone careless even about the things she liked. He couldn't understand it. He could only suppose that there was something in the nature of women that made them do things like that, set them separate and apart, making laws for themselves in their own odd republic.

Jim Collins, standing in the middle of the bare stage, was unrolling the sleeves of his shirt, and shouting valedictory thanks to two workmen who were half way down the empty hall on their way to the door. "It's all over," Jim said. "I wonder where the hell I left my jacket and coat." He found them draped intricately around the rungs of a small ladder in the darkness of the wings. "Dympna did that," he said. "She'll have to learn to take better care of her future husband's clothes."

"Has she gone home?"

"She ran home to Dinny."

They walked down the hall between the rows of empty seats. A hunch-backed caretaker was securing windows and switching off lights. They stood in the porch and looked out into the white, cold, deserted street. The snow was falling again, large single flakes drifting easily to the earth, melting as soon as they touched a hand or a face. "It'll be raining in the morning", Pat said. May, maybe, had gone home with Dympna to see how Dinny was. Maybe. "You go home, Jim," he said. "I'll walk as far as Graham's hotel."

"We'll wait up for you. Anne and myself."

"Don't, man. Go to bed and get your sleep."

"Tisn't often we have you as a guest."

They walked down the steps from the porch to the footpath. "Don't take it bad" Jim said. "Girls take notions like that sometimes."

"Christ," Pat Rafferty said, and he went off laughing at the note of wisdom and experience that Jim Collins had tried to infuse into his innocent voice.

The wind had changed. The wind from the southwest came blowing softly up the street. Under his feet the grip of the snow on the ground was weakening; and for a while he forgot about May Campbell and saw instead the white snow from the mountains melting to brown turbulent water and spreading out over the drenched withered meadows. Then he was pressing the bell at the side door of Graham's hotel and remembering what his errand was, and laughing at himself to discover his father's blood running in his own veins.

Alice Graham was glad to see him. He knew genuine welcome when he saw it; and, although he was never certain how much he liked or trusted Alice Graham, he appreciated the welcome. She made room for him to sit beside her on a couch in front of the fire, throwing heavy smooth-papered American magazines out of the way, straightening a wine-coloured cushion, rising to pour him a drink. He didn't mention May, because if she wasn't there she wasn't there, and there was no sense in asking silly questions. He reached his hands out to the heat. He said: "This is a disreputable hour to call at any house."

"This is a disreputable house," she said. She laughed softly in her throat. Her back was turned to him as she bent over the soda siphon, and through half-closed eyes he admired the shape of her, dressed in dark slacks and a coloured silk blouse, well-built and long-legged like a prize mare. If she had left three husbands behind her on the road it must have been because there was something wrong with the husbands. "You're always welcome," she said. "You should have

102

called to see me long ago," and she sank into the couch beside him, and clinked her glass against his glass, and drank it so easily at one go that he was, for the glory of manhood, compelled to do likewise. It went down like fire. She put her feet on a low stool. There was fire in the hearth and red fire in his body. Her legs curved very gracefully and her ankles were bare.

"How did the play go?"

"Very well. The hall was full. Of course it would be full anyway. Going to the play is next door to going to Mass when the proceeds are for the parish."

"I didn't go," she said. "I heard it was all angels."

"Do you not believe in angels?"

"Not in this town." They laughed together, and she said she had heard that May Campbell had the makings of a good actress."

"She has," he said. "She's very good."

"Bernard Fiddis told me she was worth seeing."

"He's a good judge," Pat said, and he reached across her, his left hand resting on her knee, to replace his empty glass on the small table. She was watching his face. She was wondering how he felt and how much he knew. He was big and as strong as three men, and still he was only an innocent boy. She said: "Bernard Fiddis has a lot of experience."

She got up from the couch and refilled their glasses. She walked to the door and switched off the light, and said: "I think it's always warmer without the electric light." But in spite of all his innocence he knew that she had switched off the light because, seen by the glow of the fire, her face was younger, the hard definite lines softened, the hard definite colours of cosmetics melted into a sultry olive that must have been the colour of her face when she was a young girl: a dark-haired, long-legged, olive-skinned girl. He tried to see her as she might have been then, but he knew that he couldn't do that without a knowledge of people and places he had never seen: mighty streets in London with the whole world passing through, busy towns built gracefully around ancient cathedrals, or the valley of an English river he had read about in a book where the clay was red and the villages were red because the houses were built out of the red clay.

She clinked her glass against his glass. She said: "Tell me, Pat, are you in love with May Campbell?"

By daylight or electric light he would have resented the question, but in the soft glow of the fire and with the honey-coloured whisky glowing in his veins all curiosity was friendly and love was a thing that could be mentioned without shame.

"I don't know," he said. That wasn't a lie but it was something less than the truth. He said: "I like her and I think she likes me. She's very attractive."

"She's dangerously attractive," Alice Graham said. "I said so to Bernard Fiddis weeks ago."

"Bernard Fiddis," Pat said, "should be able to look after himself." Slowly, as he sipped his drink, he was trying to make out why Alice Graham should warn Bernard Fiddis against May Campbell.

Alice Graham laughed quietly, a quiet laugh without fun. She said: "No man is ever able to look after himself. I should know. Ask any of the good people in this town. They'll tell you that I should know."

"I don't pay much attention to the town." Maybe Alice Graham was in love with Bernard Fiddis. It was very likely. Maybe Bernard Fiddis had a notion about May Campbell. It could happen. Anyway he couldn't go knocking at Campbell's door at this hour of the night to see was May really in the house nursing Dinny. He drank the last drop of his whisky and wished to God he had gone home with Jim Collins, and suddenly he wanted the company of Jim Collins: Jim's honesty, his belief in the honesty of little, dancing, dark-headed Dympna. Christ, there could be a terrible difference between sisters, children of the same parents. He stood up. Ten minutes walk away, at a hearth as different from this hearth as day was from night, Jim Collins and Anne were waiting on him.

"Are you going so soon?" she asked.

"I must," he said. "I just dropped in to say hello."

"Say it then," she said, "over another drink." She was laughing, laughter bubbling in her throat as the drink bubbled, dark as dark wine in the firelight, out of the bottle. She was friendly, he thought. And it wasn't her fault. And another drink wouldn't shorten his life.

She sat closer to him on the couch and he draped his left arm about her shoulders. She caught his hand with her hand and held it gently. He held his glass for a moment without tasting the drink, trying to steady the throbbing in his veins, to remember exactly why he had come to this place. He had asked May Campbell to wait for him when the play was over. He thought he had a certain right to ask her that because they had for a while been going about together, and going to the pictures together. She hadn't said yes and she hadn't said no, but she was gone when he went looking for her all the same. So he had walked into Graham's hotel looking for her, because although he liked May Campbell a great deal he didn't think she was a girl who would go straight home after the play to nurse her little brother's injured ankle. But she wasn't in Graham's hotel and he didn't know where she was. She might be at home or she might be in hell, and Alice Graham was good company, and he didn't see why he should follow like a fool where he wasn't wanted.

"You should come often to see me," Alice Graham was saying. "Life can be dull here sometimes."

He pressed her hand, slowly tightening his strong fingers, knowing that the large, purple-stoned dress-ring on her second finger must be cutting into her flesh.

"No congenial company," she said. "I often thought of moving. Only Bernard Fiddis persuaded me to stay. Often and often when I was thinking of moving he persuaded me to stay." She laughed, a short, crackling, little laugh. "Maybe I was too easy to persuade."

In the firelight her face in profile, dark hair, dark olive skin, was the face of a gipsy; and looking from her into the red centre of flame he saw a corner of the road a few miles outside the town and himself cycling home once in the summer dusk, and a dark-faced, dark-haired woman with two dark little children at her heels halting him to ask him had he seen any travellers along the road; and for a moment of misunderstanding he had thought of red-faced, whisky-sodden, commercial men; and then he remembered that the woman was looking for her own people, travelling people, gipsies and tinkers, moving from place to place and living their own dark lives outside houses and towns; and maybe Alice Graham, sitting bitter in the firelight, was feeling the want of her own people like a pain in the bowels, for in this town she was an exile, and Bernard Fiddis, in spite of his travels, had his roots here, deep under the houses, watered by the river, twisted in the earth as the little wandering roads twisted over the back of the earth.

"Now I haven't even his company," she said, "not since she got him."

He released her hand. He knew what she was talking about, but he wouldn't admit even to himself that he knew. He had only her word for it and maybe she wasn't, after all, a person you could trust. It was impossible, but then nothing was impossible. Alice Graham had been left as he had been left, but the similarity of their plight did not attract him to her. It revolted him, and all the enchantment of the fire-light was gone in a moment, and all the warm witchery of the whisky died and his blood was as cold as the snow in the street. He didn't want to belong to the vast multitude of the world's second best. He didn't want to do anything, to question May Campbell, to kiss Alice Graham, except to get out again where the little town had for a few white days covered its meanness and its pitiful little sins in a white coat of innocence.

"I must go now," he said. It wasn't the woman's fault. It was like striking somebody who couldn't strike back, a child, an old, broken man. "I'm stopping with Jim Collins. They'll be sitting up waiting on me. You know he has an invalid sister." It was like passing a dud coin to a blind beggar.

She smiled resignedly. "I don't even know Jim Collins," she said. She walked down the stairs with him, and across the hallway to the side door. "Come again," she said, "when you've nothing better to do." Standing in the darkness by the door she was very close to him, and he could have kissed her, and she stood for a long, silent minute, and he wanted to kiss her couldn't because he was a young man and she was a middle-aged woman who was beautiful only in the shadows.

Going alone along the white, silent street he felt as mean as a pointy-eyed ferret. He stood for a while in the snow looking at Campbell's house, and there was a light in the window of the room where she slept, and in there she was taking off her clothes and remembering.... what was she remembering? He could not touch her memories any more than he could reach across the cold street and through the glass of the window and touch her body. Her memories were part of her soul and he could not touch her soul, and suddenly his mouth was foul with curses and his body was shaking and breaking in sweat. He cursed her because she had left him wandering like a fool in a lighted room, empty of everything except a table and a few chairs and the shining white clothes that had covered the angels; because she had made him leave Alice Graham standing like a fool in a dark hallway, hungry for the kiss of a man who was young enough to be her son. Then walking on over the snow, warming himself with the walking, he was laughing at his madness, at his readiness to believe evil; he was telling himself that he loved her, he loved her, in spite of Bernard Fiddis, in spite of Alice Graham, in spite of snow and ice and cold wind and high water.

IV

Fiddis drove the car carefully over the slippery crunching snow. She sat beside him, and with her she had brought the odours of a theatrical dressing-room. She sniffed the air disapprovingly. She said: "I had to hurry to get away. And you don't get rid of the smell of this stuff in a hurry."

Fiddis laughed. "You smell all right to me," he said. All through the play, sitting beside the monsignor, the town behind him in the darkened hall, he had watched her moving gracefully in a lighted limited world, perfectly at home with angels and shepherds and wise men out of the magic east. Nobody in that hall knew what he knew. The town didn't know. Her father didn't know. The angels would have been shocked. The wise men would be wiser than ever. It would have given him a strange satisfaction to whisper it all to the monsignor, leaning sideways in the darkened hall, pointing to the girl on the lighted stage, telling it all to the priest, not with repentance in his voice but with the wild exultation of a man who has found a pearl or captured beauty like a bird in a cage.

She sat beside him, and they didn't talk much until he had driven the car beyond the last street lamp and the headlights showed white branches and hedges still heavy with drifted snow. He drove slowly, giving the wheels time to grip the road. She shivered slightly once. "It's colder tonight," he said. "The thaw's on the way."

"I hate the snow," she said fiercely.

"We could go to my place," he said, "only for that damned Judy. I can hardly call my place my own with her. And she's so old that I couldn't sack her."

She laughed. She said: "It sounds funny to hear you talking like that. You're the one man in this town who really is his own master."

"No man is his own master."

"I'm not cold anyway."

They crossed the bridge and turned left along the road to his house. "I'll park in a lane beyond the house," he said, "and slip in for a bottle. It's one way to keep warm. "

The lane, sheltered by high banks, guarded by a gate made of corrugated iron, was completely bare of snow. He drove the car around the first corner and parked it out of sight of the road. She slipped into the back seat and he wrapped the rug around her. "Stay here until I come back," he said. She whispered out of the shadows: "As snug as a bug in a rug," and turned her face up to him, and he kissed her once quickly, perversely restraining himself like a child playing with a delectable food, postponement increasing the expected joy.

He walked back towards the house. He walked slowly. When he was twenty he would have run like a hare, but he knew now that all delight must be approached deliberately. The great, soft snowflakes drifted out of the darkness and touched his face and melted suddenly The back of the house rose up above the road, a high, vague shadow over the white ground, no light showing in any window. Judy had gone to bed or was going to bed. Her bedroom was in the front of the house. Her sitting-room overlooked the road through a square, bay window, and he looked at the darkness of that window and thought whimsically of Judy going to bed as Judy had always gone to bed, and of May Campbell waiting in the car like Dido waiting on the shore, or the lady Helen airing on the Trojan walls.

Slipping the key into the lock of the little side door he was laughing at the comedy of that contrast. He had brought with him from the car a small flashlamp. He didn't want to fall over things in the dark and have Judy shouting down the stairs. If he did encounter her he could always say that his car had broken down a mile from the house and that he was bringing some drink to keep the life in the poor frozen mechanic who was doing the repairs. Any excuse was good enough for Judy. What did she know about cars or mechanics or life or anything? Poor Judy, slipping her brown, withered body between sheets warmed by a lifeless, earthenware jar.

He shone the lamp along the narrow hallway that led to Judy's kitchen. The door of the pantry to the left was open, and he thought even Judy nods, for Judy had a mania for closing doors. He took two steps forwards and then halted, for very distinctly from the front of the house he heard a thudding bumping noise as if somebody were beating furiously on a closed door. He stood for a second, surprised into breathless listening, and then above the bumping he heard Judy screaming, but her words melted into each other and all he could hear was the high note of raucous, half-frightened anger. He raced down the hallway, opened the kitchen door, the flashlamp in his right hand, his left hand reaching into the darkness for the electric light switch. The first blow caught him above the right wrist, as if somebody had struck him with an iron bar, numbing his right hand, sending the flashlamp crashing to the floor; and then he was grappling with somebody that he could not see, and somebody whispered: "Run for God's sake," and somebody else said: "Let me out, quick." He sensed the second blow and ducked sideways. The weapon crashed against the wall, against the light switch, for a flying fragment of something stung his face; and then with the effort of cold anger he struck into the darkness with his left hand. He felt teeth under his knuckles. He heard something between a dirty word and a sob of pain, a scurry of feet moving hurriedly away from him and out through the other door of the kitchen. A wide, stone-flagged passage went from that door to the foot of the short stairway that led up to the front hallway. Half-way along that passage a low silled window shone with the half light of the snow, and three figures struggled in the cold faint light, getting in each other's way in frantic efforts to escape. He raced towards them, grabbed the third and last as he was half way across the sill. The figure wriggled like an eel. He crooked his left arm around it, drew it back firmly, dragged it along the passage to the light switch. His hand on the switch, he drew a deep breath, listened for a moment and heard Judy shout three times, and heard her beating on the door of her room. They must have locked her in. Then he clicked the switch and flooded the passage with light, pushing his prisoner away from him against the far wall.

He couldn't really say he was surprised. Struggling there by the window, his senses, or something deeper than his senses, had told him the truth: a glimpse of a fair head by the light that came from the snow, the feel of the smooth skin of a cheek. What was the boy anyway but her shadow, something that might have been a woman like her if the accident of the womb had not determined otherwise?

He said: "Gerry, what in God's name does this mean?"

Judy was still shouting. For the first time he made out the words. She was shouting: "Let me out, you ruffians. Let me out." It was unoriginal. It was so like Judy.

Gerry Campbell said nothing. His face was very pale, and he leaned weakly against the wall, and his fair hair was in wild disorder. Maybe his voice was out there in the car, attracted by a life that was greater than its own life, waiting to be warmed by drink into the whispering of foolishness. "What happened to Judy?" Fiddis asked.

Gerry whispered: "She heard a noise. She came out of her room, and Mullan pushed her in and locked the door."

"Did she see you?"

"She saw nothing. Mullan clapped his hands over her eyes. She was in her shift."

It was a funny thought: Judy in her shift, and Mullan, whoever Mullan was, with his hands over her eyes. But Fiddis couldn't laugh. He didn't know what he could do. He couldn't tell the police. He couldn't release Judy until this boy was safely gone. He couldn't deliver a lecture on the evils of housebreaking. He couldn't even take time to think coherently. She was waiting for him in the car. Judy was beating monotonously on the locked door. If anybody passed along the road and heard her. The boy, weak with terror, was leaning against the wall.

"Did they take anything?" Fiddis asked.

"Some money. Mullan found it on the dresser in the kitchen. Then you came in."

A few more minutes and the boy would cry. And she was waiting for him in the car. She had cried a little that night in the car under the railway bridge. He struggled wildly for the few words that would end this awful interview. He caught Gerry by the arm. The boy's coat moved slightly above skin that must be soft and white like her skin. "You'd better run before Judy sees you," Fiddis said. He led the boy to the window. In a few more minutes he might cry, or plead for mercy, don't tell my father, don't tell the police. "I needn't tell you how wrong all this is," Fiddis said. "Breaking into a man's house and taking what doesn't belong to you. I don't suppose you were the ringleader." Judy had ceased hammering and resumed her shouting. Somebody might hear her at any moment. "Come into my office tomorrow," he said. "And tell me the truth. I don't want to

110

see your father's son in trouble. But I want the truth. Run now."

He almost pushed the boy off the sill, listened to the snow-muffled thud of his feet on the ground, and then closed the window. The catch and a pane of glass had been clumsily broken. His feet crunched on the fragments of broken glass. He went up the short stairway to the entrance hall, slipped into the dining-room to pocket a half-bottle of whisky from the sideboard. The fewer explanations he had to give Judy, the better. She was hammering on the door again, and he ran as quickly as he could up the stairs to the first floor. She knew his step coming along the corridor. She would have known his steps on the bright floor of heaven or the red floor of hell; she had listened for it so often, night after night, a little woman growing harder and withering, night after night and year after year, until she was bunched in a bundle like a rheumatic fist. She said: "Bernard Fiddis. Bernard Fiddis, thanks be to the blessed mother you've arrived. Oh, the villains."

He opened the door and she came out into the corridor. "Oh,the scoundrels," she said. "Did you catch them at all?"

She had dressed hurriedly, pulling on a heavy black overcoat that she wore around the house on cold nights. Her high button boots were twenty years out of fashion. Her grey hair straggled into her eyes, and she brushed it up with her hand and peered up at him short-sightedly.

"They got away," he said. "I saw them vanishing."

"The rascals," she said. "They put hands over my eyes and pushed me into the room and locked the door. The biggest hands you ever saw, and all stinking with dirty tobacco."

"Did you hear their voices?" He led the way along the corridor to his study, switched on the light, plugged in an electric fire. The room hadn't been disturbed. They were poor robbers.

"I didn't hear their voices. But they heard mine." He looked at her round, hard, pugnacious little face, and suddenly he was laughing the helpless laughter that can take tears from a man's eyes. "I heard the trampling of their feet," she said sharply, "and there must have been six or seven of them, and I don't think it's any laughing matter." He couldn't stop laughing. Finding that unfortunate boy in the passage had been a shock, and she was still waiting on him, wrapped in rugs, waiting in the car. "Judy," he said, "you're the bravest woman in the world. You'd fight a regiment."

111

She was secretly mollified. She loved his praise. But she screwed up her face still tighter and said: "You're making a jeer of me."

"God knows I'm not. I mean it, every word."

"Will you phone the police?".

"What for? You know what happened the last time. The house was never completely upset until the police came."

He was playing on her weakness. Given a choice she would have preferred burglars to policemen. He was buttoning his overcoat.

"You're not going out again?"

"The car's caught in a slippery patch a bit up the road. I came up walking to get the chains for the wheels. You'll be safe now. They won't come back."

Again he was playing on her weakness. She was diabolically proud of her courage. She wasn't afraid of ghosts. She wasn't afraid of burglars. "I have a clue," he said, "that I may be able to follow up without the help of the police."

"I'll wait up," she said, "and make you a drop o' tea."

He left her, going from room to room, armed with a poker, checking the household property—a hard little bundle of a woman whose life was part of the house, whose life was dependent on his life . After much argument she had promised to go back to bed when the checking was completed, and a corner of the dining-room table laid for his supper, and the electric kettle filled and nothing to do but push in the plug and boil the water. He wondered what her life would be like if he were to take another woman, his wife, into the house; and he was amazed at himself because the thought had never even as much as flicked through his mind until that moment.

With much ostentatious clanking he carried the chains from the garage, laughing to himself because he felt again like a schoolboy deceiving his mother. What would Judy say if she knew about the girl, wrapped in rugs, waiting in the car? What would the monsignor have said if he had known the truth about the lovely girl walking like an angel on a stage crowded with angels? What would the town say? Secrecy was the greatest joke in the world. He was laughing aloud when he pitched the chains on the snow-covered grass at the side of the road, where he could collect them on his way home.

She said: "I thought you had forgotten about me."

"Is that likely?" He held the bottle to her lips and she sipped once, twice, three times, and then coughed and laughed at the flaming heat of the liquor.

"I interrupted a party," he said. "Uninvited guests. A house-breaking party."

"Burglars! Did you catch any?"

"They had Judy locked in her room. They all got away." He told her about Judy, poker in hand, parading from room to room, until she forgot excitement in laughter at valiant Judy. He checked his watch against the clock on the dashboard. He said: "It's after midnight. They'll have a search party out looking for you." Memory of the pale boy leaning against the wall in the stone-flagged passage, or running home in terror over the snow, troubled him. Breaking into another man's house and taking something that didn't belong to you. The law saw breaking and entering, and seduction almost in the same light; and the law was wise with the dusty wisdom of centuries of sin and violence assessed and judged and balanced against punishment.

"They've all gone to bed," she said.

He had to force himself to put his arm around her, but when she leaned against him and said: "Bernard, I love you," his mood began to change. What was law but the pitiful attempt of age and experience to throw a net around the world, and in a thousand places the net was rotten and men and women came breaking through the meshes, and that was necessary because otherwise law would strangle life.

Was Judy still patrolling the house? Or maybe she was filling the kettle? Was the pale boy at home yet, shivering in his cold bed, crying to his pillow: don't tell my father, don't tell the police? Well, he hadn't anything to worry about. And the fright would do him good.

He kissed her, slowly and softly. The good people of the town were asleep, wandering from the town along all the roads opened by dreams. The monsignor was sitting in his room reading about God.

She said again: "Bernard, I love you." And then he was wondering could this secret remain a secret in such a town, or would it be like new wine bursting out of old bottles, or a flame under straw, hidden for awhile, then leaping out to brighten and scorch the world.

V

The thaw didn't come slowly, with the snow sinking or being sucked into the ground until there was nothing left but a jagged white crust on the mountains or discoloured piles in the hollows of deep ditches. But in a few hours the wind coming up from the south-west was a screaming gale, pushing the low clouds before it, and the rain began and fell steadily for two drenching days. At the foot of the town the market yard was under water and a few dozen wooden boxes torn out of some storehouse bobbed and drifted, like a fleet of lost ships, on the muddy ocean. An uprooted tree, swept in when the river burst its banks, was jammed in the doorway of the town's one and only public lavatory, which was anyway two feet under water so that Harry Mahoney said the place would be properly cleaned for the first time since it was built. In a low-lying lane on the other side of the river the flood had lifted the cover of a manhole, and a poor unfortunate wading home through two feet of water had stepped into the manhole, and that was that.

Driving to and from his office Bernard Fiddis splashed for one hundred yards along a flooded road. The roar of the river below his house was the voice of a thousand furies on a thousand different notes; and Judy, looking down at the brown water spreading over the flat, green land on the far bank of the river, said that God was surely judging the sinful world.

Unfolding the morning paper in his office he read about floods: floods in the Shannon and floods in the Severn, floods in the Mersey, floods in the Suir and Nore and Barrow, the rivers of two islands rising in wild revolution against order, and sunshine on placid water, and the everlasting monotony of flowing between two established banks. Some poet of a lost age, when poets were familiar with the mystery of rivers, could have understood and written about the secret of the revolt of the waters. But the newspaper could only tell him that soldiers had been rushed to the Shannon to help in fortifying a threatened bank; and he could see the flat farmland, green and sighing like a frightened girl, shrinking from the possibility of a terrible caress if the bank burst and the waters came down with a roar. Or at Shewsbury, the newspaper said, the Severn was seventeen feet above its normal level, and at the Welsh bridge only the tops of the lamp-posts were visible; and he remembered

Shrewsbury, and the Severn, and the wall at Worcester where the flood levels of various years were carefully marked to show how proud the English were of their rivers; and he remembered a dark-headed woman from France that he had met on the top of the cathedral tower at Worcester, and how they had talked together, looking across the Severn and the rich, level country towards the dusky Malvern Hills. She had written to him for years, and he would have married her only she already had a husband in Lyons, and he was still thinking of her when his clerk opened the door and said that Mr. Rafferty's son wanted to see him.

Bernard Fiddis liked Pat Rafferty. He liked old Rafferty. The man was alive; and from what Fiddis had seen and heard of the son he concluded that the father's undeniable intelligence had passed down to him.

"My father couldn't come in himself," Pat said.

"Couldn't tear himself away from the floods." Fiddis laughed at the thought of revolutionary man: in the shape of old Rafferty standing up to the assault of the river in revolt.

"He said this was the newspaper clipping he had mentioned. And he said it you wanted to see for yourself the harm the floods could do, that now was the time."

The son was more quiet than the father. He might learn to accept the world that the old man wanted to change. Sitting on a stiff chair, facing Fiddis across the green baize surface of a very orderly desk, he looked as tall and dark, as heavy faced and sombre as some Puritan figure in a story by Hawthorne.

"We have had bad floods ever where," Fiddis said, "but then we have only one small piece of floodable land near the town." Not a Puritan, he thought, for one evening in Campbell's house he remembered hearing May say that Pat Rafferty was fond of music.

The newspaper clipping was about a farmer somewhere in Munster who had prosecuted a County Council for failure to clean a river, and who had, moreover, won his case. It had been talked about incessantly in Rafferty's house for the last five days.

"I hear you're fond of music," Fiddis said.

"Who told you that?"

The question was disconcertingly solemn. "Oh somebody," Fiddis said. "At the moment I can't think who."

The rain recommencing suddenly whipped at the windows.

Fiddis flicked over a file of papers. "We might make a case out of it," he said. "With luck." He looked at the streaming windows. "The rain's on again."

"I like listening to music," Pat said. "I don't know much about it." He felt that he should suspect Fiddis, that he should protect his suspicion with incivility. But there wasn't much wrong with Fiddis, there wasn't a thing that would make incivility reasonable. Maybe Alice Graham was to blame. Maybe . . . but he couldn't carry suspicion beyond Alice Graham. He stood up. He said: "Can I tell my father to expect you?"

"I'll be there before you," Fiddis said. "Or, better still we can go out together."

"I have a man to bring out with me," Pat said, "to do some odd jobs about the place."

"We'll take him with us."

"I'd be glad of the lift."

Fiddis struggled into a white raincoat, lined with fleece inside the shoulders. Pat stood a few feet away looking out of a window at the wet deserted street. The shops of the town had closed for the half holiday. The shop assistants could sit in their lodgings, looking out at the rain, until it was time to go to the pictures. The town was a poor place in wet weather.

"Come out to my place some time," Fiddis said. "I've a few records that you might like to hear."

There was nothing wrong with Fiddis, nothing that Pat could genuinely dislike, nothing against him except the gossip of a woman who was—God help her—no better than she might be. Yet standing by the window Pat could not put out the unnecessary hand of courtesy to help the man into his coat. He didn't want to touch him. He didn't want to touch the coat. And going down the stairs he shrank away from him as if a touch might wound or burn, like a virgin shrinking away from the touch of a man, or a priest from the terrifying nearness of a girl.

They drove to the little house where Brass MacManus lived. Because it was the half holiday for the shops Jim Collins was there; and Jim and Brass piled into the back of the car, and Pat sat with Fiddis in the front, and they went through the rain, over the wet roads and between the spongy fields, until they saw from the top of the brae the rebellious water spread out like a sea; and the far edge of the flood was hidden in the mist of rain, sweeping low over the flood and the fields and the bare trees and the threatened homes.

VI

There were nearly twenty men talking in little groups on the street before Rafferty's house. They didn't seem to mind the rain that was still falling softly now like mist or like gentle summer rain. They were talking about the flood.

"Rafferty was right all the time. That river was a menace."

"There never was a flood like this flood."

"It's God's blessing it didn't come when the harvest was in the fields."

"Once in my father's time there was something like it, and a cotter in the bog bottom was caught in his house and drowned, and his wife and children drowned with him."

"There are no houses now in the bog bottom."

"There are three houses that are in danger this present moment."

They spoke slowly and quietly, with much patience and altogether without fear. There was nothing that any man could do except clear the fields before the invading waters. They watched the motor car coming along the road and turning towards the house.

"It's the solicitor from the town."

"Begod he'll stop the floods."

"With his fat backside."

"He'll write a stiff letter to the man that makes the rain."

"He'll sue God Almighty for trespass."

"Young Pat is with him in the car. He'll manage the boat."

"It might be as well to get the people out of those three houses."

In the great, warm kitchen Pat's father and mother welcomed Fiddis the solicitor, set him in an armchair near the hearth; and while Mrs. Rafferty made tea, the old man screwed the cork out of the whisky bottle. "As long as I remember," he said, "the high water never swamped my land. But now I've one meadow under the flood. And beyond that meadow Jim Kane's bog bottom is like the wide Atlantic."

"It's wonderful," Fiddis said, "where all the water comes from."

"It's a holy terror. And to think that all that water could be used for generating electricity. It would aggravate a saint."

"You're no saint," Mrs. Rafferty said, laughing up at her husband as she bent to balance the teapot on some coals crushed on the hearth.

Fiddis held his glass of whisky between his finger and thumb, watching it reflect the red light of the burning turf. "If we were saints, ma'am," he said, "we'd never get a drop of the stuff at all"; and old Rafferty laughed loudly and said: "If we were saints we couldn't look sideways."

Old Rafferty monopolized Fiddis, loaned him a pair of Wellington boots, led him out to view the floods. Here was a man who understood; an educated man who knew it was man's duty to fight and overcome the terrible powers that threatened his existence; a man completely different from the farmers grouped like cattle and gossiping about the flood as if the flood was God, and not the fault of the county council.

Pat and Brass and Jim aided by a few of the farmers carried the boat from the car-house where it was stored during the winter. "I have it on the lake in summer for the fishing," Pat said. It was a heavy, square, flat-bottomed boat, as broad as a battleship, a problem to steer but almost unsinkable. They carried it with effort across the street, scattering the groups of gossiping men, along the lane by the byre where cattle moved restlessly and rattled their head-chains, up the wet green slope of a hill until they could see the flood; restless, grey water fading off into the grey mist of rain. The farmers followed in a crowd. At the foot of the hill they smashed a gap through a hedge and pushed the boat out along the slippery earth until it floated. The crowd cheered.

"Nothing like it since the Titanic," a voice said.

"Mind the icebergs, Pat boy."

"If we had a bottle of stout to smash over you."

"Go first to Kane's," Pat's father shouted.

Pat and Jim pushed on the long poles, and very slowly the clumsy boat moved out over the water; and Brass MacManus, who knew as well as Pat did the humps and hollows of the submerged fields, shouted advice. Somewhere lost in the flood, Pat knew, was the course of a small stream that went sluggishly in summer between soft green banks towards the river. Remembering the green banks and the sluggish water, choked with the green leaves and yellow

118

blooms of water-lilies, was like remembering life and sunshine from the chill darkness of the grave. Checking the depth carefully with the pole Pat found the course of the stream, and for a hundred yards they followed it, poling easily, encountering no obstacles. Where a bare tree stood up like a gesturing giant above the flood they poled to the right, going straight towards the white walls of Kane's farmhouse, phosphorescent across the darkening water. The house stood on a green rise in the middle of bogland, and because the water had covered the low-lying bog, the green ground, capped with the white house, stood up like an island in some enchanted sea-wandering story. They poled across a narrow, deep valley where the water was very still and the poles could barely find a grip in the yielding ground; and looking down at grasses and bare brambles waving like seaweed, and at the dark uncertain depths of bog pools Brass said: "Christ save us, but a liner could float here."

In Kane's house the father was cutting the son's hair: a thin, yellow-faced, delicate father with seven laughing, rosy-faced sons, six of them jack-acting around the blazing fire, the seventh sitting in a chair in the middle of the floor, his shoulders draped in a torn sheet, a large bowl sitting on his head like a ceremonial hat on a Chinese mandarin; and, while the son's face screwed up in expectation of the snip that might remove an ear, the thin father methodically clipped around the edge of the bowl.

The flood didn't worry them: seven circular red sons and a yellow vertical father, and a red-cheeked, fat woman baking bread at a table in the kitchen. The father said: "If the water gets to the top of this rise it's Noah's ark we'll need and not your battleship of a boat, Pat boy."

"It might rise higher."

"It'll rise no higher, please God."

Sitting in a circle around the great fire they drank strong tea and ate thick slices of warm bread sodden with yellow molten butter. The seven crimson sons, growing more crimson with the heat of the fire and the heat of the strong tea, wanted to go in the boat with Pat Rafferty. "Me sons," laughed the mother, "want to be sailors"; and when the father forbade them they pushed off the boat with great energy, and cheered and shouted as Pat and Jim poled out again over the flood.

"We're wasting our time," Jim said.

Brass spat disgustedly over the edge of the boat. A haystack torn from some haggard went past as stately as a ship under sail, bobbing up and down with the movement of the water. "If they were up to the bellies," Brass said, "they'd still say the waters'll rise no higher, please God."

"We could go to Car's house."

"It's in no greater danger than Kane's."

"And I know what the old woman would say. She'd look at the boat and she'd say: 'I'll drown decent in me bed, Pat boy'."

"If she doesn't drown," said Brass, "she'll die of diabetes."

"She can eat two turkey eggs at one go."

Pat and Jim shipped the poles, and drifting slowly on the flood the three of them laughed and chatted and smoked. "After all our trouble taking out the boat," Jim said, "we can find nobody to rescue."

"That's the way in this country."

"I saw a flood on the Rhine," Brass said, "after the war. That was a flood."

"That was a war."

"The men that fought in it," Pat said, "never want to talk about it. If there was another war we'd have a chance to see life."

A dead sheep washed down by the water was caught stiffly in the branches of a low tree.

"You might see more than life," Jim said.

"If we want to cross where the river is, we'll cross by the shallows at the black stones."

They poled towards a round, green hill that rose out of the water near the far end of the flood. Noah in his ark, Pat thought, must have been a bloody bewildered man: familiar land changed to hostile and unfamiliar sea, not a landmark left, not a hill, not a tree standing arrogantly above the water.

The river swept them with it for twenty yards, but leaning hard on the poles they gripped the firm gravel and pushed on into calm water. In an hour the grey daylight would be gone. The rain had stopped and the wind had strengthened.

"Old Kane was right," Brass said. "The three of us are three bloody eejits." His right hand rasped over his stubbled chin. He spat again disgustedly into the water, and pointed to the house on the shoulder of the round, green hill. "Not if the heavens fell," he said, "would he be flooded up there. He'll laugh at us."

"He might come with us," Pat said. "He has a lot to live for."

"He'll never die by drowning."

They tied the boat to the pillar of a gate that was two feet deep in water, and went up a muddy lane to the house. On a lower level than the house, the barns and byres were surrounded by the flood. The rusty corrugated roof of the hay shed leaned drunkenly to the water. The door of the house was open and a hen, roosted on the half-door, squawked hungrily. The cattle and a few sheep and a goat and a horse were huddled together around a lean-to henhouse. "Like the animals in the ark," Jim said.

"If anybody else mentions the ark, I'll burn me poor boat."

The animals were silent, motionless, terrified by the surrounding silence of the water, but given by common peril a common feeling.

Pat leaned his head over the half-door and shouted: "John. John Maxwell." The squawking hen, suddenly startled, flew in to join her sisters, picking without hope around the floor of the kitchen. The wind followed them through the doorway, stirring the cold ashes on the untidy hearth.

"He's not so hot at the housekeeping."

"He should feed the flaming hens."

Pat called again. They opened a door, went down one step into a cold, untidy bedroom. The walls dripped with damp. The bedclothes were rolled in a bundle at the bottom of the dirty bed. Once, love had been in that room, giving a glow of life, maybe, to the family portraits, now stained with yellow damp from the damp walls. Pat studied the couple in the portrait above the empty fireplace: "When he was young, John was a right-looking fellow."

"We were all young once," Brass said.

They turned away from the portrait. They said nothing about the woman who stared back at them out of the portrait: sitting on a high-backed chair, her husband standing by her side, his hand resting on her shoulder. Love had been alive at that moment. Love was dead now and in a damp tomb, but the moment was still alive, a mockery of love, a denial of life. They turned away from the room. In the kitchen the hens cried with hunger. Brass found in a press the remains of a stale loaf, and he broke it and scattered the pieces on the floor. They turned away from the house; they were silent like men turning away from a grave. Love had lived on that hillside, and now there was only a dirty house, and ground that squelched under the feet, and all around was the water and the night gathering around the edges of the water. They could see the lamp lighted in the window of Kane's house: love and life and seven red-cheeked sons.

Pat cupped his hands to his mouth and yelled. The flood absorbed the echo.

"Fine lungs, God bless you."

"He went, maybe, before the flood closed in."

"He's drinking in the town."

"Or drunk."

But Brass looked at Pat, and Pat looked back at him, and they knew that what they knew they could tell neither to Jim Collins nor to any other innocent man.

Around the fire in Rafferty's they talked about floods that had been; and Brass MacManus remembered the Rhine, and Fiddis the solicitor knew that part of the Rhine like the back of his hand. Pat, listening to Fiddis, remembered Maxwell's house, and wondered did Fiddis with all his wisdom know as much as poor John Maxwell who had travelled once out of his own townland and seen the sunshine on the sea.

"It was queer, Pat, the way you couldn't find John Maxwell."

"It was, Ma."

"I hope nothing happened the poor man."

"I hope not, Ma."

Nothing had happened to John Maxwell. Nothing could happen to John Maxwell.

Fiddis was telling a story about something that had happened to him in Spain. The circle around the fire was shaken with laughter. Fiddis was good company.

Fiddis would drive Jim Collins back to the town where May Campbell lived, already asleep in her bed; there was nothing for her to do tonight. All the way to the town the road would be drying in the new wind; and in the morning the boat would be high and dry where he had left it moored in a foot of water, and his father would be lamenting about the ruined fields and the drowned cattle.

When he rang the bell, and the door opened and she was there, he wasn't able to talk for a moment. The badly lighted street was behind him, and standing to the side of the doorstep he was a shadow against a darker shadow. She peered into the darkness and said, as if she didn't know him: "Who's there?"

He hadn't really wanted to come. But a fellow couldn't go on for ever living in doubt: saying to himself in the morning that he loved her, and, maybe she loved him; doubting in the evening that she had ever given him a single thought out of all the thoughts of her mind; sore with bitterness at the fall of night because she was somewhere else, living her own life.

He said: "It's me. Pat Rafferty." He still stood like a fool in the shadows. She rocked back and forwards on her toes, a hand on each doorpost, the light behind her, her hair caught up in a great curving comb that made her look like a woman from some strange foreign country. She said: "Pat, you're welcome. I thought you had forgotten all about us."

She said "us", not "me".

He followed her into the house and took off his cap and coat, pulled the bicycle clips out of his trousers, dusted the crumpled ends of his trousers with his hand. His excuse for calling was that he had been in the town on some other business and had dropped in to see how Dinny was.

"I was very busy," he said.

"We heard all about it from Jim Collins. Sailing a boat on the floods. And then you found the old man."

All the way into the town he had felt that an excuse was essential. He must be casual. He had wanted so badly to see her that deception was essential for what dignity he had left. He had wanted to watch her face, to listen to her voice—a little deeper than the usual woman's voice but very soft and sweet—to assure himself that the words that had hurt him so much had been nothing more than the mouthings of a jealous woman on a cold night.

"Yes. I found the old man."

"That must have been exciting."

"Poor John."

Did she really think it was just exciting to find the body of a man after the world and high water had done their worst? How little she knew. And following her into the warm drawing-room the mood of his stronger moments was back with him: nothing mattered a damn, not her beauty or the way she walked, or her breasts under her white blouse, or the slow, graceful, decided way she put her feet on the floor, or the movement of her hips under her coloured skirt. She was a woman, and all women were alike under certain circumstances, and no woman was worth worrying about. In his soul he was defending John Maxwell against the world, dead John Maxwell gathered like a sopping bundle of rags in the corner of the byre, defending him against the world that had judged him, against the delusion of beauty that had damned him.

"I read about the inquest in the paper."

She said "I" not "we". She sat opposite him, leaning back in her armchair with the soft sigh of luxury.

"Were you interested in John Maxwell?"

"I was interested in the chief witness, wondering why he had become a hermit."

He felt that she meant it, that she was really glad to have him there. He had forgotten to ask about Dinny.

"Were you horrified?" she asked.

"It wasn't pleasant. He was under the water for two days."

He hadn't been horrified. The land all the way across to Maxwell's house had been horrible: crushed and flattened grass, uprooted trees, two dead sheep lying in the bottom of a drain, sand and gravel spread a foot deep over a meadow that he always thought of as yellow with mayflowers. The gravel under his feet like the bones of a slaughtered army. But the body in the byre had not been horrible.

"I wouldn't like to come on a dead man."

He would swear to God she wouldn't—not she, lying back in her chair, her soft body on soft cushions, her warm body absorbing the heat of the fire.

"John Maxwell's troubles are over," he said.

His troubles were over; dead in the byre where love had died brutally. For John Maxwell the horror was in being alive on an earth scarred as hideously as the gravel had scarred the green meadow. No, he hadn't been horrified; and trying again to see what he had seen in the corner of the byre he succeeded only in seeing her body,

124

oval face, white blouse, coloured skirt, shapely legs stretched towards the fire.

"We'll forget about it," he said.

"Poor Pat. You were a hero. And according to Jim Collins you nearly murdered the Bear Mullan."

He remembered Dinny then and asked how he was. He said lamely that he had dropped in in passing merely to inquire about the boy.

"For no other reason?"

She was laughing at him, and he could feel the blood in his veins creeping as if curdling with anger.

"I didn't know I'd be welcome for any other reason."

"You're always welcome. For any reason."

Maybe she meant it, and maybe she didn't. Maybe she was laughing at him and maybe she wasn't. She was the sort of girl a fellow couldn't be certain about; and angry and puzzled and pleased he felt for a moment that she was older than him in something that was not age, older than Fiddis or Alice Graham, older than the humpy, gossipy, old town.

"Dinny's well. Asleep in bed. But if you want to see him badly you know where his bedroom is."

Anger crackled between them for a moment like flame along a fuse, and then they caught each other's eyes and laughed.

"It isn't only Dinny," she said. "Aunt Aggie's back. The nurse is out. Gerry and Dympna are at the pictures."

A bell interrupted her, not the door-bell or the telephone bell, but a bell ringing somewhere upstairs. She rose slowly. She brushed his hair lightly with her hand as she passed. She had ways that were older than the oldest houses in the town; and, sitting by the fire and waiting for her return, he felt as if his hands and his head were growing larger with the mad pounding movement of blood away from his heart that was cold with watery fear. She had left the drawing-room door open. He heard her steps going away from him up the stairs, doors opening and closing, her voice speaking once or twice, then her steps returning quickly. The air around his chair was still restless with the passing of her body. She sat down again, and he sat on the arm of her chair, and put his arm about her shoulders.

She leaned against him. She said: "That was dear Aunt Agatha."

"Is she better?"

"She can move about a wee bit. And she can gabble. You could hardly call it talking."

The heartlessness of beauty, he thought. He had read about it in a book. The poets, God pity them, were full of it. He closed his hand over her breast, and she leaned closer to him, but he feared that at that moment there was no love in his caress.

"The doctor says now that she's all right if she doesn't get another stroke. She will though. They always do."

Very slowly his fingers were smoothing the soft silk of her blouse.

"She should have stayed in the hospital. She learned there about ringing a bell. From morning to night she keeps ringing the bell."

The cold watery fear was gone. Maybe you could only fear something that you loved without regret or misgiving. He loved Anne Collins sitting always in one chair; or John Maxwell dead in a bundle in the corner of a byre; or an old paralysed woman ringing her bell to bring beauty, smelling of life, into the room of death.

"It's all right for my father. He goes out to a political meeting with Bernard Fiddis."

He kissed her gently. She said: "Pat, you're very quiet."

There was no choking lump in his throat when he opened his mouth to speak: "Bernard Fiddis was in our house on the night of the flood."

"So he told me."

"Does he tell you everything?"

"He comes in here a lot."

"Was he in here on the night of the play?"

"Why?"

"Alice Graham thought he was."

"I wouldn't mind what Alice Graham thinks. She thought once that he would be her fourth."

He was speaking quietly, and rocking her gently to and fro. There was no malice in his questions. He kissed her again. He said: "Bernard Fiddis is not a bad sort."

"I like him. He knows a lot."

"A lot of people know a lot."

His third kiss wasn't a gentle kiss. Above their heads Aunt Aggie's bell rang, death calling to life, Lazarus lying at the gate. He pushed her down gently on to the cushions. The bell rang, at

126

intervals, for fifteen minutes, and then stopped, and then started ringing again; but she didn't leave him until Dinny's voice called from the top of the stairs: "May, Aunt Aggie wants you."

Crouching down by the fire when she had gone, he was afraid that love had died in that room as it had died in a damp room on a sodden hillside, as it had died in a dirty byre. For when he looked at the crushed cushions he saw not her loveliness, but the body of John Maxwell dead and at peace with his own withering wisdom.

5

Torch Light

I

A great wind came, singing a shrill song in bare branches, buffeting closed windows, cleaning dead leaves off the ground, making ready for the spring. Clouds banked blackly in the southwest, fell apart into white sun-soaked bundles as the wind drove them up the sky, went on over the low mountains and the fields, over the town and the shallow river. The coulter had opened up the brown, fruitful warmth of the earth. The river moved peacefully under cloud and quick sunshine, at peace with banks that glistened bright green after every shower. When the tired wind rested the earth breathed quietly, drawing in life from the sun and the soft rain.

The buds were early on the hedges. On the trees above the river and below Fiddis's house there was an early promise of green. Life was returning, a seed in the ground, a seed in the warm womb.

Brass MacManus noticed it around the edges of the quarry-hole beside his mother's house. The tall grass above the dark water was suddenly soft and green. His mother sat, in every glimmer of sunshine, on a chair outside the door, and light crept past her into the darkness of the little house where tall men with whiskers and skull-caps and tight togs almost moved in their pictures.

At the corner of Silver Lane and Tower Street the yellow-faced, foul-tongued army reservists reappeared, marking the wall with two greasy lines—one for shoulders and one for buttocks, smoking and spitting and cursing, and laughing at stories as greasy as the lines on the wall.

"There won't be a war."

"There will be a war."

"He took Czechoslovakia."

"Where the hell's that?"

"A big town in Russia."

"He'll take Poland too."

The wind, growing warmer day by day, swept in from the fresh fields, swept around the greasy corner, took with it the curses and the stories and the cheap smoke and the ignorant talk of war, swept on out of the town towards the mountains and the sea and Scotland and the sea and Norway and Russia and the frozen north.

The Bear Mullan and Joe Keenan were frequeutly at the corner of Silver Lane: Joe welcome for the sake of music; the Bear warmed by Joe's glory, but discontented and resentful because nobody paid any particular attention to himself. A new check cap covered his oiled hair. He could lean against the wall and, without jerking his head, spit right into the middle of the street.

"I get restless in the Spring," Joe said.

"So do we all."

"I know what's wrong with you. I think I'll go to England and get a job."

"And get conscripted into the bloody army."

The Spring blew around them at the corner of Silver Lane, the wind taking with it the memory of thin silvery music.

The Spring blew around Pat Rafferty working in his father's fields. He stayed away from the town as much as possible; the streets and the houses and the people had, with a few exceptions, become hateful to him. The town was a dead shell holding a pearl that shone with precious light. He wanted her and he didn't want her. He wasn't sure of her and he wasn't sure of himself. In the fields there was no doubt and no fear. The soft wind blew through the quickening thorn, and the warm rain was a blessing to the pastures and the meadows and the turned earth; and all along the river men were working, digging and dragging weeds and strengthening the banks that the flood had broken. He stayed away from the town as long as he could.

The sun shone into the little concreted yard behind Collins's house, and Anne Collins sitting in the sun gently chided Pat Rafferty for the rareness of his visits.

"We're busy on the farm these days."

"You should come often. You bring the good weather with you."

"It'd be raining, Pat, if you weren't here," Jim said. He sat on a stool in the sunshine, a last between his knees, hammering a stud into his football boots. In Collins's house there was always somebody hammering something: Chris or Jim or Jock, the lodger, who went to carpentry classes in the technical school.

"It'll soon be too warm for football."

"It'll soon be warm enough for swimming," Jim said, and he thought of the water in the lake that had always a greenish colour as if somebody had half-dissolved a green powder in it, or the black water in the river above the asylum where the pools were always as cold as springs.

There was security in the sun in that concreted yard: Anne talking, or reading quietly, and Jim perpetually making the jokes that only the simple-minded who are content with their own simplicity could make, and Mrs. Collins always fussily hospitable and always a little in awe of Pat whose father—they said— owned half the land of the country. But when he left that yard and that house and walked down through the streets of the town Pat felt as if he was moving in a strange place among alien people. Their minds and his mind were thinking about different things. Putting his hand to the bell-push at Campbell's door or walking in through the humming oil-scented garage, he felt like a man who had challenged strange, half-hostile gods to do their worst.

Alice Graham and May Campbell went up to Belfast to look at the spring fashions in the big shops. They travelled up by the early morning train to be in time for a mannequin parade in a hotel in Royal Avenue. With fifty or sixty well-dressed women they sat in a huge softly-carpeted room watching six London mannequins advance and retreat and wheel around, soft hems describing graceful circles, slim hips defined in body-fitting dresses. May had never seen anything like it before, and for an hour or two she forgot to worry about her own problem. She had been worrying about it for three days; and sitting, tired and silent, in the train on the way home, darkness over the countryside, the windows reflecting the lighted carriage, the problem returned to her. She looked at Alice Graham's face, eyes closed in half-sleep in the opposite corner of the compartment. If nothing happened to end her worry she would ask Alice Graham's advice because there was nobody else she could mention her trouble to, except Dympna, and Dympna wouldn't be able to give any advice. Alice Graham's eyelids were blue and tired, and in sleep her mouth hardened like Aunt Aggie's, not softened like Dympna's; and watching the hardness of her mouth May was afraid of her, the same fear that came to her sometimes sitting in Aunt Aggie's darkened room.

The curtains of that room were kept always drawn because the light of the early spring sunshine was too much for Aunt Aggie, life was too much for Aunt Aggie. Somebody had to stay with her all the time sitting quietly to avoid disturbing her, listening attentively because sometimes her gabble of a voice didn't carry much further than the end of the bed. May dodged the duty as often as in decency she could. Sitting in that room, doing nothing—it was too dark to read and she loathed knitting—it was possible to know fear as intimately as you would know another human being and once when fear had touched her and made her start in her chair she looked around suddenly and Aunt Aggie's eyes were fixed on her, staring steadily

The gabbling lips were saying something. She was more afraid than ever. Except for the lips and the eyes, that body was dead. She could have screamed. Listening carefully and watching the moving lips she bent down over the bed.

"Have you a pain, May?"

"No, Aunt Aggie."

"What's wrong? Are you ill?"

"No, Aunt Aggie."

It wasn't a pain. Was it a premonition of pain? Mystery was around her like the darkness of the room. Those staring eyes had in them all the life of the body; walking, and running, and sinning, and sitting down. Staring in the mysterious darkness they would discover her secret, and lips that should be dead would gabble about life that should not be alive. The darkness closed in on her, and she left Auut Aggie gabbling, and ran to sit shivering in the bathroom, and then to cry silently and uncontrollably, and to laugh as she washed the tears from her face because she didn't know why she had been crying or why she had been afraid.

On his way to a political meeting in the parochial hall Bernard Fiddis called at the house to collect old Campbell. He wore a new light-grey suit that made him look very youthful, and very much like a returned American. In the hallway he held her hand, pressed it quickly to his lips, dropped it discreetly as her father's footsteps approached the head of the stairs, coming from Aunt Aggie's room.

She said: "That's a splendid suit."

"We have our spring fashions too. We poor men even if we don't go all the way to Belfast to see six Cockney beauties waggling their bottoms."

He laughed, and she laughed with him. It was God's blessing to be able to laugh. She could tell him, and she would tell him, and everything would be all right. He would know what to do. He always knew what to do. But when the hard door had closed relentlessly behind his light grey shoulders and the black back of her father's overcoat, she realized that the one thing she wanted to tell him was the one thing she couldn't tell him.

Old John Campbell and Bernard Fiddis walked in the fitful sunshine across the Diamond and up the hill past the courthouse and on to the windy corner where the parochial hall sheltered under the high spires. Every yard they walked together reminded them of their own importance in the town. Men raised hats. Men said: "Good day, Mr. Fiddis," and "Good day, Mr. Campbell." A colleague on the town council stopped John Campbell to inquire about Aunt Aggie's health and to ask an opinion on the question of the appointment of a new town electrician. The question would be discussed at the next meeting of the council. A policeman, apologizing to John Campbell, drew Bernard Fiddis aside for two minutes of hurried whispering. One of the curates, apologizing to Bernard Fiddis, drew John Campbell aside for two minutes whispering. Three corner boys, sitting in a sheltered spot on the court-house steps, ducked their heads and touched the peaks of their greasy caps. A poor woman from Silver Lane mumbled her complaints to John Campbell, and he fumbled in the pocket of his stiff black overcoat and gave her a few coins.

They hadn't much to say to each other. Old Campbell was particularly silent, walking with his hands deep in his pockets, his big shiny boots striking the pavement with resounding solemnity.

"Worrying about Agatha, John?"

"There's not much hope for her. It would go to your heart to listen to her trying to talk."

In the darkened room he could never stop himself thinking about death: how she had died, God rest her, the autumn Dinny was born; how Aggie, God help her, hadn't long to live; how some day soon, God help us all, they would be screwing the lid down over his own face, and the four young people would be left without father or mother, without any of the benefits the wisdom of age could give.

Fiddis searched his mind for something to say, something that would give comfort, that wouldn't make him feel like the arch-hypocrite, the snake in the heart's blood warmed that stings the heart. There was pathetic helplessness about John Campbell.

"The children are grown now, thank God," Fiddis said. "May's a young woman."

"She's maybe a foolish young woman"

The poor old lips were struggling to talk to him in the shadowy room. It couldn't be true what they were trying to say. The young could die too, lovely young flesh closed in a box and buried, to hide its rottenness in a hole in the ground. For the wee while that life lasted, it was a pity to ruin it with foolishness.

"As friend to friend, Bernard, may I ask you a question?"

"Certainly, John."

"You're a long ways younger than me. But you've a wise head . . . and a quick eye."

God knew he had a quick eye.

"Would you say there was anything wrong with May?"

"Wrong? In what way?"

They halted at the foot of the steps at the door of the parochial hall. "Wrong. God, it's a terrible worry for a father to have. Wrong in a way that would bring disgrace on us."

"Good God, no." Fiddis's mind was perfectly quiet, absorbing the idea. "What put that into your head?"

"Something Aggie whispered. Something she said she noticed."

"Her imagination. Or ravings. Put it out of your head, John. May has more sense."

The idea was absorbed. It couldn't be true. There was no way in which it could possibly be true.

"I'm not so sure about the sense. Her mother, God rest her, was as lovely a woman as you'd encounter in a day's journey. But she was headstrong. She used to have me worried."

"Forget about it, John."

"Wee Dympna, now, takes after the other side. Dympna's different."

"It couldn't be true."

They went up the shaky dusty stairway, the old man in the lead, his hand unsteadily gripping the banister. His youth had been worried by headstrong beauty; his age was worried by headstrong beauty—an old bottle bursting with new wine. It couldn't be true: the ravings of a withered virgin imagining for others the life, the unseen and mysterious growth, that had been denied to herself.

Dympna was different. She weut with May to the opening night of the social club in a room above the new restaurant in the Diamond. The best people in the town were there; and in a brightly papered and pleasantly carpeted room that was a welcome addition to the town's scanty social amenities, they played cards and sang songs and had a question time just the same as it was over the radio. But for an hour at the beginning of the night the men sat at one end of the room and the women at the other and between them in the empty space was all the inarticulate awkwardness of people unused to social coutact. Their fathers and mothers had met at ease around friendly firesides; but the life had gone out of that old friendliness and only with stuttering difficulty could anything take its place.

Dympna enjoyed herself. May felt herself isolated among fifteen or sixteen young women, unmarried, ignorant of love apart from schoolgirlish notions and schoolgirlish cuddling in the corners of gateways. At the far end of the room she saw Bernard Fiddis isolated among modest men slow to marry. The air in the room was warm and dry. It was a furnace in which youth lost its sap and became resigned and slightly disappointed age; and, for a while, May was wickedly glad that, rightly or wrongly, she had used her youth, and her limbs were trembling with a knowledge that these women did not possess.

Later, in the middle of a dull card game, pride vanished and fear took its place. A young man who worked in a draper's shop was sitting beside her and pressing his knee against her knee under cover of the table. His touch meant as much to her as if his knee and his whole body had been made of wood. Maybe they were. She laughed in her heart at the idea; and then stopped in the middle of her laughter to ask herself how she knew what was going on in his mind. How did she know what was going on in any mind in the room, or what happenings had given knowledge to their bodies. All she did know was that she, like any silly skivvy, had taken her knowledge to the market once too often. Some day the people in this room would be talking about her. The thought terrified her. Her secret suffocated her.

On the way home she whispered her fears to Dympna. She said: "Dympna I've something to tell you. A dead secret." A secret was safe with Dympna.

And Dympna said: "Oh, May! What will we do, May? We must do something."

It wasn't much help. It wasn't much help to know that Dympna would lie awake all night, praying, crying to her pillow. May slept soundly. Staying awake wouldn't do any good. She thought, lying in bed in the early morning: Could I tell Bernard? If she told him anything it would have to be the truth. He would know if she told him a lie, and she was afraid he would despise her if she told the truth. There were moments when she despised herself. There were stronger moments when she thought: Why should Bernard despise me? He took what he could get. So did I. And then for a while she would hate Bernard Fiddis. She could never hate Pat Rafferty, although she tried very hard.

It wasn't much help to walk in the morning along the street and see Dinny and Chris Collins laughing together in the sunshine. She knew, for the first time, what childhood, happy childhood, really meant.

It wasn't much help to stop to talk to Tom Nixon, white-aproned and smiling, at the door of his shop. "Good morning, Miss Campbell. A lovely morning. Did you enjoy the new club? Real high society. Question time and all. The people of this town will soon know all the answers."

He sniffed the air. He said that spring was on the way. But she knew he was sniffing, not the spring, but the nearness of her body, faintly perfumed. There wasn't much she didn't know now. She knew all the answers. Except one. And any shop girl in the big city Alice Graham came from would know what she didn't know. Alice Graham? But Alice Graham hated her, as Aunt Aggie hated her, and maybe for the same reason.

The spring was on the way, billowing up with the wind from the south-west, breathing green life into bare fields and brown hedgerows, stirring seeds in the earth, scattering sunshine, bringing life.

Life was beautiful. Life was terrible. Fear came with life, and after death there could no longer be any fear.

II

Spring was the time for walking. Gerry Campbell asked Pat Rafferty to do a day's walking with him in the mountains north-east of the town, and Pat consented on condition that Jim Collins came too, and that Jim and Gerry behaved for the day like two friendly, civilized beings. He was surprised at the readiness with which Gerry agreed. There was a change coming over Gerry Campbell. Jim Collins, naturally, was ready to agree to anything. There was no enmity in Jim for anybody, least of all for the brother of the girl he intended to marry as soon as he had the money; and, anyway, Pat Rafferty would spend the night before the walk and the night after the walk in Collins's house.

They took the morning bus from the town, along four miles of road to the village of Ballyclogher. The road bridged the river within sight of Fiddis's house, went up a long slope under the arching branches of high beech trees. There was a hint of green on the branches, faint green fading into the light blue of the wind- swept morning sky. The road dropped suddenly down a steep hill into a soft, saucer-shaped valley. Above the valley on one side a half-tumbled, deserted mansion could be seen between the trees. Workmen had built a scaffolding around it, and between the valley and the mansion they were building huts for soldiers, and a sentry with rifle and bayonet stood stiffly at the end of the avenue.

"The man that owned the mansion will make money out of this."

"Nobody lived there for four years."

"The place is haunted."

Alone with its ghosts the mansion and the surrounding grounds had for four years been settling contentedly into a wilderness. Boys had played about the place with complete freedom. There hadn't even been a caretaker, and now there would be soldiers and parades and bugles blowing all the day, and man preparing to make a greater wilderness. The sight for a moment silenced their talk; it was the end of something, the beginning of change in their world as they had known it, a wind sharper than the wind of early spring and blowing from some unknown place beyond Ulster, beyond Ireland, beyond Britain and mighty London.

They were silent until they climbed out of the bus at Ballyclogher bridge. Low hills rose steeply on either side of the burn where it cut its way into the saucer-shaped valley, to twist through rushy meadows towards the river and the town. The village huddled between the hills: a church, a new, red-brick school-house, an old, white-washed schoolhouse now used as a dance hall, a few slated houses and a few thatched cottages, a dog asleep in a sheltery corner, an old man standing in a doorway; a child crying and a mother's voice chiding in one of the cottages.

They drank in the pub: cold and empty and stale smelling, colourless except for a few ancient cardboard squares advertising ales and whisky. Pat drank whisky. Jim drank beer. Gerry sipped lemonade.

They prayed in the church: as cold and empty as the pub, grit under the knees on the uncomfortable kneeling-boards, the red lamp lighted before the tabernacle on the high altar. There wasn't a sound, beyond birds twittering from a nest somewhere in the roof, or the wind moving the branches of the trees in the graveyard, or the hushed sound of the falling stream. The cold air was scented with memories of incense, burning candles, new linen.

They walked back towards the bridge. "A quiet church like that," Jim said, "frightens me."

"Guilty conscience," Pat said.

"Nothing to be guilty about in our town. I go to confession once a fortnight and, honest to God, I never have anything to tell. What can one do here?"

They left the road at the bridge and, in single file, followed a path that went upstream away from the village. The walking, the boisterous wind, the sun on the sparkling water, warmed them. Pat was singing jovially. He strode in the lead, his long arms swinging, his stiff hair disordered by the wind. He said: "Must go to confession some day soon, myself."

The thought didn't worry him. It wasn't in his blood to be gospel greedy. His father, he knew, only went to Mass on Sundays for the sake of appearances and to avoid hurting his mother. If you did not regret an action or a thought or a word then how could you, without being a hypocrite, go down on your knees in the darkness and confess them as sins. He would do it again if he had the chance, and he would have the chance; but he would know this time that these things could come about through bodily itch or even through hate, as readily as through the love that the books and the poets were filled with. He regretted only his innocence, not because he had lost it but because he had ever possessed it.

Gerry's light step came behind them on the narrow path. Gerry said: "I'm going to confession once a week now."

The stream was down below them, noisy and foamy from the points of hidden rocks. They had to shout to make themselves heard above the noise of the water.

Jim Collins shouted: "You'll be the first saint to glorify our town."

Pat called over his shoulder: "The last, too."

He looked back as he shouted. Gerry's fair hair was rumpled with the wind. His mouth, red and soft like a girl's mouth, was smiling, but his light eyes were serious, and his face was paler than Pat had ever seen it.

The path widened, went winding through a hazel wood, the trees still leafless. They walked side by side. The path ascended slowly, above the brown wood, away from the noise of the stream hidden somewhere by high banks and bare trees, until they were crossing the side of a bare hill, and they could see valley and village shining in the sun, and the flat land steaming like an animal. They followed a rutted boreen past a long, white farmhouse, held open a sagging, wooden-barred gate for a barefooted boy driving a goat away from the house, came out upon a narrow switchbacking road. For a while Pat didn't look again at Gerry. He knew that if he looked he would see her; he wanted to see her and he didn't want to see her. It wasn't love, for love—he had read and had been told—was all ideals and respect and eternal reverence and the unity of one soul with another soul. He knew nothing about her soul. But he knew that if he looked too long at her brother he would see her, smell her, touch her, taste her not like a savour in the mouth but as a burning in the marrow.

He had her step, her voice. He went once a week to confession and in the darkness whispered his sins.

The road zigzagged down a slope to the valley where the town reservoirs were: two pear-shaped lakes, one large and one small, rectangular filter-beds where brown mountain water lost a little, only a little, of its natural colour. The unwanted overflow returned, along a channel lined with slippery stones, to the parent stream. The narrow tips of the pear-shaped lakes pointed upwards to the brown mountains. Jim and Pat talked about the town and the people of the town, peopling the bare slopes with the more colourful of the characters who lived down in the green valley, in the cluster of old houses, under the shadows of the spires and the steeples and the ancient tower, their lives portioned into hours by the thin silvery chiming of the court-house clock or the brazen cry of bugles from the grey barracks. Knee-deep in brown heather that moved only slightly even to the greatest force of the wind, up in the cold quick air where the only sound was the bleat of a startled sheep or the singing of a rising lark, the town was remote, a place to be talked about as exiles meeting in a strange land talk quietly of home.

Their own lives were remote, swept from them on the great wind.

They went up and up through the trackless heather, past the green, wet hollow where the stream surprisingly burst out of the side of the arid mountain. They were souls out of the body, spirits in heaven remembering life with a little loneliness for the world they had left: for a good-hearted, laughing, little, dark-haired girl; for a tall girl whose body was a flame burning up from the ashes of an old grey town.

Gerry was very quiet. In the shelter of the cairn on the windy summit they crouched and ate.

Pat said: "Gerry, you're like a man with a guilty secret."

"I have a secret."

The wide moors were below them, a long lake its edges dark with woods, a river winding down from mountainy country to a valley of green fields and little white houses. The world was below them.

They didn't press him for his secret. For two months now he had been a different person. Even his friendliness towards Jim Collins showed that he was a different person.

"I might as well tell you fellows. You'll have to know some time."

139

"Is it that you're thinking of matrimony?"

"Did you murder somebody?"

"Not exactly. I'm going away to be a priest. This year."

"You'll be able to marry me," Jim Collins said.

"You're a slow mover, if you're not married before I'm ordained."

Pat said: "Congratulations." He said after a while: "You couldn't do better." But he was struggling fiercely with thoughts that he could not arrange in their proper order. Her brother, her shadow, the boychild that could have been a girlchild, would be a priest. Her flesh, draped with rich, heavy vestments not with soft silken clothes, the intoxicating odour of her perfume, the chaste smell of the sacristy, the hands raised to caress, the hands raised in blessing and the forgiveness of sins, the voice, his voice, her voice, the voice of a dead mother, repeating over bread and wine the awful words: *Hoc est enim corpus meum.*

The wind screamed around the ancient stones of the cairn. Men of some lost age had carried the stones up the slopes, piled them as a monument to a dead leader. You could look down into the windy emptiness and see the past and the present and the future, blown along like autumn leaves, hints and memories and whispering, half-heard voices, and all around them the unfathomable mystery of the wind, the mystery of eternity.

III

The dusty hall was crowded with desks and boys borrowed from the school. Two high, grimy windows showed a section of the spires across the street: imitation Gothic, carven figures, jackdaws fluttering and screaming around an aperture that gave access to a nest high in the timbers around the swinging bell.

Pat Rafferty and Bernard Fiddis stood in the door-way and looked in at the industrious room. Crouched over hacked, brown, ink-spotted desks nearly fifty people scribbled addresses on envelopes, folded election circulars into the envelopes, democracy speaking to the narrow streets, to the green townlands in the valleys and the brown townlands on the mountainy slopes. Twenty of the workers were big boys from the school. They had carried the desks with them; and, separated from the school and pitched iuto the political purposes of the world, the desks looked forlorn, regretting spilt inkpots and the wounds made by the sharp points of knives whose owners were seeking immortality. The desks were odorous of the schoolroom. Press an ear to the brown wood and you might hear the rhythmical hum of the schoolroom. Pat Rafferty, a grown man and an educated farmer and possessed of all knowledge, looked at those desks and was, for a moment, sick with shameful nostalgia for days of happy ignorance. His own name was cut on one of those desks. He said: "When I was at school we never got free days for this sort of carry-on."

"Brother Martin," said Fiddis, "is a tower of strength in the cause."

The irony in the words was perceptible. Fiddis didn't believe in causes, or in Brother Martin, or in Jack MacGowan, free for politics now that the season for drama had ended, rushing from desk to desk and supervising the production of accurately addressed envelopes. Fiddis was the candidate, and looked down with the ironical detachment of a pagan god on the enthusiastic efforts that might give him a seat in Stormont on a hill above Belfast, and in Westminster by the wide Thames.

"What does it feel like to be standing for parliament?"

"They wanted a moderate man who could combine all the nationalist votes. They have him in me."

Jack MacGowan was standing with his back to the fire at the far end of the room. He held in his hands a heavy black book filled with the names of men and townlands and the numbers of houses in streets.

"I won't be elected, of course. This always was and always will be a Unionist constituency."

"They say the new Labour candidate will split the Unionist vote."

"They say the end of the world will split the sky. Politics don't develop in Ulster. The Orange farmer votes Unionist because he's told if he doesn't he'll have to learn Gaelic and become a Roman Catholic. The Catholic votes Nationalist because the priest tells him to, and because he wants to see Ireland free and united and Gaelic, whatever that means."

Jack MacGowan was reading from the big book: "Tower Street: James Hunter, Michael Kelly, Andrew MacFaddan, Owen

Ward, Peter Donnelly, Joseph Given, Henry Cassidy, Peter MacCaffrey ..."

The monsignor in the pulpit read out the same list after every church collection. Tower Street would go in a body to the polls and vote for the Nationalist candidate, just as Tower Street subscribed to the upkeep of the Catholic Church.

"You'll head the poll in the town," Pat said.

"We will. And we'll have a torchlight procession afterwards to celebrate, just exactly as it has been for the last sixty years. We're great people for tradition. In politics, in religion, in morals."

"My old man says that like Paddy-go-Easy we're content with whatever contented our fathers."

"What time does he expect us?"

"Four o'clock in Drumquin."

"He's one of the few revolutionaries in Ireland," Fiddis mused. "He really wants to change things. Ireland's mistake always has been to think that the best revolutionaries are the fighters."

Jack MacGowan was reading from his big book: "Drumquin, Fintona, Clogher, Ballygawley, Castlederg, Newtownstewart...."

"We'll be beaten to hell in the small towns," Fiddis said.

You could listen to Jack MacGowan's voice and see the small towns. Any other country would honestly call them villages: a few streets and a few lanes scattered on a green slope between a ruined castle and a gravelly bend of a river; or one street a hundred yards long, stretching from a corrugated iron garage to a humpy fair green. Heads looked out over half-doors. People gossiped lazily and at length about little or nothing. The pattern of life was the same in one little town as in another.

"Poor Jack," Fiddis said, "is a talker. He'll never change anything."

"Except his shirt. Once a week."

"He can't even get a rise of pay. Slevin the Republican is a fighter. But he'll never do anything except get himself into jail."

Jack was reading out the names of the townlands: "Aghee, Aughanamerican, Dunwish, Edenderry, Fireagh East and Fireagh West, Garvaghey...."

You could see the townlands: green valleys, brown mountain, dark bog, damp meadows, freshly-opened ploughland airing in the spring wind, little white-washed houses, two-storeyed slated

142

houses, every man living as his father had lived before him, reading week-old news in the stodgy local newspapers and wondering would the mysterious European powers make a war over some place with a name as long as your arm.

"It's places like that your father wants to change."

The workers at the desks were checking their own lists against the list being read out by Jack MacGowan.

"My father wants to clean a river," Pat said. "All his life is a river."

Fiddis laughed. "An epigram. By a son about his father. He masters the river and he masters life. There's something every man must master. A fear or a bad habit or a horse or an enemy or a river or a woman."

They stood shoulder to shoulder in the doorway. Papers shuffled, feet scraped the floor, pens scraped on envelopes, voices mumbled. They stood together now like friends and talked trivially and illogically as friends could afford to talk, and Pat knew that the next time Fiddis said: "Come out to my house and hear my records," he would go gladly, and he and Fiddis would be friends for ever like men who had shared a cup of water in a desert. And then Woman was mentioned, and Woman was just one woman, all the legends of beauty and all the beauty alive at that moment essenced in her body; and the memory of her body, was between them and driving them eternally apart.

"In Spain," Fiddis said, "your father would have been an anarchist." But the heart had gone out of their lazy idle talk. Pat wasn't listening and Fiddis knew he wasn't listening. It had been pleasant to stand there together, looking at the people and still apart from the people, sharing the secret of a common detachmeut that made them more than brothers. A chance word, like a stone through glass, had broken the dream. They shared one secret that they could never mention to each other. They only knew that they shared it because there were momeuts when they were more than brothers. If it was ever mentioned the world wouldn't be wide enough to hold the two of them; if it was never mentioned there would always be silence and suspicion and moments of sickening understanding.

Jack MacGowan was coming towards them, weaving his way between the badly-arranged desks, dusting document dust off hands and clothes, calling to Harry Mahoney to keep the show going uutil he came back from the meeting. Pat was glad of the interruption. They went down the stairs to the street and into Fiddis's car. They drove out of the town, picking up John Campbell on the way. He would stand on the platform with Fiddis and Pat's father and a few of the village shopkeepers and a few of the promineut farmers from the district around the village. Sitting in the front of the car with Fiddis Pat could close his eyes, shutting out the passing countryside, seeing the village they were going to, and his father, always punctual, waiting by the platform at the foot of the fair green. The humming of the engine melted in his ears, and changed, and became the shouting of an enthusiastic crowd. The crowd would be enthusiastic because only the people who were going to vote for Fiddis would come to his meeting; these people would as soon expose themselves to a killing fever as listen for five minutes to the other man's argumeut. The voters who were convinced, as their fathers before them were convinced, would cheer Fiddis until the village echoed from the garage at one end to the fair green at the other: Who is he at all? It's Mr. Fiddis from the town, the solicitor. Doesn't he speak like a book? Small wonder, isn't he an educated man with two university degrees to his name? Isn't he a lawyer that could get a man off with murder itself? They say he had a lot to do with the release of John Maxwell that was drowned in the flood. Poor Maxwell. God break a hard fate.

Pat would sit in the car, waiting for the end of the meeting and the time to take the reins of the trap and drive his father home. He would listen to the making of speeches and the shouting, asking himself his own questions about Bernard Fiddis, failing hopelessly to find the answers: Could I be his friend as he wants me to be, as I want to be? Could I forget what Alice Graham said? Was it the lie of a jealous woman? Did May leave me that night to go somewhere with him? Has he touched her as I've touched her? Is she an open field that any man can tramp across? Does she love him? Or me? Or anybody?

Sitting in the car beside Fiddis, eyes closed against the passing fields, Pat turned the questions in his mind. Sitting in the car beside Pat, eyes intently open to every curve of the road, Fiddis wondered at the strange demented thoughts that could come to a dying woman in a dark room. Twice he had meant to mention the matter to May, to put her on her guard against any awkward questions the foolish

144

old man might decide to ask. Twice he had stopped, the words trembling on his lips, and afterwards laughed at himself for the tomfoolery of shyness, it was shyness, that prevented him from using cold words to outline the warm secret she shared with him.

The third time he would tell her. There wasn't any necessity. But no wise man left anything to chance.

He jolted Pat Rafferty with his elbow. "Pat's asleep," he said.

"Dreaming," said Jack MacGowan.

"The young can afford dreams," said old Campbell.

Pat laughed. Christ, he thought, it was comic.

The fields rippled past like a green flood, round hills rising and falling like waves. The village was ahead in a green hollow, wet roofs shining in the sun, the people and the platform and Pat Rafferty's father waiting for the candidate.

IV

The thin music was like a thread of sunlight creeping into the darkest corner of the old deserted house. Tangled grass and the trees around the house deadened the delicate sound so that it never reached beyond the orchard to the red-surfaced road, to mystify or terrify passing people, to set them thinking of the ghost of a crabbed old man and the ghost of a gentleman goat and the thin silvery ghost of music.

The Bear Mullan was sitting on the window-sill of the room upstairs, listening to the music made by Joe Keenan who squatted tailorwise on the table. The Bear beat time to the music, his long feet hitting the floor, his thin hands rhythmically flapping on his knees, as he had seen negro minstrels doing in the pictures. He wore—and was very proud of—a new, tight-trousered, navy blue suit, a pale blue, silk handkerchief emerging from the breast pocket, a muffler wound around his lean neck, his new cap cocked on the back of his head. He said: "You could make a fortune, Joe. Playing that thing."

"Tell me how," said Joe Keenan. "Tell me where."

"At concerts and things."

"On the pavement for pennies. People from our alley never play at concerts."

"It was in the paper about a girl in Dublin playing the fiddle on the street and some famous fellow came along and heard her."

Joe blew a last, long, angry blast on the mouth-organ, his black eyebrows stiff in a straight, intense line. He said: "That was in Dublin. Nobody hears you in this town. I've been at this for years and who ever heard me that was worth the dung on his boots?" He tapped the mouth-organ against the palm of his hand. "There isn't a wall in the town that I haven't drawn something on. But who ever made a remark on them except the poxy sergeant that threatened to clink me if he caught me drawing any more girls in bathing suits. Disfiguring the town, he said, with naked women."

The door of the room swung backwards and forwards, gently creaking, in the draught. The Bear closed it firmly, then stood looking out of the window. The branches of the trees were touched with a delicate green. Joe stayed squatting on the table, his fingers plunged in his mass of thick black hair. "In this town," he said, "if you're from the alley you're damned. You can become a message boy. You can join the bloody army. That's the height of it."

"The bloody army. I suppose they'll take this place the way they took Ballyclogher mansion."

Their souls bled at the thought: heavy wheels turning on gravel newly-laid before the house, the crash of trees falling to make room for cylindrical huts of corrugated iron, stiff voices shouting orders, nailed boots tramping and bugles blowing. Each in his own way and for his own reasons loved the house. It was a place of escape, a fortress, a part of the soul, a chapter of boyhood, a green silence against the black and white squalling squalor of Crawford's Alley.

"I'll go and get a job in England," Joe said, "in a factory."

If the house was taken from them, the town's claim on them would be as weak as water.

"Over in England," Joe said, "they'll never know where I was born. I can say I lived in a big house in the Diamond. That me father was an artist or a musician or owned a garage."

The Bear raised his right foot to the edge of the table. With his silk handkerchief he shone the long pointy toe of his patent leather shoe. "Nice boy Campbell," he said, "left us in the lurch anyway. I'll get even with that twirp before we go to England."

"Forget about him. He wasn't our kind."

"Christ, he wasn't. He told the whole story to Fiddis, I'm certain sure."

146

"Even if he did, Fiddis didn't do anything. So why worry."

The Bear changed feet, and polished rapidly. "Didn't do anything. And I know why, Joe Keenan. I know why."

"Why?"

"I saw what I saw. The two of them in a car in a lane off the Belfast road. In broad bloody daylight. No wonder he wouldn't say anything that would put her pansy brother in a fix."

Joe whistled slowly. He said: "Leave it to Fiddis, the solid man. First home every time."

"If he ever says a word about us, begod, I could say a mouthful about him. The dirty old blackguard."

"You'd only make a cod of yourself. It's not our business. Maybe they're going to get married."

The Bear's eyes were little lumps of black stone. He fixed the blue silk handkerchief back in his breast pocket. He said: "Down in the alley you have to be well married before you can carry on like that."

Joe whistled again. "Hot stuff," he said.

"She's a hot bit all right. Wouldn't mind entertaining her here. Meself and Andy Jim Orr and the goat."

"Control yourself, Bear," Joe said. "England's full of them." He leaped down from the table, yawned, stretched himself. "Big cities," he said. "Big factories. Thousands of girls." He was laughing. The Bear's eyes glistened. "We'll be late for the match," Joe said. "And it's the last match of the season."

They closed the front door of the house as firmly as they could, and then climbed out through the small, low, kitchen window. Every visit now might be their last visit, and some day or any day they might stand on the roadway and hear the crash of falling trees and the roaring of the engines of military lorries, and the blaring of bugles. Whoever came would have to smash the front door to pieces, and Andy Jim Orr and his ghost of a goat would have time to escape. Something was happening to the world when a ghost couldn't even be sure of his peace.

With a bucket of whitewash and a brush Brass MacManus had made ready for the spring. The walls of the wee house, he said, would be a credit to the ground they stood on, and every day now the deep water in the quarry hole shone with a new life, and the grass that surrounded the shining water was a new fresh green. He whitewashed the inside of the house; with his mother's help carefully removing the photographs and carefully restoring them to their proper places when the work was done. He was proud of all those photographs of tall, solemn, athletic men, and looking at them he could see also smooth fields and running figures, could hear the thumping of quick boots on the ball, or the thin restraining whistle. He handled those photographs as carefully as a devout pagan might have handled his household images. They were more than photographs. They were memories of victory, records of achievement, trophies won, white cups and gold cups and sets of medals. His mother's life was in those photographs.

He whitewashed the outside of the house making it worthy of the earth, worthy of the view. He was proud of the view. No man, rich or poor, barring Fiddis the solicitor, could stand on his threshold and see a view like that: the ground sloping down to a road that was always lively with traffic, beyond the road a railway cutting through the fields, going on towards the mountains, and beyond the mountains, he knew, were the seabreakers rolling in on the strand at Bundoran.

The air in the house was scented with lime. The place was as fresh and clean as a new flower. Jim Collins came, bringing Dympna with him, to see the results of the spring-cleaning.

They sat around the red hearth and drank strong tea and ate thick soda bread, still warm enough to absorb the yellow strong-flavoured butter into every crumb.

"Your bread's a treat, Mrs. Mack," Dympna said. "Will you give me the recipe?"

"I will, and welcome, dear."

"She's thinking of the housekeeping, already," Brass laughed, slapping his knees with delight, proud of Dympna and Jim and his mother and her bread and the white house and the sunshine outside on the grass. His face was black and stubbly, Dympna thought, but his heart must be all the colours of the rainbow.

The old woman refilled the teapot, settled it again on a small circle of glowing coals. Jim Collins helped himself to another cut of bread, bit with silent savage enjoyment, said through a full mouth: "Thank God I'm not playing in this match. I'd be too full to run."

"It's the last match of the season." There was regret in the voice.

The warm sun returning brought to Brass always that one sorrow.

"We'll soon be swimming."

"Not me. But I'll take down the old fishing rod."

"It's a quiet sport," Jim said.

"It gives a man time to think." Sitting there in the kitchen Brass could look into the fire on the hearth and see not the hot flames but the cool, musical river, chattering over shallows, solemn in deep pools.

"I get too much time to think," Jim said.

He really meant it. He really meant, too, that he was glad he wasn't playing football today. The soda bread wasn't worrying him. He could eat tweuty scones, digest them as a turnip cutter digested turnips, and still run like a hare. But when you played football your mind must be on the game, and your eye on the ball. Sitting there by the fire, or walking to the match with Brass and Dympna, his mind wasn't on the game. Without looking at Dympna he could see her face, white and troubled, her lips moving to tell him the terrible thing about May. Dympna had to tell somebody.

It was all very well to say as Dympna said: "I blame that Graham's hotel." But, holy God, a girl that walked with her head as high as May Campbell should have had more sense.

May was hiding something. Even innoceut little Dympna knew that May was hiding a name, keeping to herself a secret that must some day soon be the property of the whole gossiping town.

Maybe it had all happened because of bad company and a few drinks and a strange man in Graham's hotel. But the town never believed stories about strange men, not any more than the town believed that the queer illness that had a year ago afflicted three young men was really the fault of a mysterious Jewess who had, according to the three young men, spent her summer holidays in Bundoran.

Jim Collins knew the town, and the people there didn't believe in fairies, and if May mentioned no name the people would do it for her with a heart and a half.

What name would they mention? He would make certain that Anne never heard a word about this. He would make certain sure that if it was ever meutioned to him he would lay the blame heavily on Graham's hotel. What was that woman, anyway, but a foreigner from some backstreet in some unknown city?

Gold of the scores of candles. Perfume of vases of spring flowers. Their slippered feet were as quiet as cats on the cold mosaic as they walked from the sacristy to the high altar. The clock in the organ loft chimed the hour. Easing himself down to the prie-dieu on the gospel side of the decorated altar Dinny told himself that in sixty minutes Chris and himself would be free again in the sunshine and the last match of the season would be beginning, with a shriek of a whistle and a boot on the ball and hundreds of people shouting with one voice.

The altar was a coloured burning mountain, a soft mountain of flowers and flames, the softness broken here and there by rigid outcroppings of white marble, and the centre of the mountain was the golden monstrance, rayed like the sun and holding the white Host God looked down from his golden throne, from his perfumed flickering mountain, and saw two boys in white surplices and red soutanes, kneeling and watching while the clock in the organ loft ticked away the hour, and down in the body of the church a few people prayed, and Tom Nixon's beads rattled against the wooden pew as he asked of God success for his undertakings.

Dinny liked his hour on the altar. It didn't happen so often, a few times in the year when there were special devotions and the altar was specially decorated, and the monstrance, with the white Host from the darkness of the tabernacle, was raised high among the flowers. God could see everybody and everybody could see God. Dinny liked the silence, the slow burning of the candles, the smell of flowers and the smell of melting wax, the little noises: feet shuffling on the tiled aisles or bumping on the wooden floor, the ticking and the chiming of the clock, the rattle of rosary beads against the pews.

Chris Collins thought his hour on the altar was a very long hour. Dinny knew that the book Chris had half-concealed between his elbows on the prie-dieu wasn't a prayer book, or even a red-backed copy of the *Messenger of the Sacred Heart*, which was a sort of a prayer book even if there were stories in it, but a twopenny Buffalo Bill with a coloured picture on the cover. The picture showed Buffalo Bill, in a pointy hat and a brown suit, sitting straddle on a log laid across a bottomless chasm, a bear at one end of the log, at the other end a lurid Indian wickedly chopping with a hatchet. Chris was hopping from one knee to another, was twining and untwining his thin ankles, in an ecstasy of excitement. He was miles away from the altar and the flowers and the candles, finding out whether Buffalo Bill faced the Indian or the grizzly bear lost so completely that one of the two relieving altar boys had to nudge him sharply.

Their hour of prayer was over. Walk from the altar, hands joined, eyes modestly cast down, the great adventure of Buffalo Bill tucked securely under the left oxter.

Bundle surplices and soutanes into brown wooden presses. Exchange soft slippers for hard boots. Run, run out of the church into the sunshine, the rooks crying around the spires, the sleepy streets as empty as the empty barrels trundled down the cobbled slope from the side door of Brady's pub.

The whole town was at the match. Run, run, for this minute the referee was putting the whistle to his lips, the centre forward was touching the ball, and the whole town was cheering.

"We've no money."

"We'll climb the tins."

Run like hares, down Tower Street, over the red metal bridge, along a quiet road of big detached houses, along a quieter lane with the black tins to the left hand, and over the tins the shouting.

"It's a sin, Chris Collins, to read a Buffalo Bill on the altar."

"Be your age, Dinny. Me brother Jim used to do his Latin exercises when he was on the altar."

"All the same."

"Don't annoy me. And me breathless."

Hard scrambling and hard climbing and hard boots on the tins. The green ground, the quick players, and all around them in a great circle the shouting people, alive and roaring, the town, the world, in a great shouting circle as round as the world.

"Holy mackerel, Dinny, I tore me coat on the tins."

"I skinned me knee."

"The ma'll kill me."

"I'm lame for life."

Jump down and run into the crowd. Escape the man who's paid to watch the tins, but who's watching the match instead. Run across the grass into the crowd, into the shouting world.

Half way down the stairs the nurse met old John Campbell. She wasn't running. She wasn't excited. She was cool and careful and professional, bending a little and speaking, almost whispering, into his ear, holding his arm in case he would go rushing up the stairs, damaging himself, doing no earthly good to the dying woman. Men were like children who got excited easily, and death was nothing to get excited about; it was the end of excitement.

Still he was very good, dear old Mr. Campbell, he did everything the nurse told him to do—telephoned the priest and the doctor while she ran down the back garden to find May resting in the sun, her face as pale as a ghost even though the sun in that corner was as hot as a furnace. That girl, whatever it was, wasn't as well as she should be. Then the three of them walked up the stairs together, and old Campbell put his head out of the landing window and called to one of the hands who was hosing a car to run full pelt and bring home Gerry and Dympna and Dinny, wherever they were.

In the room they spoke to each other in whispers. The nurse gently pulled across the curtains on one of the two windows. It didn't matter now. She was gone too far into the shadows for the light from the window to overtake her and trouble her with the memory of life. The table was ready beside the bed—a crucifix, a blessed candle, a bottle of holy water; the table was bright with white linen that caught the light from the window. She lay so quietly she was almost invisible in the bed. Now and again she sighed, very quietly.

They weut from the room when the priest and the doctor came. Father and daughter stood on the landing and waited for the nurse and the doctor to join them. The front door had been left lying open and old Campbell tiptoed down the stairs to close it, and when he came back May was gone. A drink of water, he thought, would clear the dust of agony and suspense from his mouth and throat, so he walked to the bathroom and opened the door and saw May there, and he closed the door instantly and tiptoed back to wait for the nurse and the doctor. He was trembling, as weak as a kitten, sweat breaking out all over his body. He gripped the banister and leaned against it to steady himself. Old people, particularly old people of his family, couldn't afford shocks.

She came back to him. Her face was very white. She was wiping her lips with a small, lace-fringed handkerchief. She didn't know that he had seen her hunched up over the washbasin, her shoulders contracted, her body trembling with the retching. It might have been more than twenty years ago, and she might have been another woman, and he might have been discovering for the first time the secret of the pain and the revulsion that was a prelude to life. A man knew nothing until he was married. Why didn't she trust him? Why didn't she tell him?

The nurse and doctor tiptoed out of the room. The doctor shook his head, and grasped old Campbell by the hand.

But then how could she tell him? She was young and ignorant and afraid of what had happsned to her and afraid of his anger. As if an old man could be angry.

The nurse looked sharply at May and said: "Are you well, child?" That nurse was a wise, kind woman.

Gerry and Dinny and Dympna were coming on tiptoes up the stairs, and Dympna was crying softly, and Dinny was holding on to her hand.

She was in there now, the priest bending over her, and she was whispering her sins. John Campbell tried not to see her poor, dry lips, moving with effort, whispering her own sins this time, her poor, dry sins that had never ended in foolishness, the sins of a woman who had given her life to another woman's children, sins of the mind, sins of the thwarted heart. He said, as if the words had been torn out of him with a grapple: "Poor Aggie. Poor woman. 'Twas little she knew."

After that there was deep silence. You couldn't even hear Dympna sniffling. You could hear only the noises of the street, muted as if they had sunk down to you slowly through calm, deep water. May thought that never before in that part of the house had she heard the noises of the street.

The priest opened the door and beckoned, and they went in single file into the room.

V

It poured from the heavens on the day of the funeral and the people crowding, dripping and steaming, into the church, dipped wet fingers in the holy font and said to each other: Blessed are the dead that the rain rains on. The other line of that jingle, Jim Collins thought—moving from knee to knee to give his trousers a chance

153

to dry—was: Blessed is the bride that the sun shines on. He looked up at the chief mourners kneeling together in the front seats, and saw Dympna among them —dark hair and dark mourning cloth and head bowed between her little hands. He was sorry because of Dympna's sorrow, weeping among weeping people, and outside the skies weeping on the earth. Blessed are the dead. The black-vested priest on the bare lenten altar raised his hands in supplication; and for Dympna's sake Jim imagined some Easter day bright with sunshine, and golden vestments on the priest because Christ was risen like the sun, and Dympna dressed in white walking the aisle towards the cheerful altar. Blessed is the bride. Maybe it wasn't right to be thinking that way and the poor old woman locked in a box before the altar, waiting for her last journey, and in bloody awful weather too. She never had been much of a friend to the cause of Jim Collins, but she was dead now, and blessed were the dead, and his trouser legs wouldn't be dry this side of Christmas.

Chris Collins was the altar-boy who carried the stoup of holy water when the priest came out to pray over the coffin. The priest sprinkled the coffin with holy water. Chris pulled his left ear with his left hand. In the front row of the block of chief mourners Dinny Campbell pulled his right ear with his right hand. It was a secret sign. It meant understanding and sympathy and the conspiracy of two against the whole wide world, against the living and against the terrors of death; and when the time came to sit up for the sermon Dinny was as content as any body could be, surrounded by black, solemn uncles and black, weeping aunts and poor Aunt Aggie's coffin six inches from his nose.

Resting the palms of his hands on the edge of the pulpit the priest said: "And this is the Will of My Father that sent Me: that every one who seeth the Son, and believeth in Him, may have life everlasting: and I will raise him up on the last day."

Gerry Campbell crossed his legs and squeezed back into the narrow space between his father and his uncle Andrew. The thought of the last day was a thought that always gave him the shivers: angels flying and trumpets blowing and graves opening and the awakening dead rubbing the clay out of their eyes, and everybody knowing everything about everybody else. Aunt Aggie would find out something about him that she hadn't known all the times she kept telling him that the highest ambition a man could have was to change bread and wine into the Body and Blood of God. Maybe she had found it out already. Maybe dead there in her coffin she knew his secret as Fiddis knew it, and he was more afraid of Aunt Aggie dead than of Fiddis alive. There was something awful about Aunt Aggie, the length of her, her yellow face, her small, shiny, dark eyes like the eyes of the Bear Mullan. Still the dead were dead, and blessed were the dead, and he was finished with Aunt Aggie and the Bear Mullan, and it was a good while to the last day. He would be a priest then anyway, able to face fifty aunts and all the bears in the zoo.

"She gave her life," the priest said, "to protect and rear four orphan children. She was a mother to them in place of the mother they had lost." Old Campbell swallowed noisily and Dympna looked almost angrily at the preaching priest. "By that sacrifice she has stored up reward where neither rust nor moth consume, nor where thieves break in and steal." The Bear Mullan, Gerry thought, would never rob Aunt Aggie.

Brass MacManus at the back of the church moved his lips in unison with every word the preacher said. His eyes were upturned and glazed with the effort of listening. Long practice had made him a great hand at memorizing sermons, at estimating the ability or lack of ability displayed by preachers. The poor mother's heart would never allow her to sit in a church for the duration of a sermon, and back in the little kitchen Brass would repeat almost word for word what had been said, the merits of the manner of saying, the gestures that had gone with or grown out of the words. All the way through the dripping town, walking silently in the funeral procession, he remembered what the priest had said about poor dead Miss Campbell: a model for Irish womanhood, a mother to helpless orphans, a pillar of the church, an active worker in all good causes.

It was a long procession. Why wouldn't it be? And every blind in the town was drawn and every shop closed. Tho town, Dinny thought, had closed its eyes and gone to sleep; except Graham's hotel, with eyes wide open and Mrs. Graham, the queer woman wiping the inside of the streaming panes of a window so that she could have a better view of Agatha Campbell's coffin passing on the way to the graveyard.

Mr. Nixon the grocer was in the same car as Dinny, and Mr. Nixon said: "What could you expect from one that learned her manners on the London pavements?" But somebody else nudged his elbow and indicated Dinny, and Mr. Nixon said no more about Mrs. Graham.

The rain fell straight and steadily, no wind moving it, and only the hardy walkers and the people in cars went the whole way out the Dublin road, past the white house where the saddler kept pet jackdaws, past the gasworks and the technical school and over the railway bridge and past the golf links, to the graveyard. The rain hissed on the gravelled walk, and statues and crosses were ghostly with the mist rising again from the warm earth, and the clay fell with a damp dull sound on the coffin, and Dympna suddenly cried so loudly that Jim Collins could hear her where he stood, half-sheltered by a marble statue, and moving patiently from one wet foot to the other.

The rain lasted all day and all the day after, and in Campbell's house relatives by the dozen were shaking hands and hoping to see each other soon: at a wedding or a christening or maybe, God help us, at another funeral, for we all must die, and God rest poor Agatha who sacrificed herself for the young, and God give the young the wit to realise all she had done for them. Then they were gone, taking the bad weather with them, and everybody, even old John Campbell, was highly relieved.

He sat in an armchair in the drawing-room, his back to the window and the sunny street, his slippered feet to the fire, his heavy long face turned to his elder daughter. The room was too warm, with the sun through the window and the heat from the hearth, and his mind and body relaxing in the heat left him at peace with all things, with death that couldn't be avoided, with disgrace that could be hidden if a man had money and a bit of gumption. He must consult Fiddis. Fiddis was a man who could keep a secret.

He said: "The house is quiet now, May."

"Yes, Father."

She was stitching a laddered stocking, her left hand hidden in the thin fabric, her lips pursed, her eyes intent on the movemeut of the shining little needle. She had a face like a picture. She was a daughter that any man might be proud of, might tell lies to protect her from the tongues of the town, cutting into her life like knives cutting through butter.

"She was a good woman."

"Yes, Father."

156

"She gave up a lot to look after you all when your poor mother died."

Silence. May thought: they all said that, all the relatives, again and again until she almost believed it herself, until she was almost ready to think of Auut Aggie as a holocaust, a whole-burnt offering. Nobody had said what exactly it was that Auut Aggie had given up. A man? Had any man ever wanted her? A career? A vocation in the convent? Aunt Aggie's sacrifice was a family legend.

"She's gone now," her father said. "But isn't she well dead? Isn't she safe from misfortune or disgrace? When you think of the misfortune that followed that poor Maxwell man. . . ."

She sat opposite him and sewed her stocking and said nothing—his eldest child; and he remembered how fear and revulsion could change into love and pride once the ordeal was over and the child was born. Her shame was his shame. Her secret was his secret. She was afraid of his anger but how could an old man be angry and ah God she was lovely. He said: "May, child, I know your trouble."

She didn't lift her eyes from the quick needle and the thin fabric of the stocking. She said: "What trouble?"

"When I married your mother she was young and innocent. But she was as wild as a hare. Times were different then. There was more innocence in the world."

She said nothing. Her blood was cold for a momeut, knowing that he knew, and then she wanted to run to him and throw her arms around his neck, and cry and cry like a baby. Many a father would have cursed and roared and shouted and threatened to throw her out on the street; but he was so good and so quiet, his white hair, the clumsy knot on his tie, that she was sick with sorrow for him, and softening towards tears she would have told him everything if he hadn't spoken first.

"Who is he?"

"I'd rather not say."

She couldn't say. She couldn't afford to soften into tears, to weep out two words that would tie her for ever to one man and shut another man for ever out of her life. She would have to think very coolly.

She said: "Don't be angry with me. I know the harm I've done."

He wouldn't be angry with her. How could an old man be angry with something that was a very large part of his own withering life?

"I won't force you one way or the other. But think it over. Why shelter someone who isn't worrying about you?"

She couldn't tell him that she was sheltering nobody; that she had thought it over and over and over again; that she was protecting herself as well as she could, sewing up the rent in her life as carefully as she was sewing up the rent in her stocking. One folly was enough for a lifetime. If she must have a husband she would have something more than a husband.

He gripped the arms of his chair very tightly. He wouldn't be angry. He said: "The young will be foolish. I blame myself."

Through the window she saw Bernard Fiddis's car pulling up at the kerb.

"If your poor aunt, the heavens be her bed, had been at herself, she'd have told that woman to mind her own business and leave innocent girls alone."

He was almost angry. He said: "The painted hussy." But his anger had passed like a harmless wind over his daughter's head, to battle vainly around distant and irrelevant obstacles. And the door bell was ringing, and Jinny's heels were hammering along the hallway, and Bernard Fiddis was at the door.

VI

Jim Collins said two or three times every week that it must be a bloody great thing to own your own motor car. Jim was speed-minded and machine-minded.

Dympna said that her father had promised to give May an Austin ten for her last birthday but that Aunt Aggie's death must have put it out of his head.

It was Jim's idea to borrow a motor car for the first really sunny Sunday and to drive with Dympna the pleasant fifty miles to the seaside at Bundoran. Dympna couldn't go and leave May at home in a house that had lately been a house of mourning, and Jim suggested that Pat Rafferty should make up the foursome. He had told Pat Rafferty what Dympna had told him about May, and Pat had never moved a muscle of his hard face, never even flicked his eyes sideways with shock or surprise. Thank God anyway that Pat Rafferty wasn't the guilty man.

"That Graham's hotel was no place for a young girl," Jim said.

"I suppose not."

"What will she do now, do you think?"

"God only knows."

God only knew. What was the use in telling Jim Collins the truth? Jim was innocent. Jim was foolish.

Jim drove a motor car with reckless headlong skill. They left the town after early Mass. The fields were wet with a heavy dew. The sun was struggling up the sky away beyond the straight trees of Clanabogan planation. It would be a warm day.

"If there's a war,' Jim said, "I'll join the Royal Air Force. Up in the air a man has room for speed. Squadron Leader Collins."

He made a shrieking siren noise with his mouth, stepped on the accelerator and with his finger on the horn swept past a roadside church where the people were gathering for Mass. The road cleared before him. A man leaped from a trap and ran to the head of a frightened prancing horse. Another man leaped on to the grass margin and stood shaking his fist at the vanishing car. Dympna was alarmed. She said: "Jim, they'll take your number."

"Let them. I haven't killed anybody—yet."

May was laughing. She was enjoying the speed, the hedges whizzing past, the dark, smooth road rushing to meet them, the discovery of a positively poetic recklessness that she had never suspected could exist in the prosaic Jim Collins. Aunt Aggie had never liked him, and that was a point in his favour. Pat Rafferty sitting beside her in the back of the car liked her again for her laughter and her courage that didn't mind missing death by a touch on the steering wheel. A crash, and four sudden deaths would solve some problems, but this morning, with everything green and blue and the air dripping with sunlight, life was too good to lose; and softly he touched May's hand, and her fingers closed around his and she moved nearer to him until their bodies touched.

Little towns and level crossings, slow streams reflecting the sun, a great lake studded with islands and beyond the lake mountains in the western distance, a customs hut with yawny men in unbrushed uniforms, a great river going down over rocks, down as the road was going and they were going to the blue battering sea. They had their first sight of the sea when the road topped a green ridge spotted with white tents, and Jim halted to give a lift to a green-uniformed soldier tramping perspiringly towards the town. In green or in khaki his heart went out to soldiers. The sea was eternity around time, blue infinity around one small green-and-brown island, around four million islanders and the joys and sorrows of four million separate Sundays.

Making room for the soldier May sat very close to Pat and he held his arm around her waist; and when the soldier thanked them and left them at the edge of the town they still sat like that, warm against each other, his hand cupped over the beating of her heart. Brightly dressed people crowded the pavemems. The music of a band came floating up on the wind,·and through a gap in the houses they saw the surf and the sand. Two lives, at least, out of four million islanded lives would for this one day know no separation. Afterwards when you turned your back on the sea and your face to the life you lived on the island, anything might happen: the sun might die, the sky fall in rain.

"First stop Rougey," Jim said.

For this one day their faces were to the sea, and the sea was about their bodies, their souls lost in blue water, their eyes on a blue horizon that might be the beginning of another world.

Jim drove down to the edge of the strand, and taking togs and towels they crossed the crowded sand to the high black rocks of Rougey. Beneath the cliffs and sheltered by a jutting elbow of high rock the sea moved crisply in a wide deep pool, where good swimmers could exercise at peace, sheltered from the trampling rush of the breakers, cut off from the crowded strand and the patient little donkeys and the children building castles in the sand. The four of them were good swimmers, and, afterwards, fresh and rapidly growing hungry they lay on the sun-warmed rocks and looked back over the crescent-shaped strand to the square solemn mountains beyond the straggling town.

"I like this place," Jim said.

May breathed deeply the Atlamic wind. .She hadn't felt so well for weeks. She said: "Except it's always filled with people from our town."

"They have their rights," Dympna said. "We can't keep them out."

Pat laughed contentedly. He knew no reason why he should feel so happy. By all that he had ever heard he should feel like a man in the condemned cell for she was in trouble and he was the cause of her trouble, and unless a miracle happened the scandal-mongers of the town would have their names in the mud in two months' time. But lying in the sun or swimming in the water she didn't seem to be unhappy, and with her in the sun and in the cool water he was infected by her happiness.

"Brass MacManus was here once," Jim said. "He's talking about it still."

"Poor Brass," said Dympna.

May was combing her hair. It was like warm silk in the sun. "1 don't know what you people see in that unshaven specimen."

Pat laughed. He was ready to laugh at anything because there was a secret between him and that lovely girl, and a secret, innocent or guilty, was still something that the rest of the world didn't share. "John Maxwell," he said, "came here on his honeymoon."

Dympna shivered. The noise of the hobbyhorse organ came, in a lull of the wind, across to them over red sand and shouting children.

"The people I mix with," May said. "When they're not talking about tramps they're talking about murderers." She stretched out her arms and stood facing the roaring sea, her fair hair blown backwards by the wind, a goddess offering herself to a god. She said: "I'm hungry." Three partially-dressed men on a lower level of the rock looked up at her and shouted their appreciation, but the wind maliciously jumbled their words into a vague sound, the shivering cry of a world desiring beauty. Then Pat was beside her with his arm about her waist, his great body towering over her, leading her gently down the terraced rock to the sand and the edge of the sea. Jim and Dympna followed. They were puzzled, but because they were innocent people their puzzlement was as passing as foam on the tossing water; and anyway, with the world as clear as crystal under the bright sun, it wasn't a day for worry.

They lunched in a hotel and Dympna nervously sipped her first sherry, and Tom Nixon coming in with two men who were as red-faced as himself patted Dympna on the shoulder and said: "That's right. I always like to see young people enjoying themselves." He wore a white straw hat and a brown tweed suit. He was the image of joviality and he never even seemed to remember Pat as the man who had called him a dirty name across the counter of his own licensed premises. When he was safely seated at a distance at his own table with his two red-faced companions, Dympna said: "He'll go home an' tell my father he saw me drinking in Bundoran."

May mimicked the voice of Tom Nixon: "There's no doubt in the wide world, John Campbell, it would open your eyes as wide as a barn-door to see the fashion of these modern young women an' their cocks tails." Tom Nixon always called them cocks tails. They laughed together. They were happy. They had all agreed this time on the topic of Tom Nixon.

"Something wrong with a man,' Jim said, "who's forever making jokes at other people's expense."

Pat said nothing. He saw John Maxwell standing in the middle of a public house floor, talking foolish, and the world enjoying the fun. But he put the memory away from him, for this was a day of sunshine and sea and agreeable happiness: bathing in the pounding surf when the effect of lunch had worn off; acting like children at the hobbyhorses and the rifle range and the chairoplanes and the bumping cars; sipping tea in a hot little restaurant that seemed to be made up completely of sizzling plate-glass windows; eating ices in a cool little restaurant with people that you knew and people that you didn't know coming and going softly over the carpeted floor; dancing in a crowded dance hall and leaving its perfumed heat for a last walk by the cool sea. There should have been a moon, but there wasn't. The wind was less boisterous than it had been during the day but it was edged with cold to remind the world that this lovely weather was little more than something stolen from winter. May and Dympna took their coats from the car, and all together they walked past Rougey, higher and higher along the tops of the cliffs, the wail of the sea somewhere in the darkness below them. In spite of the coat May shivered. Jim and Dympna ran somewhere to shelter from the wind, and Pat and May were walking alone.

He looked down at the sudden flash of light where a wicked pointy rock had ripped phosphorescent whiteness from the restless water. He said: "Jim told me what Dympna told him." If there had been a moon to soothe the terrible ocean into silver, if the wind had been warm, he wouldn't have said that. He would have thankfully taken the whole day as a day daringly stolen from seriousness.

She said: "Dympna's not so good at keeping secrets." In her soul she cursed herself for telling Dympna, and Dympna for telling Jim, and Jim for telling Pat Rafferty. A sudden terror, colder than the wind, gripped her. "You didn't tell Jim the truth?"

"No," he said. "I'm not a fool. . . ."

They stood close together sheltered from the wind by a high dry-stone wall. Somewhere in the darkness, cattle were cropping the short grass.

"What'll we do, May?"

"We'll do nothing. I'll handle this. I know a way out."

"But it's my fault."

"It doesn't matter whose fault it is. What do you want to do? Go to my father and say: "Mr. Campbell, I'm the villain.""

"That's the usual thing," he said. "That, or run away to England."

She was laughing a hard laughter that was terrible to hear. He was too young to know that that laughter would remain with her for ever, remaking her soul in its own image and likeness.

"I asked advice," she said, "of Alice Graham." She had learned so much of Alice Graham, all sorts of lessons. Alice Graham had a new pair of red shoes to match the colour of her polished finger-nails, as long as claws, the cruel, jealous bitch. Suddenly May shivered so much with the memory of her hate that Pat held her more closely and said: "Poor May. You're frozen. We'll go back to the car."

How little he knew. Men were so much younger than women, weaker, more foolish, yet there were times when their stupid physical steadiness could give comfort as a warm fire or a comfortable chair—things without any life or soul or understanding of their own—gave comfort. She leaned against his great body, as steady as the stone wall, and without weakness and without tears she remembered and hated Alice Graham. Every word the woman had said had been like a stab to the heart from one of those red pointed claws.

"So you want help do you? My dear child, think where you are. This town! This country! Now it would be different in London or in Glasgow. I know people there. Civilized people. . . .

"Don't tell me Bernard Fiddis was such a fool. I know. You can't tell me any cowboy stories about Bernard Fiddis. . . .

"That's the worst of playing about with clumsy couutry

schoolboys. Let this be a lesson to you as long as you live. . ."

"Tell your father the truth, the whole truth."

No, there was no help in Alice Graham, nothing but plotted wickedness behind her painted face and her shiny eyes that were sometimes brown and sometimes black, nothing but the hope that if May's father forced her to marry Pat Rafferty then the field would be clear for Alice Graham to canter home to her fourth and last, to a big house and comfort and wealth where she could grow old with dignity, forgetting the days of her wandering from husband to husband like a tramp wandering from house to house.

Pat was urging her gently back towards the strand and the car. He was talking continuously, a low soft voice, a sound as meaningless to her as the sound of the wind and the sea. Vaguely she understood that he was trying to comfort her, to tell her not to worry, that everything would turn out well. She wanted to laugh at him and, at the same time, to hug him, the poor, old, know-nothing of a circus clown. How little he knew! How little, for all her wickedness, did Alice Graham know!

Did Alice Graham think that Bernard Fiddis would risk his livelihood and the favour of the town by marrying a foreign woman who was no better than a tramp? Friendship was one thing. The town winked at that. Marriage was another, and marriage to a woman who had husbands scattered everywhere from hell to Connaught wasn't marriage as the town saw it. Bernard Fiddis wanted a woman who could be a credit to him, a woman who belonged to the best people in the town. Did Alice Graham really think that May Campbell would worry her poor old father with the truth, or that her father would force her anywhere she didn't want to go? Alice Graham's soul was as transparent as weak tea; a woman to be pitied, three husbands and nothing to show for any of them.

She stumbled over a stone in the darkness, and he caught and held her with a frantic gentleness, and she pressed eagerly against him; he was warm and strong.

"Are you all right? You must take care of yourself."

Anxious husbands who wanted eight-pound sons safely delivered spoke like that to young wives. And she wanted to say goodbye to him in the only way that her body understood but she could not make him understand.

164

They sat in the car, looking forward into two completely different futures.

"We'll always be able to stand up for each other."

"Promise me, Pat, you'll say nothing until you have my permission."

He promised, hesitantly: "I don't want you to sacrifice yourself protecting me."

"Pat. Poor Pat." She stroked his hair gently. She was a mother from that moment. "I'm not the sort to sacrifice myself."

They waited for Jim and Dympna. The wind gently rocked the car. Unseen spray fell like frozen hail on unseen, sea-battered sand. She said: "I'm not protecting you," and thought that the words might be her last truth for a long time to come. He leaned forward and switched on the headlights. He said: "They'll see where the car is." In the white light the wind gravely twirled wreaths and ropes of sand.

VII

In the big room at the back of Gormley's secondhand clothes shop Tom Nixon was organizing his new joke. Two weeks ago he had given jalaped chocolates to the fattest man in the town. Five weeks ago he had sent a telegram to the meanest man in the town to tell him he had drawn the favourite in the Irish Hospitals Sweepstake, and the man had been for four hours going from pub to pub and throwing money around him like chaff before he discovered he had been hoaxed. The new joke would be a political joke, almost a political satire, a mock celebration complete with torchlight and speeches to steal the thunder of the celebration inevitable when the Nationalist candidate headed the poll in the town. It would be the joke to end all jokes. It would rock the town with laughter.

Tom Nixon had assembled his politicians for a dress rehearsal. The speeches were ready and written out: one speech about the state of the public lavatory in the market yard, where the tree washed down by the flood was still jammed firmly in the doorway making admission the monopoly of the agile; another speech about the industrial possibilities of the cowdung left on the streets after the fair day; a third speech taking libellous liberties with the names of several decent townspeople.

For three speeches there were three politicians: Big Rory the drover, and Lame Joe who sold laces on the street, and Bacon Peters who was one of a large family of half-brothers and half-sisters all bearing their mother's surname.

"My name," Big Rory said, "is Lord CowCommons." He closed his eyes, and soothed with his right hand the stiff grey stubble on his circular, protruding chin: a big hump-shouldered man, as uncomfortable as hell in tight and unfamiliar evening dress but ready to go to bed in chain mail if Mr. Nixon was fool enough to make it worth his while.

"Me name," Lame Joe said, "is General Sir Laces Joseph." In evening dress he would have looked, with his thin face and black drooping moustache and weak nervously gesturing hands, like a timid professor compelled by duty to preside at an undergraduates dance. In tight military trousers and flaring crimson coat, his chest rattling with ancient medals, he was like a ghost victimised by cruel schoolboys. He moved nervously from foot to foot. His fingers vainly searched for the reassuring touch of a bundle of bootlaces.

"Me name," Bacon Peters growled, "is Viscount Skitter Alley Row." His eyes were vacant and stupid; his big feet turned inwards; his forehead and nose were narrow, his jaws fantastically square.

"Your names are correct according to our publicity agent," Tom Nixon said. The few helpers that he had admitted into the secret sniggered encouragingly. He consulted a printed handbill and read the three names out loud. He said: "Remember your names and your speeches, for God's sake. The opposition party may heckle us." The sniggering hardened into laughter.

"General Sir Laces," said Gormley the secondhand clothes man, "will have another run at his speech."

Lame Joe stood up timidly on a chair, and read quaveringly from a sheet of paper: "Fellow countrymen and gentle ladies, born honestly and reared decently, I come before you to stand behind you to tell you something I know nothing about."

It was the sort of fun that would rock the crowd with laughter.

"As one who has at heart the welfare of the people, and one who has always in his public life supported the fundamental freedoms including the right of every man to a seat in the house . . . "

Lame Joe limped his way over the long words. Tom Nixon and Gormley and the other organizers of humour laughed like horses.

". . . it is only the truth to say that this obstinate tree has long caused an obstruction in the life of the town. . . ."

The meanest man in the town was there with Tom Nixon, laughing as heartily as if he didn't know that Tom had fooled him into spending money in the expectation of plenty. The fattest man in the town was, under doctor's orders, still in bed.

"You couldn't do a better thing," Bernard Fiddis told Gerry Campbell. "You'll find the life severe at first, but you'll be very happy when you settle down."

He spoke without much conviction. Encouragement was cheap, but he doubted if this handsome, smooth-skinned, fair-headed boy would settle down and be happy in the life he had so surprisingly chosen.

Gerry's eyes wandered to the window, his ears absorbed the sound of papers shuffling as Fiddis set his desk in order after the day's work. He could never find it possible to look Fiddis directly in the eyes. "The monsignor told me that when he first went to Maynooth he thought he wouldn't stick it for a week."

"A common experience, I believe," Fiddis said. He locked the drawers of his desk one after the other, very deliberately, knowing that he could only get Gerry out of the office by leaving the office himself. Gerry shouldn't call to see him so often, and certainly shouldn't stop so long when he came. For some reason, that had nothing to do with Gerry's escapade as a burglar, the boy, or young man or whatever he was, irritated Fiddis: the smooth skin, the delicate hands, the fair hair. "I read a book once," Fiddis said, "about Father Willie Doyle, the famous Jesuit. He was killed in the war you know. Taking his hat from the rack near the window, he looked across the street at the coloured window of one of the town's three bookshops. "The Jesuit noviceship is a very severe test, and when novices used to feel like quitting and going home Father Doyle used to advise them to wait until the next meal time."

Gerry laughed; but leading the way to the door Fiddis wondered if Gerry had seen the point in the Jesuit's wisdom: the interdependence of body and spirit, the mingling of humour and mysticism, sacrifice of the body and a good appetite for food. Maybe Gerry had seen the point, and maybe, also, he would stiffen his will as Father Willie Doyle had done, as every man had done who genuinely intended to make the sacrifices that life as a priest demanded.

Anyway, who was Bernard Fiddis that he should judge in his soul the capacity of any other man for making bodily sacrifices?

"As for that other thing," he said, "forget all about it. It'll never come against you. It's about as serious as robbing an orchard."

Gerry blushed and mumbled something and looked away. He would have been happier if Fiddis's tongue had abused him like the lash of a whip, for this nonchalant forget-about-it tone established between them a detestable man-to-man equality.

"Every man has his wild moments," Fiddis said, knowing that with Gerry Campbell wildness had much less to do with the case than the attraction of colour for the colourless, of the evil character for the character that swung hesitatingly between good and evil. "Still you're lucky to be clear of that Mullan fellow. From what I hear, he's a bad lot."

They came to the bottom of the stairs and the hallway leading to the street. With the gesture of a man suddenly remembering something he had previously forgotten Fiddis clapped his hand to his forehead. "Heavens, I was afraid I'd forgotten something. And I've some instructions to give to the typist."

"Will I wait?"

Fiddis was already half way up the first flight. He said: "No, don't bother. I'll be a good while. See you later." He waved a hand and disappeared round a corner of the stairway. He sat down in his office, still wearing his hat, and methodically picked and polished his nails, giving Gerry time to move on down the street.

When Joe Keenan and the Bear Mullan came in with a message for Gormley's assistant, Bacon Peters was standing on a chair delivering his speech about the industrial potential of the cowdung left on the streets after the fair day. The speech was a satire on the inadequate arrangements of the town council for keeping the streets clear of refuse, but Bacon Peters hadn't the voice for satire. His lips slowly opened and closed, his jawbones moved creakily like unoiled machinery, and words came forth like stones rolling down a hard hill.

Tom Nixon studied the Bear's thin face, the ridge of his nose like the edge of a knife. He said: " Do you want a job, young fellow?"

168

The Bear looked at him and said nothing.

"Doing your messages for five bob a week," said Joe Keenan.

Somebody in the room laughed. It might have been the meanest man in the town. Tom Nixon, with visible effort, smiled a false smile.

"I'll make you a politician, Mr. Keenan," he said. "You've the tongue for it. I wouldn't dare to offer a job to a quiet gentleman like Mr. Mullan."

The Bear turned towards the door. He said: "Shag off to hell." Joe Keenan looked at the two figures in evening dress, the third figure in flaming uniform. "You should be content, Mr. Nixon, with three poor eejits that don't know any better."

There was an uneasy silence as Joe walked out through the shop. Tom Nixon could think of nothing to say. But then Bacon Peters recommenced reading and the fun went on as merrily as ever.

Standing on the steps of the town hall, waiting for Fiddis, Gerry saw Joe Keenan and the Bear coming together up the street. He moved to meet them because he didn't want Bernard Fiddis to find him talking to the Bear. He said: "You're a powerful swank, Bear."

"An uncle in America," said Joe, "died and left him a new suit."

The Bear surveyed Gerry stonily. "We haven't seen you for a long time."

"I've been busy."

"We're going away," Joe said. "To England. To work in a factory."

"I might be going away myself."

"See you in Andy Jim's some Thursday before we go."

"Sure thing," Gerry said. He wanted to get away for he was afraid that at any moment Bernard Fiddis might come walking down the street. "I'd like to see the old place again." He really meant that. He liked the quiet, damp walls, the dark, whispering protection of the trees. The house would be something to remember when he was living under discipline in a cold college. "Some Thursday," he said, and he walked on down the street.

Gormley and Tom Nixon stood talking in the shadowy shop where the walls were curtained with suits of clothes and the air dry with the smell of old cloth. They watched Bernard Fiddis going slowly along the footpath on his way home from the office.

"If he only knew," Gormley said, "what General Sir Laces Joseph has to say about him."

"It wouldn't worry him. I'll say it for Fiddis that he can take a joke. Like his father before him."

Gormley sighed. He had a precarious income and a family that wouldn't stop increasing. "I suppose like the rest of us Fiddis has his own worries."

Fiddis walked slowiy along the footpath, mechanically raising his hat to people he knew, remembering Alice Graham and wondering about May Campbell. He had called in to see Alice on his way from the office. Sitting in an armchair, mopping his brow with a silk handkerchief he admired her new black costume, the skirt buttoned up the front, new glossy red shoes to match the colour of her enamelled finger-nails.

She said: "I'm glad you like them."

"It's warm today."

Her words were unusually clipped and hard. "You're such a stranger."

He knew he had neglected her for a long time, but he had called in with friendly intentions and she wouldn't give him a chance.

"The colour of that enamel makes you look predatory."

"I feel predatory."

She offered him a drink and although the day was too warm for whisky he drank it for the sake of friendliness. She lowered her own whisky at one gulp. "A girl called in to me," she said. "A lovely girl in trouble." She went on talking, and he realized that that whisky had not been her first for the day, and he knew that she wanted him to assure her that the lovely girl's troubles had nothing to do with him, that he was as free as the free air. He listened and said nothing, and when she had finished he looked at his watch and said he'd have to hurry to get back into the town for a political meeting.

She barred his way to the door. "Didn't you hear what I was saying?"

"Quite clearly." He had heard the malice and jealousy in her voice snd it had made him feel sick.

"You're a fool. Don't you see that that brat wants you as a husband?"

It would have been too cruel to say: "So do you." He settled his tie before a mirror. "Wouldn't I make a lovely husband?"

She was suddenly weary, helplessly weary, leading the way down the stairs to the front door, but he felt no pity because the greedy and the malicious deserved no pity.

"I'm thinking of selling the hotel and leaving the town." He scarcely heard what she said, for he was looking up and across the street at Campbell's house and the cars coming and going around the garage, and wondering why she hadn't told him instead of placing herself at the mercy of a woman who hated every bone in her body. The poor girl had been afraid.

"I'm thinking of leaving the town."

He shook her hand. He said: "I'll see you before you go," and walked past her into the street.

He would have gone straight to her house, but at this time of the evening he wouldn't have a chance of finding her alone. Guilty or not guilty, this was his responsibility, this was the end for ever of his detachment. How could he blame her? If she had given herself to the whole world, he had still been preferred to all the world; and his mind was confused with antique images about trampling flowers and plucking morning stars. In a great city you could do that sort of thing and get away with it, but not here, not in this town now moving around him in the gentle evening, feet on the pavement, wheels on the street, whispers in cool doorways, and beyond the houses the green fields and the tinkling, shallow river.

The telephone in his hand, he thought that responsibility came to a man as casually as a cold in the head: a word or a chance meeting, a moment of desire, a moment of folly, and there you were tied hand and foot to the destiny of some other person.

Jinny answered the phone and he asked for Miss May. A moment of silence, an unknown man talking somewhere about the price of bullocks, and then her voice, a lovely voice.

He said: "Alice Graham was telling me something."

"Yes." She had known that Alice Graham would tell him, presenting May Campbell's case to Bernard Fiddis as only an enemy would or could present it.

"Is it true?"

"Yes."

"Why didn't you tell me?"

"What good would that have done?"

Did she hate him and love that other unknown man? Not so

unknown, because he knew now what it was that he felt when in Pat Rafferty's company: a peculiar attraction, a peculiar revulsion.

"Who was he?"

"Does it matter?"

He couldn't blame her. He had neglected her as he had neglected Alice Graham. Of course he had been busy with politics, but the real reasons were that novelty had worn off and that he had the soul of a gipsy; and now responsibility had replaced the sense of adventure and novelty and discovery. Maybe he had a certain responsibility to Alice Graham: encouraging her to stay in the town when she might have returned to England or Scotland, encouraging her by that encouragemeut to hope for something that could never happen. For Alice Graham had, also, the soul of a gipsy, and besides she didn't belong to the town. There was only one thing he could do.

He said: "Listen carefully, May. If I asked you, would you marry me?"

"Are you asking me?"

"Yes."

"Give me time to think."

"We'll talk it over," he said. "And in the meantime don't worry."

He put down the telephone. Desire was reawakening in him—her voice, her soft, lovely voice. With the sense of responsibility came the desire to possess perpetually, the sense of property. He couldn't help it. It was in his bones. It was in the old stones of the town.

VIII

Two soldiers walking in the dusk towards the town and the barracks heard the girl screaming. They remembered the time exactly because a bugle was blowing from the distant barracks, and her first scream happened so suddenly and so sharply they couldn't say whether it was a human voice or an exceptionally shrill effort by the bugler. Then the bugle stopped, and through the silence she screamed again, and again and again, until she was screaming unceasingly and they were running towards the house, across the lawn and between the monkey-puzzle trees, battering and ringing at the unresponsive front door, running around to the back in time to see a man bursting through a hedge and running away from them, across the fields and into the darkness. They ran as far as the hedge but he had already vanished. The girl was still screaming in the kitchen. For a while the two soldiers were afraid that somebody would come in and blame them for tearing her dress to ribbons, and leaving the marks of thumbs on her throat, and giving her as nice a black eye as a man ever gave to a nagging wife. Then she stopped screaming and started crying. She was a bony, red-headed girl. So one soldier patted her on the back, and she said something about a man, with his face covered, standing there when she opened the door. The second soldier said that a girl living in a lonely place should never open the door to strangers, and she began to laugh suddenly and said she hadn't been expecting a stranger. Then one soldier looked at the other soldier, and on the way back to the barracks they told the whole story to a policeman of their acquaintance. She was a funny girl and it was no harm to be on the safe side.

In the morning the news was all over the town. It wasn't often that anything like that happened. Brass MacManus heard it when he was in the butcher shop buying a half pound of mincemeat for the dinner, and when he told his mother about it she said the world was away with it and nothing like that had ever happened when she was young. Later in the day when Brass was carrying a bucket of water from the well in the field beyond the quarry he met Chris Collins and Dinny Campbell coming looking for him, and his first question was: "Have they caught the mystery man yet?"

Dinny and Chris didn't know. Their faces were troubled. "We want to ask your advice," Chris said.

"Fire away." Brass rested the full bucket on the ground. Pat Rafferty and Jim Collins were in the house and his mother wanted fresh water to make tea.

"It's about Gerry," Dinny said. "He didn't come home last night."

"Does your da know that?"

"Nobody knows it except us," Chris said.

"He makes his own bed now," Dinny explained. "And he rises early an' goes to Mass. Nobody noticed he wasn't at home last night except myself."

"Maybe the mystery man murdered him," said Chris with a gruesome relish.

"Why didn't you tell somebody else before this?"

"Because we know where he is, and they'd kill us for not mentioning it sooner."

"Because you worked with Andy Jim and you're not afraid of the ghosts."

"What ghosts?"

"Because if we got him back without anybody knowing, there wouldn't be any row."

"Because Joe Keenan could do it, and you're very friendly with Joe Keenan."

Brass restrainingly raised his hands. "Take it easy, men. For God's sake, take it easy. One move at a time is the way to score goals." He lifted the bucket from the ground and turned towards the house. "Come in with me an' tell your story. I'll let nobody say a word to you."

They followed him with hearts at peace. There was a great comfort in Brass MacManus: in the easy way that he carried the heavy bucket, in the clump of his boots on the flat flagstone at the door of the house, in the way he bent sideways through the door although he was a small man and didn't need to bend at all, in the way he hunkered down on a stool at the fire, waiting for the kettle to boil, and cracking jokes as they told the whole story to Jim and to Pat Rafferty.

Brass and Pat went down Crawford's Alley to find Joe Keenan. The sun was bright at the mouth of the alley where the whitewashed houses were high enough to need three steps up to the front doors, but around the first corner they were walking in the shadow cast by the houses of Devlin Street and on their left hand the alley dwellings were low dark caves, two steps descending to each clay-floored kitchen. Children played and laughed and screamed and shouted, and fell now and again on the rough ground and cried agonizingly. The warm air was sticky with the smell of suds and dishwater spilled in the gutter. Behind them in the smithy at the corner of the alley hammers rang on a steady anvil. They went through a dark kitchen, said good-day to a bent-backed, wrinkle-faced woman, and found Joe Keenan sitting on a stool at the back of the house. His coat was off, his shirt-sleeves rolled up, and, sitting with folded arms, he looked into infinity.

174

"I'm looking at the gardens," he said. "Aren't they lovely?"

"The hanging gardens of Babylon" said Pat, "couldn't hold a candle to them."

The gardens were a desolate expanse of black grassless clay, spotted with occasional heaps of stones and rusted tin cans, criss-crossed with fences of sagging wire. In a few places the desperate industry of alley people had conjured from the surly earth a patch of cabbages or potatoes.

Brass was standing at the back door, shouting to the woman in the kitchen. "The granny's as deaf as a post," Joe said.

"Do you know anything about the Bear Mullan?"

"He's the greatest gentleman in Ireland since he got his new suit."

"Was he the man the soldiers chased last night?"

"Who knows?" Joe said. He liked Pat Rafferty but he understood the Bear.

"Gerry Campbell didn't come home last night."

"Maybe it was Gerry was the mystery man."

"Gerry Campbell's going away to be a priest."

Joe was impressed into thoughtful silence.

"Brass and myself," Pat said, "are going out to Andy Jim Orr's. Will you come?"

"The Bear had a spite against Gerry," Joe said. He went into the kitchen, unrolled his shirt sleeves and slipped on his jacket, changing his mouth-organ from the hip pocket of his trousers to the inside pocket of his jacket. "I got a job to do that made me a few bob and I couldn't go out there yesterday. We were having a farewell party."

"Going away?"

"What do you think? Would you want to look at that all your life?"

He pointed at the black, untidy earth of the gardens. He said: "We can look at the back windows of the Diamond and dream we own the town."

"You get tired dreaming."

"You're telling me."

They walked along the alley to the tinkling smithy where Jim Collins was waiting.

"I might be going away myself," Pat said.

"We'll all go," Joe said. His face, pale and small, under his bushel of black hair was suddenly alive with an idea. "There'll be nobody left in this bloody place. It'll be a ghost town, like something you'd see in the pictures. Maybe over there if you drew a picture on a wall people would stop to look at it. Or if you played a tune they might stop to listen to you."

Over there was the whole world: towns, cities, great harbours strange people speaking in strange tongues. They walked without much talk past the town's last house. If you listened carefully, Pat thought, you could hear through that green spring silence the movement of life over there, a restless giant turning in his sleep. Was Joe Keenan listening to the same attractive, terrible sound?

"The Bear's a bloody madman," Joe sighed. "I hope he did no harm to that pansy."

On the road within view of the house Brass and Jim debated whether they should approach unseen from different places or walk boldly together up the grass-grown lane. The evening was stretching the shadows of the trees. Joe Keenan leaned against a gate and hummed the air of the song about red sails in the sunset. "Swift wings we must borrow," said Pat, and Joe Keenan laughed helplessly as if he had seen some side-splitting joke in a song about red sails and swift wings. "Be serious, boys," Brass said. "This might be murder."

"If it's murder," Pat said, "he's well dead and buried by now," and he climbed over the gate and strode up the lane with Joe Keenan by his side. The trees in the orchard were green with fresh leaves. Brass and Jim Collins followed.

"How many years," Joe said, "before apples become crabs?"

"Don't know."

"You should know. You're a farmer's son."

"There's many a thing a farmer's son doesn't know."

The house was before them, one attic window red with the sun.

"I have that record," Pat said. "Red sails in the sunset. Come out and hear it some time."

Patterns repeated themselves. Different people exchanged the same words. Come out and hear my records, and he could have gone only for the fear that two men who had a lot in common, had one experience too many in common.

"Come up and see me, some time," Joe said. "You forget that

176

we're all going on our travels." Then, without a shout or an exclamation, he ran forward, around the corner of the house, and Pat, seeing no reason for running, ran with him, shouting over his shoulder to Brass and Jim to search the house for Gerry. Behind the house a green lane began, going between high unkempt hedges, a place for early primroses and lovers meetings; and fifty yards along the lane was the Bear Mullan running away from them. Joe Keenan shouted, and the Bear glanced over his shoulder, waved an angry fist and went on running. He ran a few steps and leaped a few steps. "Like a kangaroo," Joe said, and they ran in pursuit over ground that at first was soft and squelchy, but that hardened into green firmness as they went up the sloping land, and when they came panting to the top of the ridge the Bear was putting his foot on the first of the slippery, brown, moss-grown stepping-stones across the river. They were at the edge of the water before he was half-way across, and Joe Keenan shouted: "Wait on us. We won't eat you." He didn't look around. He shouted: "Keenan, you bloody traitor," and scrambled recklessly towards the far bank, slipping once and plunging a leg into the water, so that Joe Keenan, with genuine regret, shouted "Ah God, his new suit!"

On the fisherman's path on the far bank Pat gained steadily. At the wooden stile he was only a few yards behind, and when he came to the road and the grey stone bridge below the ancient graveyard the Bear was leaning helplessly against the parapet, his mouth open like the mouth of an exhausted hound, his face a sickly white. They stood on the narrow roadway and looked at him. He had lost his splendid cap and his hair had come unstuck to fall like a fence of meshed wire before his eyes. One trouser leg, sodden to the hip, clung closely to his thin leg. He struggled for words. They came with staccato difficulty. "Joe," he said, "I never thought you'd do it."

It was the voice of Caesar calling to the friend who stabbed him, and Pat Rafferty, feeling out of place and unwanted, saw Joe Keenan and the Bear Mullan moving together in a world of brotherhood and sworn friendship. It was a world to which he did not belong. Not even Jim Collins meant as much to him as Joe Keenan did to that tired string of misery leaning for rest against the old grey stone.

"I told nothing," Joe said. "They know all about you."

"That's the truth," Pat said. "Joe Keenan was no traitor."

"You're mad as a hatter," Joe said. "Why couldn't you leave skinny Lizzie alone? She might as well 'a' been a packet of razor blades. Anyway she didn't want you."

"She wanted pansy Campbell. She thought it was him when she opened the door. She was all smiling, and then her face changed when she saw me an' I couldn't stick it any more."

"What did you do to him?" Pat asked.

The Bear had turned his back on them. His shoulders were shaking. It was terrible to watch him crying. Joe touched his shoulders and said gently: "You didn't damage Campbell, did you?" The thin body was shivering with sobs. The voice said brokenly: "Rafferty, I never did anything to you, and you battered the face off me one day."

It was God's truth. Pat couldn't deny it. He could only ask again: "What did you do to Campbell?" and wait fearfully for the answer and know that his fear was not for Gerry Campbell, dead or alive, but for the outcast leaning against stone and crying like a child.

"I tied him up in the barn. I gave him the paintbrush. Joe, will they give me the cat for that?"

But Joe Keenan was laughing the laughter of relief and genuine joy, laughing loudly enough to take echoes from the steep hill on one side of the river, to disturb the dead in the ivy-swathed graveyard around the ruins of the ancient church. "Begod," Joe said, "I wouldn't doubt you. I knew you'd never leave this town until you painted somebody. There's an artist lost in you," and his laughter went on until Pat was affected by it, and until the Bear stood up straight and looked at them with hysterical wonder in his eyes. In the silence that followed their laughter they were conscious of their surroundings, the dusty road and quiet fields, the steep hill, the graveyard, as if the things around them had come alive and shared their joke, as if the dead in the graves had shared their indecent laughter.

"Is it right," Joe asked, "that Cromwell put guns on that hill, and that Colmcille built that church?"

"Neither Colmcille nor Cromwell were ever next or near this place."

"Would you blame them," Joe said, "for keeping away?"

Their irrelevant words dropped, pebbles into a bottomless pool, into a deeper silence. "What now," Joe asked, "the police?"

"The police don't know who the mystery man was."

"They won't know if we don't tell them."

"We're not God," Pat said. "We're not God."

The girl had smiled, expecting Gerry Campbell; and then her face had hardened when she saw the Bear, and for one awful moment the outcast had rebelled against his isolation.

"We're not God," Pat repeated. "We're not God."

The money in his pocket had been given him by his father to pay a bill in a shop in the town. He counted out five notes and handed them to the Bear. "You know the way to the main road?"

"I do." The Bear's eyes were furtive, timidly raising themselves to the prospect of escape, his mind still suspecting a trap, too suspicious to be grateful.

"You'll get the Belfast bus there. You'll be in England before you're missed."

"He'll never be missed," Joe said. "None of us will ever be missed."

The Bear's lips shivered like paralysed lips feeling the first painful tremor of returning life. He said: "Thanks." It was a strange word.

"Run, before Jim Collins comes. Remember you painted his future brother-in-law. And when you get to Belfast buy yourself a new cap."

The Bear said nothing. He shook hands with Joe and Pat and then with Joe again. He sniffled, and wiped his nose between finger and thumb. "I'll overtake you in England," Joe said. "Tell them I'm coming. Tell them to have the band out." He had to shout the last words because the Bear was trotting away from them, his wet trouser-leg flapping dismally. They looked after him. "Some day," Joe said, "I'll pay you back that money."

"I don't want it."

"The poor eejit. He never had a chance."

"Nobody ever has a chance."

"Oh, some people have," Joe said. "Some people get all the breaks." He leaned on the parapet and looked down at the water spreading out from the narrow arches of the bridge, gently touching the leaning grasses and the overhanging bushes. "You're a funny fellow, Pat Rafferty. I always thought to look at you, you were law and order."

"Was Campbell making a fool of the girl?"

"Her own imagination. All imagination."

The quietness settled around them. The fisherman's path was before them, and the brown, slippery stepping-stones, and the sloping, green lane, and then down to the house to tell lies about the Bear's escape.

"I suppose it's all a lie," Joe said, "about the guns on that hill." The river was beside them, going like the Bear Mullan towards the sea.

"A bloody lie."

The steep hill was behind them, looking across the river to the place where the dead had slept for centuries around a broken shrine.

"If you had guns on that hill," Joe said, "you could swivel them round and blow the town to hell."

IX

Brass and Jim found Gerry in the barn, sick with shame, weak with hunger and exhaustion. They didn't question him for details, but from the disjointed sentences that he dropped on the way home they gathered that Mullan had clubbed him from behind, that he had returned to his senses to find himself tied to one of the tarred posts that barely supported the sagging roof of the barn. It might or might not have been the truth. Who cared? The main thing now was to keep the whole unfortunate business a secret; and after a while the people of the town would stop talking about the mystery man, and the Bear Mullan would be somewhere over the water, working in a factory, earning his living honestly for the first time in his life. So Gerry walked quietly home to tea, met the suspicions of May and Dympna with a few glib excuses, found that he had not to meet the suspicions of his father because the old man had gone to bed before lunch with a bad cold.

"That wet day in the graveyard," he told Bernard Fiddis, who called to see him when Gerry was having his tea. Fiddis and May whispered together in the hallway for a while, and, although Gerry, sitting in the dining-room, listened as carefully as he could, he didn't hear a word they were saying.

"A wet day in a graveyard killed many a man."

"Don't worry, John, you'll outlive us all."

The old man—what of him was visible—didn't look so good: a heavy body huddled helplessly under piled bedclothes, two hands that were suddenly aged and gaunt, a face pale with illness but still blotched with remnants of its normal floridity, grey hair squashed untidily against the pillow. The air in the room was tingling with the smell of disinfectant.

"It wasn't only the wet day, Bernard. There was Aggie's death, and now May. All this worry."

"What worry?" It was a cruel question, but there was nothing as prudent as cruelty.

"You remember a question I asked you one day, Bernard? About May. We were going to a meeting in the hall. And God knows you have your own worries with these damned elections, without listening to my wailing."

"Politics don't worry me. And we're old friends."

"You remember the question?"

"I do."

"Well, Bernard, I'm sorry to say the answer was yes."

This was the difficult moment. The shocked, surprised face would be easy, too easy. A facile assumption of knowing all about it all the time might look suspicious, even to John Campbell. Fiddis's face was motionless. He nodded his head slightly. He said: "I was afraid of that for some time past. I noticed a few things. I was worried for your sake, John, and for hers."

"I blame myself," the old man sighed. "That Graham woman was bad company."

"Blame nobody, John. Young people have been foolish before this. There's nothing new in nature."

Platitudes staggered like wooden-legged men from the man in the chair to the man in the bed and back again: friends in need were friends indeed, nothing was bad but could be worse, least said was soonest mended, what the town didn't know the town couldn't talk about. Staggering, wooden-legged men led the way to the moment for which Fiddis had planned. The air was fertilized with friendship, the mind rendered less acute by all the sawdust of philosophy.

"What in God's name will I do?" asked the old man, and the question was the pistol shot releasing the big attack, not wooden-legged men but active armed soldiers, up and over, relentlessly advancing through all the floating smoke of friendship, pipes playing, drums beating, bayonets poised, confident of victory.

"I've thought it over from every angle, John, and I think I see a way out."

The big body stirred in the bed.

"Supposing you forced her to name the man. Did a marriage like that ever turn out well?"

"Not often."

"Never, John. Never in human history." That, Fiddis thought, was what you meant by a sweeping generalization.

"Now look at me, John. You know me. You know everything about me. You know that the one thing I should do is go and get married."

There was a long silence. The clouds of sprayed disinfectant were still visible in the corners of the room. The old man moved his body restlessly and looked up at the white ceiling. "You'd sacrifice yourself, Bernard. I couldn't let you do it."

"Sacrifice be damned. She's a lovely girl. In a million years I'd never find a more suitable wife. Can you or I or any son of Adam blame her for one foolishness?"

Another long silence, restless turning in the bed. Fiddis stood up and walked to the window. Pat Rafferty had just chained his bicycle outside the gramophone shop and was walking slowly across the street towards Campbell's house. The slow easy swing of his arms and legs was the dangerous approach of a relieving army. It was now or never, bayonets ready, leap down into the enemy trench.

"You know what the town will say if you do this?" It was a feeble protest.

"Is there a man in this town will lift a finger or a tongue against me?" The town! I am the town! If his soul had not been sick with something close to panic Fiddis would have laughed. But Pat Rafferty must be on the doorstep by now. So close to complete possession, and was everything to be ruined by an old fool who couldn't make up his mind and by a young fool who wanted to tell the truth? Now for one last great effort.

"I'm really asking *you* to do *me* a favour, John."

"Will she be happy?"

"We'll leave that to her own free choice."

The door-bell was ringing, but the bugles were blaring over a

182

conquered field. Fiddis closed the bedroom door gently, walked slowly down the stairs, his face grave, his heart smiling. In the hallway May was remonstrating with Pat Rafferty. "I asked you to wait," she said. "I asked you to wait."

"I must see him," he said. "I must tell him the truth . . .", and he stopped abruptly as Fiddis come nearer.

She said: "How do you think he is, Mr. Fiddis?"

"He'll be all right. But he needs rest. On no account should he be disturbed."

"Pat here wants to see him."

"It's important," Pat said hurriedly.

"I wouldn't disturb him just now. The heart, you know. If it's advice you want maybe I could . . ."

"Maybe you could," Pat said, but his voice was as dull as lead.

They left the house together. She closed the door behind them, and leaned her forehead for a while against the cold hard wood. They crossed the street, Fiddis's hand softly resting on Pat's forearm. Pat scarcely felt the hand, scarcely heard the soothing friendly voice. His feet seemed as big and clumsy as butter-boxes.

"There's something I would like to ask you about," he said. "When you have time." If she really wanted him she would go with him when he went to speak to her father: that was what love meant if it meant anything, two against the world, Jim and Dympna; or even friendship, Chris and Dinny, Joe Keenan and the Bear Mullan.

"The election count ends before noon tomorrow. I'll naturally be beaten, but I'll head the poll in the town, and the tar-barrels are ready to celebrate. You'll be in the town?"

"My father wouldn't miss it."

"Go out to my place about nine o'clock. We'll have time for supper and a few records—and your troubles." And after that, Fiddis thought, I'll drive May Campbell away for a while from this curious town and when she returns she'll be my wife. I wonder how Judy will like another woman in the house.

It was, he supposed, sitting down alone in his office, dishonest, deceitful, and a dozen other mean and scurvy things. But it would be better for everybody in the end. Pat Rafferty would live to bless the name of Bernard Fiddis who saved him from a hasty, unfortunate marriage.

He dialled very slowly the number of Graham's hotel. He said:

"Is that you, Alice?" She was the sort that would want to know the best or the worst. He said: "If you're thinking of selling, I've an offer. Tom Nixon is considering the hotel business."

"That little scab."

"His money's good."

"Better than his breath. Or his jokes."

He laughed: "Don't be catty. And, by the way, I'm going to get married. John Campbell has given his consent."

"Congratulations," she said. Just that one word, and then something clicked and the line was dead.

That at least was the truth. You could say in favour of lies that they were easier to tell, because, among other things, the effort of the imagination acted like wings and lifted you over the lumpy ground. But whether lies or truth did the more good or the more harm, who knew, who could tell?

X

The crowd was gathering outside the parochial hall when Pat left his bicycle leaning against the railings and went into the church, out of the dusk into shadows where the only lights were one red lamp before the tabernacle, three gas lamps burning near the three confessionals, and high above the pointed arches of the nave the last greyness of the dying day filtering through the clerestory windows. The penitents knelt in stiff silent rows. He stayed at the confessional nearest the door, patiently waiting his turn, hearing the rattle of the wooden slides opening and closing as the priest turned from one penitent to the other: "Go in peace, my child, thy sins are forgiven thee." "Bless me, father, for I have sinned."

The number of men ahead of him decreased steadily. He prayed a little, but most of the time he was rehearsing what he would say to the priest. Telling the truth was hard work, but it had to begin somewhere, and, after the priest, there was still her father, when he was well enough to be seen. It was no news for a man with a weak heart.

The thunder of the brass band playing its way up from the Diamond broke in on his meditations, sending his carefully arranged words whirling away like leaves in the wind. They were bringing Fiddis up the town to make his speech from the top of the steps in front of the parochial hall, and in an hours time he would be sitting in Fiddis's house, eating supper, listening to records, discovering the truth. But first of all there was the priest. A few penitents distracted by the approaching noise had abandoned their good intentions, and as he pulled aside the heavy curtains and edged his way into the cramped darkness the band suddenly stopped playing. In the silence that followed, the sound of the wooden slide moving across was like a brattle of thunder coming unexpectedly on a sultry day. Now was the time for truth.

A profile half seen through the grille. Breath straining noisily through old nostrils. A grey head nodding in sorrow and in understanding of the ancient weakness.

"Do you intend to marry the girl?"

"Yes, father."

"Do your part then like a man. Tell the truth then, like a man."

"Yes, father."

A burst of cheering from the street. Fiddis was making his speech.

"These pleasures are given by God for a purpose. Not to be misused. Not to be dragged in the gutter."

"Yes, father."

A hand raised in forgiveness. God knew all. God pardoned all. A burst of cheering from the street. Go in peace, my child, thy sins are forgiven thee.

After the darkness of the confessional the dimly lighted church seemed bright. Noise no longer muffled by a heavy hanging curtain, he could hear Fiddis's voice like the sound conveyed through a long, thin needle from a worn gramophone record; and every burst of cheering ran up the nave like a horde of ill-mannered school children, and the echoes clattered about among the brown, carved angels on the high shadowy rafters. It wasn't easy to pray, to keep the eyes steadily on the pinpoint of red light glowing in the sanctuary, to speak, without hope of audible answer, to the presence hidden behind the golden door of the tabernacle, behind the wall of white bread and the sea of red wine; and all the time his voice, muted and absurd, but still his voice, speaking to shouting people a series of foolish phrases. Bernard Fiddis didn't mean those phrases, didn't believe one word of all the words he was throwing to the cheering crowd. But somewhere at some time he had uttered words that he had meant, body and soul, hot foolish words whispered only to one other person, secret words setting two people together against the whole world. Go in peace, my child, and kneel before the sacred tabernacle, and torture yourself with wondering about her and Bernard Fiddis, and free of your own sins speculate on the sins of others. No, it wasn't easy to pray if you weren't used to praying, and how could he be used to prayer when his father worshipped a river? The days were dead when men could, with hope in their hearts, pray to rivers.

He left his bicycle where it was and walked away from the church, manoeuvring his way around the fringes of the crowd. The torch lights burned steadily around the raised place where Fiddis stood, a square of red light surrounding the orator, the chosen man, red light reflected in the brass instruments held by the silent bandsmen, patiently waiting until the speechifying ended and the marching recommenced.

"They may gerrymander the country districts," said Bernard Fiddis, "but we defy them to gerrymander this patriotic town. Once again we have shown them that, beyond all doubt, this town stands for an Ireland free, united, Gaelic and democratic."

The crowd went wild. A bandsman solemnly blew a note on a French horn. Even out on the edges you could feel the enthusiasm like the beating of a monstrous heart. Pat fled from it. His father was somewhere in there, probably holding a torch and cheering like twenty men for an Ireland in which every river would be properly drained. Pat halted for a moment and heard Bernard Fiddis: "They'll tell you about Nazi Germany. They'll tell you about Soviet Russia. But what did Hitler or Stalin ever do that Lord Craigavon hasn't done?" The crowd roared again. The French horn bellowed like a bull. Pat ran across the silent Diamond, on down the town, away from all the tomfoolery of a man saying what he didn't believe, of people cheering what they didn't understand. Then turning the corner at Graham's hotel he halted, and rubbed his eyes in wonder.

There was a platform erected on the other side of the street. It wasn't a normal meeting with sensible dishonest speeches, and cheering as regular as a mighty, slow-beating pulse. It was more like a gathering of the world's drunk men and the world's ragged people: dancing and capering and shouting, playing mouth-organs and melodeons and blowing into shrieking tin whistles, waving

186

flaming torches until the light was dancing as madly as the people, crying crude witticisms at the three fantastic figures on the platform. One of the three read something from a scroll of paper as solemnly as if he were reading the proclamation of a king, undisturbed by the antics of the crowd: "No longer then shall we suffer this unnatural restriction on our liberty. No longer shall a tree washed down from nowhere stand between us and the exercise of our natural rights." He raised his right hand solemnly and for a moment the crowd was almost silent. He intoned sonorously: "Have we a remedy?" And the crowd with one voice answered: "We have," and the figure in uniform held on high an antiquated, cracked chamber-pot, and all the tumult of the crowd resounded at once, shouts, catcalls, melodeons, bugles, as if a jungle people had been shown a mystic symbol.

Pat stared in amazement. It was as if you had looked at a serious picture by a serious painter and then, turning the page, there was the same picture distorted by a whimsical, half-malicious caricaturist. Behind him and above him, as he stood staring, a window opened and the voice of Alice Graham said: "Why do you stand here amazed?"

"What is it all about?"

"It's wit. Irish wit. It's Tom Nixon and his troupe of town imbeciles."

She came down quickly and opened the door for him, and they sat together at a window in a room overlooking the street. She switched out the light, and, unseen, they could study the capering crowd shouting around the platform and the three figures of fun. Her breath smelt heavily of drink, and now and again her tongue stumbled and missed a word, or her mind refused to supply the right word at the right time. He had never seen a woman really drunk until that moment. He stared at her, and could find nothing to say, could only wonder why he was here at all when ten minutes previously she had been as far from his mind as if she lived in the moon. She leaned towards him, the smell of whisky- scented breath hot about his nostrils.

"You're a shy boy," she said confidentially. "You've a retiring disposition. You haven't been to see me for ages and I've practically to go and drag you in off the street." She had been careless with her make-up, and even by the little light that came in from outside he could see loose lumps of powder and daubs of rouge and naked, pitiless wrinkles.

He said: "I was busy."

"Don't work too hard. You look worried."

"I am worried."

For a flickering moment he wondered could he tell her his trouble. She was a woman of experience, but then he remembered that May Campbell had already, to no purpose, asked her advice. What could she do? What help could she give? The only help could come from telling the truth. Anyway she was drunk, too drunk to notice that he had said he was worried, or to do anything but stumble, as a drunk mind does, from one idea to the other like a man falling over furniture in a dark, unfamiliar room. Her right hand was stroking his face, smooth, scented fingers slipping down one cheek, around his chin, up his other cheek, fingertips tapping his forehead, not an unpleasant sensation, and all the time her tipsy voice rambling on: "Your big, long, black, worried face. You're like a picture of some old Scottish preacher. Don't let her worry you. Don't believe what she says. She'll blame you because you're young. He's too old for her. She doesn't want an old man. But don't believe what she says. She's a liar and worse than a liar. It so happens that I know the truth. It could have been you or Tom Nixon or the man that sweeps the streets or the lame man that lights the lamps or the loafer who holds horses for the farmers on a market-day. . . ."

He was on his feet, horrified. The smell of whisky might have been the smell of brimstone. Hell was in the room; and the fools shouting in the street, and the brass band leading the procession around the Diamond.

"What do you mean?"

"What do I mean? Guess, lovey." She was standing also, her hands on his shoulders, blowing hell into his face. "Guess a big house and a yellow motor car. Guess a man that was playing about with little girls when you weren't even a gleam in your father's eye. Guess . . ."

He pushed her away from him and ran for the door as she staggered and grabbed at a chair and fell heavily. She screamed once, and then her lips opened wide and the gutter came out at one gush; but he was half-way down the stairs and almost out of hearing,

188

running towards the uproar of the shouting fools and the brass band leading the triumphant procession down the street. He slammed the door behind him. The bandsmen, marching four deep and blowing vigorously enough to rattle the windows in the houses, were cutting through Tom Nixon's meeting like a disciplined column of police through a disorderly mob of rioters. The three fantastics on the platform shouted and waved their arms in protest, but nobody could hear what they said, and the whole crowd, laughing and singing and waving torches, fell in behind the band. He was caught hopelessly in the crowd. He couldn't cross the street. He couldn't even stand peaceably in one place. He couldn't see sight or sign of Bernard Fiddis. Somebody thrust a burning torch into his hand and he found himself in the middle of the street, hemmed in by the crowd, handling the torch as carefully as he could so as to avoid dropping burning fragments on his frantic neighbours; and looking up at Graham's hotel he saw in horror that she was leaning out of an open window, waving her arms like a lane-woman in a barging match, screaming words that nobody could hear, that only Pat Rafferty could understand. He knew she was telling the town about May Campbell and Bernard Fiddis, that she was mad with drink and jealousy, and for one moment of bitter malice he hoped that the noise would stop so that the whole world could hear clearly the terrible things she had to say.

A man in the crowd chanted: "Go hame, Missus Graham, wash your ass in milk and crame."

They thought she was objecting to the noise and the fun, and a stone went whirling through the air and a pane of glass splintered. A fat man in pyjamas opened a window and shouted in protest, and a voice in the crowd bellowed: "Himself and Missus Graham can't sleep a wink," and another stone went spinning through another pane of glass. The man in pyjamas and the shrieking woman withdrew quickly. The windows were slammed. The procession moved on, the band playing and the people singing:

An outlawed man in a land forlorn,
He scorned to turn and fly. . . .

High up or low down he couldn't see Fiddis. He held his torch steadily, and sang with the marching crowd. He was a good head above any man near him and an old woman on the footpath called to another old woman to look at the statue of liberty coming down the street. . . .

> But kept the cause of freedom safe
> Upon the mountains high. . . .

Fiddis would be too cute and too superior to be caught in this riot. Set the fools shouting and singing, and then drive home in your big car and laugh yourself sick every time you remembered their folly. Joe Keenan wanted to blow the town to hell. With this torch I could burn the world. Oh, leave it alone and it would burn itself. . . .

> Oh, leave your cruel kin and come
> When the lark is in the sky.
> And it's with my gun I'll guard you
> On the mountains of Pomeroy

At the bridge at the bottom of the town the procession turned a corner and he slipped out of his place, heaved the torch over the parapet, watched it die with a fierce sputter of protest as it touched the water. He waited until the crowd had passed and the place was quiet and he could hear the cool river talking around the piers of the bridge. The band was playing a different tune. The crowd was singing different words:

> For Rody MacCorley goes to die
> At the bridge of Toome today.

The words, the music, faded into the distance. He walked slowly by lanes and then by little roads towards Fiddis's house; there was no hurry now, and if he ran the wind would scream in his ears, like the drunk, jealous woman screaming from the opened window, telling him what Bernard Fiddis was, what May Campbell was. And Bernard Fiddis might have been his friend. And May Campbell might have been his . . . The thought set him shaking with dry joyless, tearless laughter.

Fiddis opened the door and reached out the right hand of

welcome. Pat didn't even see it. He was looking at the man's face, and suddenly it seemed flat and featureless, an egg of a face.

"A long-awaited pleasure," Fiddis said. "Come on in. Supper's ready."

"Thanks. I won't be stopping." He stood just over the thresholde calm and cool now, all the frenzy of twenty minutes ago quenched as the water had quenched the sizzling torch.

"Is anything wrong?"

"You know about May Campbell?"

"Yes." A lingering, reluctant yes.

"I called in on Alice Graham on the way through the town. She told me I needn't worry. She said you were the man who should worry. Is that the truth?"

A long silence. Then: "You're young yet. Life is a strange thing." The dead sentences were like the vain steps taken in a nightmare flight from something unseen and swift and horrible.

"I don't want a sermon. I want the truth." The truth. The truth. In the darkness behind a curtain with God's priest. In a dark room with a drunken, jealous woman.

Another long silence. Then Fiddis said: "Alice Graham told the truth," and Pat closed his fist and swung his arm and struck the featureless face, not the face of any man he knew, a heavy sickening blow.

Fiddis stood without moving. A lie was easier to tell than the truth. A lie meant blows, but the truth would mean three lives for ever twisted out of shape. There was blood in his mouth, but the blow had scarcely stirred him. He waited for the second blow, but Pat Rafferty turned and walked out over the threshold, across the gravel to the gate, and out on the road he cried as he walked, and didn't know he was crying. So that when he put his hand to his face and found it wet with tears he was surprised and then angry and then ashamed.

Something had been born between them, something more lasting than the love between man and woman, but a blow had sent it, not crying into the complexity of life, but down and down for ever into death.

She sat well-wrapped in the back of the car. Dympna sat beside her and Fiddis drove them away from the town. At the top of the high hill beyond the barracks Pat Rafferty was caught by the headlights, monstrously tall, his long shadow against the high hedge, pushing his way home. Fiddis slowed up, then changed his mind and drove on. When a lie was told and heard and accepted it became something like the truth—as antichrist was like Christ. The book was closed. The taste of blood was in his mouth. Out of all the frenzy of life, places seen, people spoken to, food and drink and books and music and enjoyment and pain, would he remember only that blow?

XI

His father, sitting with his back to the lamp, read aloud from the local newspaper. His mother sat on a low chair far away from the fire and carefully cleaned henhouse marks off eggs that were meant for tomorrow's market. He tried to close his ears to his father's voice, to close his eyes to the sight of his patient mother, to know by imaginative effort what the world would be like lacking them. He tried to listen only to the wind swishing in the orchard boughs, to see only the night gathered outside the house, because the night was nothingness, and life and the world were nothingness.

His father read: ". . . to have the catchment area take its proper place in the list of works . . . to immediately implement this long-drawn-out agitation by receiving and thereby hearing the views direct from the farmers concerned in this most vital issue. . . ."

There was no escaping from that voice: ". . . and in the meantime to have trees and other obstructions removed, i.e. as an interim relief measure inaugurated so as that the river can take without obstruction the original course nature and providence designed, and not to be taking short cuts owing to these impediments, thereby flooding valuable fertile land. . . ."

"That's the talk," his father exclaimed. "We have them in a cocked hat."

His mother said: "You're very quiet, Pat."

"I'll live to see that river cleaned," his father said.

"I'll live to see it running as clean as a new canal."

"Was there a big crowd at the meeting, Pat?"

192

"Yes, Mother."

"Fiddis the solicitor's as good a speaker as ever stood up in that town," his father said. "What's your opinion, Pat?"

His father didn't expect an answer, for he was hidden again behind the blotchy pages of the newspaper. So Pat opened slowly the book that lay on his knees, a book of translations that a poet in Dublin had made from the poets of dead-and-gone Gaelic times.

> Once I saw a girl
> Take a man in play

The old teacher who had loaned him so many books would never loan him another. He would return this one through the post. It was easier to say goodbye that way.

> Love he never knew
> Till his dying day

Well, he knew now that he had loved her all the time, and yet he had never known love: two people, his father and mother, sitting in the same warm radiance.

His father readjusted his spectacles, laboriously turned a page. A loose sheet slipped out and slithered across the floor. "There'll be trouble with that Hitler boy yet," he said. "He won't be content with Czechoslovakia"

"God preserve us from war," his mother said. "We had enough war in this country. That Hitler's a proper rascal."

"Still you can't deny he did a lot for the German people. He raised them from the dirt. A man like that would do this country a lot of good."

"Praise be to God we're not in the dirt. And isn't Hitler against the Church?"

> Love he never knew
> Till his dying day

It was pain, burning pain, to sit and watch them, because even when they disagreed they were in perfect agreement. He wanted to rise up and run out into the darkness, to grip with his hard hands on the secret of the night and the future, to meet whatever it was that was coming his way, to do something that would set a great clock striking somewhere higher than the court-house or the spires or the highest mountain in Ireland; to set the whole world turning restlessly in what the prayer books called the sleep of life; to make for ever a beginning and an end.

6

A Picture

SHE said: "I can remember so clearly the day that photograph was taken."

She remembered that John Maxwell had been released on that day because the jury had disagreed for the third time, that an American priest had come to her father's house for his tea. What had that priest been like: tall or short, dark or fair? Do you remember, Bernard?

No, he couldn't remember. But he remembered the hot gospellers singing across the street, and the line of her breasts above the high, old-fashioned, dining-room table.

"Gerry and his pals were raging mad that they had to stand-in to balance the photograph. They thought they were grown men. That was their last month at school. I remember that."

He took the photograph from her and walked slowly up the stairs to his study. Her finger had lingered for a second, a fraction of a second, at one spot on the yellowing surface. He knew before he had shown it to her that that would happen, and he had anticipated precisely what his own feelings would be; but he couldn't say now whether those feelings were pleasure or pain.

When he had bought the photograph in the poorly lighted shop the little photographer's finger had lingered on the same spot. "That's the boy there, Mr. Fiddis. That's the poor lad. The first from this town to go, but not the last. Not the last. It's a dreadful business. His poor father."

"Yes, I know."

The boy's poor father had brought Fiddis the news: "Sunk in the salt sea, Bernard. No grave nowhere. It'll kill his mother. What under God ever possessed him to go away the way he did? Isn't there the whole world full of English and Germans well able to fight their own war? Wasn't he content at home?"

A man who had aged ten years in one year. A shadow of a man lost in his clothes. A man who didn't care if every river from the Amazon to the Volga was blocked with sand and gravel and roots of trees. Is that my doing? Is that my sin?

Pin up the photograph on the wall above the writing-desk. Every time you sit at the desk it will be a remembrance of sin, remembrance of a blow, of her lovely finger lingering for a fraction of a second on the yellowing surface. Masochism?

She doesn't know he's dead, but some day she will know, and will hate me not because he's dead but because I hadn't the courage to tell her he was dead, hadn't the courage to mention his name, to assure her that all was for the best, that nobody had sinned, that we didn't believe in ghosts. She needs my assurance.

Sit and write in your diary about the social changes that war has brought even to this town: hungry conscripts walking the streets and eating dry bread by the handful, hundreds of workmen building factories and military camps, monstrous aeroplanes passing and re-passing. The joy of being a diarist, an educated man capable of expressing his thoughts in writing, an acute observer of the social habits of lesser people! There on the wall is a picture of fifty-nine boys to remind you that a world at war is, for you, only one death.

Sit at your ease and write about the day you cycled with her up into the lonely places in the hills, where the young river falls over slabs of limestone that are cooler than ice, where the old man in the house by the bridge didn't know that a war was happening, but he had heard of a great scheme on foot to clean the river from its source right down to the sea and it would be a godsend to the poor farmers. You were afraid to look at her, and you knew that she hated you because you were afraid.

Close the diary suddenly, as if you felt that somebody was looking over your shoulder. It isn't a ghost; it's only a child laughing child's laughter in the sunshine before the house, and Judy's voice, like the voice of a girl, speaking to the child. How good to be really old, for only the aged can recover childhood, all memories dulled, all sins forgiven.

The hand that struck me lives in the child, and I love the child.

How good to be courageous and ruthlessly able to break things:

to point to the picture, to say that he stood there, and now he is dead under the sea, and all the time you loved him, and every time the child laughs or cries or moves about the house his ghost is between us and we are hating each other and loving that ghost.

Sweet child, is the blood in your veins suddenly chilled because it is lost under the sea?

He looked out of the window. The child and Judy played together in the sunshine. His wife walked across the gravel to visit her father and sister in their house in the town. The river flowed, between dark green trees and bright green grass, towards the grey town and the blue sea.